MW00588284

JINN HUNTER

Book One: The Prism

TAHIR SHAH

JINN HUNTER

Book One: The Prism

TAHIR SHAH

SECRETUM MUNDI PUBLISHING

MMXIX

Secretum Mundi Publishing Ltd
PO Box 5299
Bath BA1 0WS
United Kingdom

www.secretum-mundi.com
info@secretum-mundi.com

First published by Secretum Mundi Publishing Ltd, 2019

JINN HUNTER: BOOK ONE – THE PRISM © TAHIR SHAH

Tahir Shah asserts the right to be identified as the Author of the Work
in accordance with the Copyright, Designs and Patents Act 1988.
A CIP catalogue record for this title is available from the British Library.

Visit the author's website at: www.tahirshah.com

ISBN 978-1-912383-28-3

This is a work of fiction. Characters are the product of the author's
imagination. Any resemblance to persons – living or dead – is entirely
coincidental.
All rights reserved. No part of this publication may be reproduced, stored in
a retrieval system, or transmitted, in any form or by any means, electronic,
mechanical, photocopying, recording or otherwise, without the prior written
permission of the publisher.
This book is sold subject to the condition that it shall not, by way of trade
or otherwise, be lent, re-sold, hired out or otherwise circulated without the
publisher's prior consent in any form of binding or cover other than that in
which it is published and without a similar condition including this condition
being imposed on the subsequent purchaser.

This book is for Tarquin Hall,
my steadfast friend through thick and thin.

Peer into the eye of a jinn and see your future.
Hear the whispering of a jinn and go insane.

Moroccan proverb

PART ONE

NEQUISSIMUS

One

THE VAULTS BENEATH the Bank of England, on London's Threadneedle Street, were utterly silent, as they were on any other night.

The only sound was the muffled hum of the neon tube lights, and of the duty guards' rubber-soled Dr Martens shoes pacing deliberately over the even cement floor.

Like most of the guards on patrol that night, Mortimer Baskart had worked at the Bank so long he was blasé about what he was charged with guarding. He rarely gave it a second thought – that the contents of the vault he patrolled were worth more than fifteen billion pounds.

A mountain of bullion was housed there, arranged on bright blue shelving, as it was in each of the Bank's eight cavernous vaults.

Half a million bars of the purest gold – belonging to governments, companies, and some of the wealthiest individuals on earth.

Security was tight but, as Baskart liked to joke, in the age of cyber-crime, only a madman would bother stealing five thousand tonnes of bullion. After all, far easier pickings could be carried off with a few clicks of a mouse.

At twelve minutes past two, he radioed the duty

officer locked in the control booth three levels above. One by one the other guards followed suit.

All eight vaults were secure.

Nothing unusual to report.

Baskart was about to go back to his crossword, when he heard something.

Frowning, he looked up.

There it was again.

A faint hissing sound, like gas escaping from a hose.

Turning slowly as he listened, Baskart took in the prim stacks of golden bricks, reflecting fluorescent light.

The hissing grew louder, peaked in a crescendo, and faded. As it did so, an intricate interlocking pattern was traced over the walls and floor. Covering every inch of available surface it etched itself into the cement.

Perplexed, Mortimer Baskart looked on, as something yet more unfathomable took place.

The bars of bullion began to tremble.

Then, without any sound or apparent heat, they melted.

Dripping down onto the floor as though they were molten wax, they seeped into the cement.

Within a minute and a half, every ounce of gold was gone.

Two

THE LIGHTS HAD been lowered in the main lecture theatre at the Courant Institute of Mathematics, a stone's throw from New York's Washington Square.

Seated at the back, dressed in a crumpled button-down shirt and frayed chinos, was Oliver Quinn.

With honest hazel eyes, dimpled cheeks, and a smile that never seemed to leave his lips, there was a mildness about him... as though he wouldn't – or couldn't – harm a fly.

Regarded as a dreamer by everyone who knew him, Oliver was zoned out far more than he was zoned in – his mind churning day and night with an endless stream of ideas, images, and fantasies.

The course on Advanced Pattern Theory was taken by the department's senior professor, Dr Fred Moss. There wasn't a more demanding course on the subject in the country. Two-thirds always flunked. Those who didn't, rarely did better than scrape through.

Oliver was different though.

For him the coursework was such a breeze, he was zoned out even more than usual.

But, on this particular day, the challenge presented to the class was so intriguing that it sucked in his full attention.

Dr Moss had projected a gritty black-and-white

image on the wall and was asking for a volunteer to explain it.

An awkward silence hung heavy in the classroom. Oliver looked up.

In one precise movement, he fished out a red polka-dot handkerchief, opened it out, and dabbed it thoughtfully to his left nostril. Folding it once, then again, he slipped it back into his chino pocket, and sighed.

In the six seconds it took to do so, Oliver's gaze never strayed from the curious image projected on the theatre's wall.

Focussing, he took in the seemingly random connected and interconnected white lines, set against a bleak grey desert-scape. His right hand roamed back through the mop of unruly blond hair, the fingers splaying as they reached the back of his neck.

Still his focus didn't flinch.

Oliver might have been sitting in the lecture theatre, but his mind wasn't there.

It was on the open seas.

He was navigating a ramshackle dhow across an ocean conjured from dragon's blood. Hanging in the lizard-green sky above, a pair of twin suns was roasting him, as they had done day after day for many weeks.

The dhow's keel tore through the dark waves.

As he guided the craft toward the horizon, Oliver

thanked Providence. The odds of escaping the Kingdom of Avenged Hope alive had been so slim the mission had been tantamount to suicide.

A stray cough eased Oliver's attention back to the lecture theatre.

Dr Moss motioned to a pinprick of black somewhere near the middle of the projected image.

A pinprick lost in the maze-like grid of lines.

'This speck's been identified as an automobile,' he said. 'So that gives you some sense of the size we're dealing with. The question is why such a vast matrix would have been laid out as it was in the Gobi.'

The professor clicked to the next slide, and then to another.

Each one bore a similar random image.

'Ancient man must have done them,' pronounced a strait-laced Russian girl at the front. 'You know, like the Nazca Lines.'

Dr Moss held up an index finger, wagging it left, then right.

'There's no doubt these are modern,' he replied. 'US spy satellites have identified abandoned military equipment near each of them.'

'What about aliens?' another student broke in.

'What about them?' probed Moss.

'Well, you know, reaching out to some other dimension.'

Oliver didn't catch the comments or the questions.

Leaning forward, his eyes strained on the third image, his mind struggling to make sense of the pattern.

As he gazed at it, zigzag lines with no symmetry at all, his mouth opened a fraction, and he breathed silently in.

The other students were all engrossed on the pattern – a pattern they each saw the same.

Random lines arranged in two dimensions.

But what Oliver witnessed fused into something completely different.

A vast and complex matrix of white lines – some converging; others not. Some were trembling as though they were alive. Yet more were psychedelic – every colour imaginable. Forming a kaleidoscopic labyrinth, they cavorted around one another, as though acting out a pre-programmed sequence.

But far stranger than the lines, was the space around them. It had consciousness – the kind occurring in insect colonies.

A consciousness known to entomologists as 'group think'.

Oliver counted the dimensions…

All eleven of them.

His mind buzzing as it made connections, he got a flash of the dhow's keel racing through waves.

Waves of unctuous dragon's blood.

Three

THE PRISM WAS a vast inverted pyramid, fashioned from triangular sheets of impregnable glass.

A mile wide, and twice as high, it lay at the heart of the Abyss, divided and subdivided into an infinity of octagonal cells.

Rotating on its vertical axis, it clattered, lurched, and screeched, as it swept round and around, powered by the fugian wind.

Three pairs of immense iron sails kept the Prism turning, by powering an elaborate machinery.

Cantilevers and clockwork bearings.

Oscillators and mainsprings.

Drive wheels, cams, and coaxial gears.

And, most important of all, the pendulum of the great escapement.

The mechanism was as dependable as time itself. Because of it, never once had the Prism stopped turning. So the rogue jinn remained as prisoners – trapped in their cells by the penitentiary's cloak of metamagnetism.

As a result, there was peace.

Before the Prism's conception, through centuries of fear, jinn had terrorized every dimension. A dominant life form since the dawn of time, jinn had ruled the Realm – with rogue jinn the preeminent masters.

But, gradually, they were pursued.

Outwitted, then trapped, they were imprisoned by the bravest and canniest legion of warriors.

The Jinn Hunters.

The balance of good and evil was maintained by the fact that so many rogue jinn were interned within the Prism's transparent walls.

But the prison was only strong if it turned.

Cease for a fraction of a moment, and it would lose its impregnability. If that were to happen, the jinn convicts would gain their freedom.

Escape was unthinkable though, because the Prism was managed by an army of guardians devoted to an ancestral cause.

Known as 'malbinos', their fraternity had been bred in antiquitas – in a time before records began. Duty was hard-wired into them – the duty of ensuring no imprisoned jinn ever escaped.

Living as long as three centuries, malbinos were short in stature, and blessed with extraordinary physical strength. On either hand they possessed five fingers and a pair of thumbs. Their hunched forms were obscured head to toe in coarse white bristle, over which was secreted an unctuous lilac slime, which they knew as 'fusilia'.

Set all the way round each malbino head was an arrangement of oversized eyes.

Nine of them, each one a different size.

Multiple eyes made the malbino custodians especially suited to the guardianship of the Prism. Nothing escaped their untrammelled gaze. Yet, despite such perfect sight, no malbino had ever possessed an ear, let alone a pair of them. Through a complex telepathic faculty they could discern most sounds.

Only the musings of jinn were out of range. The lack of ears meant malbinos were immune to the constant whispering of their prisoners.

It was the perfect arrangement.

For, listen through ears to a rogue jinn whisper, and even the most attentive malbino would be instantly driven insane.

Four

As the students filed towards the door at the end of class, Dr Moss motioned a hand towards Oliver Quinn.

'Got a minute?'

As usual, Oliver was lost in his own world.

'Um, sure,' he grunted hesitantly, once the question had been repeated.

'What d'you make of the images?' Moss asked.

'*Huh?*'

'The images – the ones up there on the wall.'

Oliver combed a set of long fingers back through the mop of rowdy blond hair. He got a flash of the dhow, and of the blood-red sea.

'Wild,' he said doubtfully.

'*Wild?*'

His gangling form leaning back against the wall beside the desk, Oliver managed an anxious grin.

'They were like gateways,' he said.

'*Gateways?*'

'Yup.'

'Gateways to what?'

'Dunno. Just that they were amazing.'

'Any idea what they were designed for?'

Oliver shrugged.

'Have a guess,' prompted Moss.

'Something to do with spying, maybe.'

'Spying?'

Oliver yanked his daypack from the floor, up onto his shoulder.

'They were obviously somewhere remote,' he said. 'Even though they were related to high-tech, it was kind of low-tech high-tech, if you see what I mean. Something outdated. But kind of cool.'

Moss looked at Oliver hard.

The Institute had never had a student like him. Oliver Quinn may have been lost in a dream world much of the time, but he could recognize patterns hidden to everyone else.

10

'Have a go,' Dr Moss coaxed. 'Guess what they were designed for.'

Oliver pinched the end of his nose.

Glancing down at the floor, his eyes took in the worn felt furrows in the low-grade carpeting. As he thought of the random patterns he'd seen projected on the classroom wall, his mind was mapping the beige carpet square.

However hard he tried to prevent it, the pattern returned him to the dream world, and to the Kingdom of Avenged Hope.

Professor Moss's voice broke through, jerking Oliver back to the present.

'Oh, er. Um. I'd say they were a way of calibrating satellites,' he said. 'Chinese spy satellites. It's outdated technology. These days you'd be able to make the calibration with a pattern on a postage stamp.'

Moss took a step back.

'How did you know that?' he enquired incredulously.

Oliver looked up from the beige carpet square.

He smiled.

'A lucky guess,' he said.

Five

OF ALL THE malbinos, none was more trusted or expert in the dark and devious ways of rogue jinn than Morrock.

The most experienced malbino of all, he had toiled at the Prism for a century and a half, and hailed from a preeminent line of ancestral guards. He knew every inch of the Prism's labyrinthine passages, just as he did its deepest secrets. But, most importantly of all, he understood how rogue jinn thought.

Revered by his fraternity, and even by some of the prisoners, it fell to him to train the new generation.

Morrock didn't care for youth.

He regarded it as a dangerous condition – one more likely to lead to calamity than it was to success. A long career of guarding the Prism had proved that youthful zeal was pointless without a solid foundation – one of understanding.

At dawn the newest trainee reported for duty at the stone cleft – the point at which all careers in guardianship began.

Bright-eyed, eager, and enthusiastic beyond belief, he had dreamed of pursuing the ancestral calling from childhood. From the moment Morrock caught sight of the boy, he knew he would have to begin at the beginning.

'What's your name?' he spat gruffly, his spoken words seeping telepathically into the lad's head.

'Jaspec, son of Sofulec.'

Morrock let out a grunt.

'What do you know of rogue jinn?'

'That they're a threat to the Realm and mustn't be trusted.'

'D'you fear them?'

Arching his back perfectly straight, young Jaspec swallowed hard.

'*No!*' he called out, his face snarling. 'I have no fear of them at all!'

Morrock frowned, each of his nine eyes colder than the last.

'You must always fear the prisoners!' he bawled. 'If you do not, they will get the better of you. Do you understand?!'

Jaspec blinked awkwardly.

'Yes, Brother Morrock. I understand.'

'You must learn to think like the prisoners, because only then can you know what they are planning.'

'But, Brother Morrock, how do rogue jinn think?'

The veteran malbino raised a hand.

'I'll tell you everything,' he said. 'I will speak and you will listen. Do you understand?'

The student blinked a second time.

13

When all nine of Jaspec's eyes had closed, then opened, Morrock grunted.

'First things first,' he said. 'Follow me.'

'Where are we going?'

'To see the reason you must fear,' said Morrock.

'Are we going to the Prism?' Jaspec asked eagerly. 'Are we going to where rogue jinn are trapped in the cells? Am I to see them for myself?'

Turning, the veteran malbino limped off through the stone cleft, the young trainee guard close on his heels. Jaspec's questions came thick and fast, but all were left unanswered.

Limping through the twists and turns, as though the route were second nature, Morrock caught a flash of himself making the journey for the first time so many decades before: bright-eyed, a slender waistline, nimble feet, and an insatiable zest for life.

It was hard to believe, but even he had been young and sprightly once – a time when he hadn't set eyes on the creature destined to become his nemesis.

All of a sudden, Morrock stopped, the sheer stone walls rising up on either side, their shadows as cold as death.

Half a pace behind, Jaspec froze.

'What is it?' he asked urgently.

'Listen to everything I tell you,' Morrock countered. 'Remember every detail, so that the knowledge becomes you as much as you are yourself.

Most of all, sense my fear, and learn from it.'

'But why must I fear, Brother Morrock?'

'Because if you do not fear the prisoners,' the veteran malbino said, 'they will swallow you whole, spit out your bones, and dance on your soul.'

Six

IN THE COURANT Institute's afternoon session, Dr Moss dropped the lights again and projected the morning's lead story from the *New York Times* website on the back wall.

Scrolling beyond a headline blaring news of the Bank of England heist, he paused on a photograph – a detail of pattern.

The pattern etched into the walls, ceilings, and the floors in each one of the Bank's now-empty bullion vaults.

'Have a good look,' he urged the class.

'What the heck?' blurted the student who had suggested aliens during the morning session.

'As you can see, they're calling it the "Heist of the Century",' said Moss. 'Billions in gold bullion evaporated, and nothing but this pattern left in its place. No intruders, and the alarms didn't even go off. What do you guys make of it?'

The prudish Russian at the front put up her hand.

'Reaction-diffusion pattern sequence,' she said.

The professor nodded.

A Chinese student near the back called out:

'A diagonal matrix of diffusion coefficients.'

Moss paused.

'I'd say you're both right.'

He nudged the side of his hand towards his star pupil.

'What do you think?'

Until then, Oliver had been silent, his mind zoning in and out of fantasy.

'Hmm?'

'The pattern found at the London bank heist,' Moss recapped. 'What's your take on it?'

Pushing a hand back through his hair, Oliver scanned the newspaper article and then the pattern. With the entire class waiting for his answer, he took a moment to reflect.

Conclusions tended to come to him effortlessly, even to the most complex problems. But, for the first time in a long while, Oliver had no answer. He just sat there, while the class waited for him to deliver another dose of characteristic genius.

On the surface, he appeared calm, if baffled like everyone else.

Yet, deep down, something was stirring inside him.

Something as unexplainable as the bullion heist.

Seven

LIMPING DOWN GULLIES little wider than himself, Morrock led the way to the low vaulted tunnel that formed the gateway to the Prism complex.

The colour and texture of rock-hewn lapis lazuli, the walls were dark blue, covered in quastular bats. Hanging in clusters, they squealed in alarm at intruders, their wings glowing gold from fear.

Pacing after the old malbino guard, Jaspec shot out a fresh volley of questions.

Like all the others, they went unanswered.

At the end of the tunnel, Morrock halted and turned sharply.

The eyes on the front of his brow regarded Jaspec with disdain.

'We have reached it,' he snapped. 'From here you must do exactly as I say. Do you understand?'

Less confident than before, Jaspec nodded.

'Very well,' Morrock replied. 'We shall begin.'

Lowering himself onto the tunnel's flooring, he squeezed through a tight aperture, groaning and grunting.

Inches behind him, Jaspec took the last stretch of the shaft with ease.

All of a sudden, the passageway came to an end, opening out into a space.

The Abyss.

Desolate, vast, and utterly mesmerizing, it seemed to defy the laws of scale and possibility.

At its heart lay the Prism.

Rotating on its vertical axis, as it had done for centuries, the great glass penitentiary clattered round – powered by iron sails, the sails driven by the fugian wind.

Jaspec's lower jaw dropped at the sight.

For as long as he could remember he had heard tales of the Prism. Like all other malbinos, he had been weaned on them.

Until that moment, having not seen it for himself, he'd never understood the scale.

Peering round at the young trainee, Morrock felt a twinge of nostalgia, as he remembered the first time his own nine eyes had feasted on the sight.

The veteran malbino limped up to the glass bridge spanning the chasm – from the tunnel to the Prism itself.

'There are seven levels to the penitentiary,' he mumbled, as though the information was almost inconsequential. 'Each one is reserved for an order of jinn. Do you understand?'

Jaspec nodded.

'Yes, Brother Morrock.'

'The uppermost cells contain Species One,' the elder explained. 'They are dull-witted, and can't think more than fifteen seconds ahead. As a result, they're hopeless, hapless, and are easily trapped.'

Reaching the end of the bridge, Morrock leaped down onto the Prism itself.

'When we go past,' he whispered, 'do not look at them directly.'

'Why not, Brother Morrock?'

'Because they scare easily and, when afraid, they swallow themselves.'

The Prism's impregnable glass surface stretched out until it touched the darkness. Brilliantly illuminated from within, it was rock solid, like the surface of a planet, gyrating through space.

Raising the tip of his nose with a thumb, Morrock sniffed the air long and hard. Then, having let out a grunt of satisfaction, he disappeared down a foxhole between the sheets of triangular glass.

Unnerved, Jaspec followed, doing his best to appear brave.

The hole emerged into a long galleried passage.

Identical octagonal cells spanned out on either side, above, and below. The lighting was bright, the air tinged with the faintest touch of haze. A pungent smell lingered there – a mixture of burned honeysuckle and sworp-sworp soap.

Morrock gesticulated at the cells.

'Species One,' he said with loathing. 'All of them imbecilic.'

Jaspec held up a hand.

'What are they here for, Brother Morrock?'

The old malbino cocked the side of his face at the first cell.

'That's a wart jinn from the Kingdom of Smod,' he replied. 'Been here for as long as I can remember. A danger to society, and to himself.'

'What was his crime?'

'Devoured the royal family, after mistaking them for a bowl of mos-mot.'

'*Mos-mot?*'

'The porridge wart jinn like to feast on in the season of Candlemas.'

A creature was curled up behind the glass, its iridescent skin pocked with suppurating warts. Either side of a long bristled snout, a dainty eye was welling with tears.

'How long will he be in here?' Jaspec asked.

Morrock scowled at the question, his back teeth exposed in rage.

'That is no concern of ours!' he roared. 'We are merely guardians in the service of Zonus. You would do well to remember it, do you understand?'

Dipping his head in terror, Jaspec bared his jugular – the malbino way of signalling subservience.

Growling and grunting, Morrock limped on down the passageway.

Either side of it, the glass cells were uniform and empty of anything but the inmates. The cubicles may have been identical, but the rogue jinn prisoners they housed were anything but similar.

Some were as small as marbles, while others were far beyond gigantic. In the same way that an immense black hole is compressed in on itself, even the most unwieldy jinn were contained in a standard-sized cell.

Jaspec followed in Morrock's footsteps, his apprehension doubling with every pace. For the first time in his life he experienced real fear. Suffocating, perplexing, and utterly grim, it was bitter as the sourest grapes from the Kingdom of Kríx.

Peering into the cells, one by one, he was struck by the rogue jinn's astonishing range in form and size.

Some seemed vaguely like malbinos – two arms, legs and a single head. A great many more bore features for which jinn were often known – serpentine scales, barbed fur, serrated talons, hooves, horns, tentacles, and row upon row of shark-like teeth.

They ranged wildly in colour.

A few were pinkish-grey, while others were the shade of pickled walnuts, or blazing red, or any other of ten thousand hues – constantly changing, depending on their mood.

Having passed dozens of cells, Morrock paused, and motioned to the glass floor between his feet.

'That one in there was caught by Epsilius,' he whispered.

21

Jaspec frowned.

'*Epsilius*?'

'The greatest living Jinn Hunter,' Morrock replied. 'Remember the name and honour it as you honour your own ancestors!'

The young malbino peered down into the cell.

Inside, nudged up against one wall, was a trembling mass of turquoise fur. Somewhere near the middle was a single eye, resembling an ostrich egg cracked into a soup tureen. Off-centre below it was an oversized mouth, filled with drool and uneven-shaped teeth.

Moving down along the glass wall, Jaspec's gaze reached the fur and the yellow eye.

Without meaning to go against Morrock's orders, the young malbino found himself drawn in. Before he knew it, he was staring into the pupil, sucked in, as though hypnotized.

Having limped ahead, Morrock froze.

He swivelled round.

As he did so, the turquoise jinn opened its mouth as wide as it could. With teeth gnashing and amid a tidal wave of drool, it began ingesting itself.

Nothing in his wildest dreams could have prepared Jaspec for the sight of a rogue jinn swallowing its own body.

Crying out, the young malbino pounded at the glass with his fists.

Face flushed with rage, Morrock dived forward and punched an octagonal emergency button set into the floor.

Within an instant, the jinn was paralysed.

A moment later and a dozen malbino guards were on the scene, armed with giant callipers, tridents, and nets.

'I didn't mean to,' moaned Jaspec despondently. 'Didn't mean to look at him, but I couldn't help it.'

Morrock spat a salvo of orders at the guards.

Then, stepping close to Jaspec, he sighed.

'Young malbinos like to think of me as cruel,' he intoned tenderly. 'I'm not. But the way I view life in the Prism has been shaped by experience. These nine eyes of mine have witnessed the most terrible sights – the kind which no malbino should ever see. Memories so fearful they haunt my waking life and all my dreams. I have witnessed terrible events take place because of simple mistakes. Mistakes that spiralled out of control.'

Morrock reached out a hand and touched a pair of thumbs to Jaspec's shoulder. 'Never disobey me again,' he said. 'If you do, unthinkable terror will befall you.'

Eight

HALFWAY THROUGH THE afternoon session, Oliver excused himself and made a beeline for the restroom.

Hunched down over the washbasin, he soothed his face in a stream of cool water. He was feeling both hot and cold, focussed and awry, elated and downcast, as though something had tampered with his internal settings.

All of a sudden, he caught sight of himself sitting on a brick wall with Bill Lewis, his best friend since fifth grade. They must have been about twelve. Bill was showing off a prized baseball mitt bought with his savings.

'It's awesome!' Oliver gasped. 'I'm green with jealousy.'

The words had hardly left Oliver's mouth when Bill jerked the mitt off his hand and passed it to his friend.

'For you,' he mumbled.

'What? No! I can't take it! You delivered papers for weeks to earn that!'

Bill's face soured.

'You have to accept it,' he said. 'And you must remember something and never forget it.'

'*What*?'

'That I'm always here for you, just as you are always here for me.'

Nine

JASPEC CLOSE BEHIND him, Morrock slipped down a second foxhole.

After twists and turns, they emerged in another sector of the Prism.

'This is where Species Two are kept,' the veteran guard explained. 'A little more intelligent than the ones above, they're easily trapped. They're panicked by small objects – like grains of sand, buttons, and even by little jinn. There's very little remarkable about them, except their expertise in shape-shifting.'

Jaspec peered into the first cell, in which a lugubrious rodent-like creature was sprawled out. As soon as it spotted the malbinos, it transformed itself into a steel strongbox.

Morrock motioned towards a lumpy odd-shaped protrusion on the side.

'Take notice,' he said.

Jaspec leaned in towards the glass.

'What is it?' he asked, squinting.

'A kind of nostril,' said Morrock. 'Every Species Two jinn are born with an olfactory gland on the bottom of their left foot. No amount of shape-shifting can ever conceal it.'

'Why's it there?' asked Jaspec.

The seasoned malbino guard shrugged.

'Why is any of it as it is?' he replied. 'No one

knows – not even the fopula slugs… and they know everything… or, at least, everything worth knowing.'

'Fopula *who*?'

Morrock turned to the young trainee, his multiple eyes wide.

'You don't know anything, do you?' he snapped.

Jaspec didn't reply.

'Have no fear,' said Morrock, leading the way towards another foxhole, 'you will learn everything soon enough.'

As they descended through the layers of octagonal cells, the Prism's glass grew thicker, and the guards on duty more seasoned.

On every passageway, malbino sentries were stationed at regular intervals, each one alert for the tell-tale signs of dereliction. Checking and rechecking the cells in an endless routine, they regarded every-one and everything with suspicion.

Such was the ingenuity of convict jinn, especially those housed on the lower levels, that nothing was taken for granted. Fifty times a day, the inmates and their cells were inspected. The malbinos on duty were checked as well. After all, the most likely way to escape would be for a shape-shifting jinn to assume the identity of a guard.

Morrock and Jaspec descended deeper into the depths of the Prism.

Every duty guard and official they encountered

saluted the malbino elder, before bowing down low in respect.

'How do they know you're not a jinn in disguise?' asked Jaspec, as he strode slowly down the short passageway.

Morrock felt his back warm with anger at what he regarded as youthful insolence. But, rather than lash out, he replied:

'They know it is me because of the secret.'

'*Secret*?'

'The secret known only to them and me.'

'Will you tell it to me?' Jaspec squirmed. 'Will you tell me the secret?'

Again, the veteran's back warmed and, again, he calmed himself.

'With time you may learn that secret and many others,' he said.

'How long will it take before the secrets are revealed?'

Morrock was tiring of the trainee and the perilous condition of youth.

'A wise malbino would never wish to know any secrets,' he answered, frowning hard.

'But why not, Brother Morrock?'

'Because secrets are accompanied by grave danger.'

Pushing his shoulders back, Jaspec remembered how brave he had claimed to be.

'I'm not frightened,' he said.

27

'*Really?*'

The young malbino did his best to appear defiant.

'Yes.'

'Not frightened of anything?'

Jaspec shook his head.

'Nothing.'

'Then I'll show you something,' said the old malbino calmly.

'What?'

'Come with me.'

A warren of interlinking furrows, passages and gangways came and went, as Morrock and Jaspec clambered further and further into the Prism.

As they descended, the atmosphere grew heavier, as though it was somehow weighed down with terror.

With each level, the passages were shorter, until they were hardly passages at all.

Eventually, they reached the lowest point, where the Species Seven jinn were housed.

The nadir of the inverted pyramid.

Drinking in Jaspec's youthful vigour, Morrock turned to the cell and blinked.

'Go on, have a look.'

'What's in there?'

'The jinn I guard.'

The young malbino craned his neck to look inside.

All he could see was the faintest outline of a form.

His eyes scanning the creature slowly, Jaspec felt

28

a force pressing down on his chest.

'Can't breathe,' he choked, doubling over.

'Is that all you feel?' asked Morrock.

Panting, Jaspec looked towards the cell.

As he did so, he was overcome by a second sensation.

Slipping into his muscles and flesh, it coursed through capillaries and veins, across synapses, and into every fibre of his fur-covered frame.

The sensation was fear.

Pure, perfect fear.

Shaking, Jaspec collapsed onto the glass floor, all nine eyes bloodshot, his palms streaming with sweat.

'*Whhhhhat... what... what's that?*' he wheezed, fighting to make the words audible.

Morrock retreated from the cell's wall, as though even he were not safe.

'It is Nequissimus,' he said.

Ten

THE BANK OF England had been cordoned off, while forensic teams began their work in searching for clues.

Locked down, the City of London was awash with military vehicles and personnel, with both army and police helicopters thundering overhead. Every imaginable government agency had become hastily involved, each one vying for the moral high ground in a post-heist blame game. The Prime Minister was demanding answers, and a name.

The name of someone to hold accountable for the greatest bank robbery in history.

Shortly after eleven a.m., Mortimer Baskart was taken under armed guard to a secure interview unit south of the river. His face was drawn, his lips dry, and his clothing damp with sweat. With only a couple of years before retirement, he worried easily. As his doctor often warned, the stress of guarding bullion was the last thing a man like him needed.

Five minutes after arriving in Interview Room C-6, Baskart was perched on a standard police-issue chair. Across from him was a plain-clothed officer. His accent was private school, and his half brogues handmade.

'I need to know exactly what happened,' said the officer. 'It's as simple as that.'

Mortimer Baskart sighed.

'You might as well lock me up for being a nutter,' he said. 'Because what I saw… and what I'm gonna tell you… it doesn't make any sense.'

The officer glanced at the clipboard in his hand.

'Mortimer,' he said reading the name, 'we just need information. No one's accusing you of anything.'

While Baskart went over what had happened – how

the gold melted like wax before disappearing into the floor – a team of special officers was raiding his flat. Every guard was given the same interrogation, as their lives were ripped apart and thrust into blinding light.

Meanwhile, at the Bank of England, the bullion vaults were subjected to every conceivable forensic test. The patterns etched into the ceilings, walls and floors were run through every known database.

Along with the CCTV footage, and the duty guards' interviews – they provided no clues at all.

Eleven

CLIMBING UP THROUGH a narrow foxhole between the cells, Morrock grimaced in pain.

His right foot was swollen and sore, the upper edge bruised.

For years the veteran malbino had walked with a limp – ever since a clumsy sloth jinn had crushed his foot while being moved from one cell to another. But the pain seemed to be coming from the foot's flesh rather than the bone.

Pausing to rub it gently, Morrock thought back to his childhood dream – becoming a guard at the Prism. Unlike the other malbino offspring, he had always yearned to be stationed in the lowest depth –

at the Seventh Level. The desire to guard the most dangerous rogue jinn came about through ancestral devotion.

For six generations, Morrock's family had served in guarding the most dreaded jinn of all. So respected were they by the other malbinos, it was said they, and they alone, could contain the evil held in the lowest cells. The reason was not special knowledge, but rather that their bloodline had been selected by King Solomon.

Ascending through the passageways, Morrock paused time and again to rub his foot, which was growing more painful all the time. Eventually, he emerged onto the Prism's upper surface.

Night shrouded a group of young malbinos who had kindled a fire. Huddled around it, they were slurping bowls of stew made from the spiced meat of ghost venison. The delicacy was hunted in the cloud forests at Wipiliā and sent to the guards twice yearly by the king.

Sweeping through the heavens above, the vast iron sails clattered round, powered by the fugian wind.

Flames licking the darkness, Morrock took his place across from the youth. Superiority prevented him from sitting too close to the young guards.

As soon as he arrived, the others paused, waiting in respectful silence until he had finished a second bowl of stew. Only when the old malbino had eaten his fill, did they dare raise the beaten bronze ladles to their lips.

Flames sparking and spitting, faces bathed in the glow of expectation, the young guards looked over at Morrock. All of them had heard the tales of evil, terror, and artifice.

Tales containing a single recurring name.

After a long interval of silence, Jaspec put down his empty bowl, closed his mouth, and asked:

'Brother Morrock, will you tell us about *him*?'

'About whom?'

'About the one they call "the great jinn".'

Young faces washed in firelight, the malbinos turned as one. Each of them was well aware how the old jailer abhorred youth.

Lowering the bowl slowly, Morrock burped.

Then, staring into the fire, he rubbed the back of a bristled hand over his bruised foot. Consumed in concentration, he allowed his gaze to range upwards with the sparks, onto the iron sails as they arced slowly round.

'Evil is not dangerous,' he said, the words cold and empty. 'What is dangerous is to forget.'

'To forget what, Brother Morrock?' Jaspec asked.

'To forget the fact that evil has no limit. In its perfect form, pure evil is absolute. It is a circle... a circle of wickedness.'

Plucking up courage, a young malbino on Jaspec's left raised a pair of thumbs.

'Brother Morrock,' he said, his voice shrill, 'will you tell us about the great jinn… about Nequissimus?'

The name hung in the freezing air, as though too corrupted to dissipate into the darkness.

A hand soothing his foot, the old guardian took in the bright young faces. While envying the physical youth, he regretted the communal lack of experience.

'Nequissimus will only rest when he has escaped,' he said. 'When he has brought terror to the entire Realm.'

'But surely, Brother Morrock, there is no chance of him ever getting out,' whispered Jaspec.

The old guardian's gaze descended from the iron sails, back into the flames.

'How wrong you are,' he declared ruefully. 'There is one certainty, and it's that Nequissimus will eventually be free. It is only a question of when and how.'

Twelve

TEN MINUTES AFTER leaving the Courant Institute, Oliver was strolling through Washington Park on his way to visit Uncle Sinan.

A strong late September wind had stripped the

elms of their foliage. Interwoven and forlorn, the leaves covered the path in a thousand shades of golden yellow, bronze, and brown.

Without thinking, Oliver mapped them as he walked.

His mind calmed, it searched for patterns.

All of a sudden, he was in the dhow again, adrift on the sea of dragon's blood.

A young mother had paused beside the Garibaldi statue, a baby in her arms, swaddled tight against the breeze. Straying out from her feet, a long shadow spanned far across the patchwork of fallen leaves.

As he passed her, Oliver observed the freckles on the woman's face, illuminated perfectly in autumn sunlight. Taking a mental snapshot, his subconscious counted them all in a fraction of a moment.

Three hundred and ninety-four freckles.

Two moles.

A small crescent scar on the left side of the chin.

Feet pacing much faster, Oliver found himself contemplating the pattern left during the heist at the Bank of England vault.

How could half a million bars of gold simply disappear?

His mind moving fast, Oliver crunched a sequence of unrelated objects and ideas – like a series of snapshots. They began and ended with the same three mental slides:

Gold bullion.

Chinese satellites.

A tapestry of fallen leaves.

Abruptly, Oliver observed himself from a height.

It was as though a camera in outer space was tracking him as he rounded the circle, and made his way towards the Washington Arch.

To anyone else, the sensation might have been bizarre, almost dreamlike.

But, to Oliver Quinn, it was disturbingly ordinary.

An illusion spilled over from fantasy.

A fantasy that echoed his life.

Thirteen

POISED IN THE corner of his octagonal cell, Nequissimus slipped into an insentient state – a state known to the malbino guards as 'moöl'.

Glowing in putrid grey-green, slippery scales shimmering like algae on the Ocean of Fecund Fear, the great jinn closed its many eyes and began to brood. He was considering the terror he'd wreak on escaping, and the pathetic frailty of the malbinos who guarded him.

As he brooded, he began to tremble ever so slightly.

A trembling that grew, fragment on fragment, until

the octagonal cell's floor and walls were vibrating. Captive jinn in the cells above might have protested, but none dared. They knew full well Nequissimus could snuff out their lives, or drive them to insanity with a single whisper… a whisper hissed in the blink of an unblinking eye.

No creature however mighty was protected from the murmurs of Nequissimus.

No one except for the malbinos.

For three days and nights, the trembling went on.

With each moment, it grew in pitch and volume, until the entire Prism was pulsating. Every last sheet of impenetrable glass was shuddering and grinding, swaying back and forth, the cells ringing with the crazed, screeching clatter of fear.

The senior malbinos held a conclave, as they did at times of crisis. An elderly guard named Spowla suggested petitioning the maragors for help. As the judges of the Realm, it was they who had sentenced the rogue jinn in the first place. The suggestion was overruled by the other members of the conclave. As malbinos, they preferred to reach a solution from within their own ranks.

Dozens of ideas were put forward and discarded.

Eventually, with no agreement, the malbinos turned to Morrock, regarded as the wisest of the clan. As Nequissimus's jailer, the others pleaded with him to come up with a solution.

The veteran guard listened, even though his mind was on his sore foot more than it was on the conclave.

'I will go and speak to the great jinn,' he said, 'and will report back to the conclave within a day and a morsiminal hour.'

'But what if he doesn't stop?' asked one of the malbinos gruffly.

'Then we will draw the matter to the attention of Councilus,' said Morrock.

'*Councilus*?!'

The veteran guard nodded.

'But they are too busy to give a care to us, or to the Prism.'

'Too busy?' quipped another. 'They're not too busy – just too old!'

Holding up a hand, Morrock clicked his thumbs together.

'I would correct you both,' he responded curtly. 'There's no matter quite so important to Councilus, or to anyone or anything in the Realm, as Nequissimus.'

Bidding the others a good night, Morrock limped away.

Level by level, he descended through the passages, until he came to the lowest one.

The level which bore a single cell.

The muscles of his throat swelling with blood, he ordered Nequissimus to cease his disturbance.

But the juddering didn't stop.

So the guard did something he always warned his malbino brethren never on any account to do.

Stepping up to the thick glass wall, he pressed both hands hard to its surface. From long experience he had found the action sometimes calmed wayward jinn.

But touching was perilous.

As he stood there, all ten fingers and four thumbs flush against the glass, the old malbino guard sensed his bruised foot throbbing all the more. The skin beneath the slime-soaked bristle already raw, it began to bleed.

Morrock struggled to snatch his hands from the cell wall.

But they were stuck.

He couldn't move them.

All the while, sheets of glass trembled, shook and quaked, as though supernatural rage was being vented. Through centuries of incarceration, the great jinn had mastered patience, waiting for the right moment to hatch the perfect plan.

Both palms fixed to the cell wall, Morrock peered down at his right foot. As he watched, the bloodied bristle and skin fell away.

Gradually, a growth sprouted.

Developing little by little, it grew into a curled, shell-like form.

Strangely familiar, it resembled a large pink ear.

An almost human-looking ear.

Reclining sedately at the back of his cell, Nequissimus glowed grey-green, his emerald eyes wide and unflinching. Only when the ear had reached maturity, did the great jinn – the most despotic in all existence – allow his three lips to part.

Fighting to free himself from the glass, Morrock had guessed what was about to take place.

But it was too late.

The whispering had begun.

Fourteen

IN A FOREST beyond the gristial rainbow stood a tree so ancient its wizened trunk was half-petrified, its boughs weathered and bleak.

Under the tree, in a pool of perpetual shadow, lay a granite rock neither remarkable nor large. None of the creatures in the forest, nor even the tree itself, had ever noticed the object.

But, under the rock lay a cavern.

A cavern of stupendous size.

A cavern filled floor to ceiling – and from rock-hewn wall to rock-hewn wall – with pure gold.

Gold thrones from the court of Nebuchadnezzar, and golden shields from the age of Seti I; cutlery and vases, chests, ingots, and mounds of plates – all fashioned from solid gold. Too many sacks of pure gold coins to ever be counted. Gleaned from every imaginable minting, they were embossed with the profiles and monograms of princesses, emperors, queens, and kings.

There were gold bars, too – millions upon millions of them, cast hastily into the cavern by the owner of the hoard.

Reclining on a golden chaise longue at the back was an amply built aduxa jinn, named Soulia. In each of her three paws was clutched a solid gold plate – from a service made for Louis XIV.

With eyes wide, her huge mouth drooling, she sank her front teeth into the first dish, feasting on the yellow metal.

Like a good many jinn of her species, Soulia was slothful and attracted to shiny objects. Her own unrivalled obsession was with the precious metal. It was the only thing she ever thought about, and the only food she ever ate.

For decades, she had kept a watchful eye on the vaults beneath Threadneedle Street, biding her time until the perfect moment.

The moment at which sloth was overcome by greed.

Fifteen

An Aladdin's cave of exquisite Oriental carpets, Ozymandias & Son was sandwiched between a pair of proud brownstones on East 8th Street.

Owned by Oliver's uncle, Sinan, it had been in the Quinn family for four generations. On the run from creditors, his ancestor, Cem, had set out for the New World, stowing away on a packet steamer as it took on supplies on the banks of the Bosphorus.

The storefront was modest, its painted sign peeling, the woodwork around the large window battered by the elements. But, inside, the salon was packed with woven treasures from Samarkand, Anatolia, Bokhara, Shiraz, and beyond.

In all Manhattan no connoisseur of Oriental textiles was quite so learned as Sinan of Ozymandias & Son. His reputation was the stuff of legend, his name whispered in elevated circles. Sinan Quinn, it was said, could describe a carpet and its provenance blindfold, merely by holding it to his nostrils.

At three that afternoon, Oliver pushed open the door. A Tibetan temple bell chimed gently inside, signalling a customer.

Pacing through the salon, Oliver dropped his daypack down, and sat cross-legged on a fabulous Turcoman carpet. Hand-knotted by nomads in the Karakum Desert a century before, it was adorned with an intricate design, a kaleidoscope of colour – deep reds, blues and indigo. Yet it was not the colour or even the pattern that was most mesmerizing, but the smell.

The carpet had a scent like nothing else. Dark crushed spice, fragrant tones of sandalwood and driftwood, sulphur, and the sea.

A sea of dragon's blood.

No one in the world was closer to Oliver than Uncle Sinan. Since his parents had vanished on a frozen winter morning sixteen years earlier, the elderly uncle – who had always seemed timeworn – had brought up his nephew. A figure shrouded in mystery, Uncle Sinan was intensely private, deeply eccentric, and unlike anyone else.

As a young child, Oliver perceived that his uncle understood him in a deep-down way, as if from the inside out. While other parents were teaching their kids facts and figures, Uncle Sinan was raising his nephew in what was regarded by most as a world of nonsensical fantasy.

The shop's door may have been unlocked, but its owner never appeared at first, not even when Oliver arrived. Uncle Sinan believed a customer, a friend, or even a member of the family, should have time to savour the atmosphere in silence, while alone.

Powers of observation were at their height in solitude, he said.

Still seated on the Turcoman carpet, Oliver leaned back against a stack of Berber carpets from the Moroccan Atlas. Knitting his fingers together, he allowed his eyes to close. When they were blind, he inspected the shop, as Uncle Sinan had taught him to do.

First, he gazed up at the ceiling, all cracked and blistered. Panning slowly down, he took in the rows of neatly furled carpets – Turkish kilims and Afghan tribal rugs, fabulous suzanis from Uzbekistan, silk carpets from Persia, and woollen ones from the Caucasus.

So familiar to Oliver, he had committed the patterns to memory. Even with eyes closed he could see them in absolute detail – remembering when a weaver's fingers had slipped and missed a line. Or, when an intricate pattern recurred, feeding back into itself.

But it wasn't the carpets which held Oliver's attention most.

On the salon's back wall an array of objects was arranged on shelves. A treasure trove gleaned from all continents and all times, a collection that was in itself the seed of fantasy.

Even before he was tall enough to inspect the objects, Oliver had been obsessed with them. Eyes closed tight, he examined his favourites.

A corroded astrolabe, recovered from a sunken dhow.

The carved molar of a narwhale.

Six phials filled with flying ointment from a Magian court.

The pickled left lung of an albino ostrich.

An iron box filled with powdered antimony.

Breathing shallow, his eyes opening, Oliver raised a hand to his brow.

The sunlight was blinding.

Twin suns roasting from a purple sky.

The dhow's keel coursed through blood-red waves towards the horizon.

'Expected you an hour ago,' said a low, deliberate voice.

Oliver blinked, the waves melting into the rugs.

Uncle Sinan was climbing up the stone steps from the basement, leading to a hatch at the far end of the salon. His stout form was dressed in a blue tunic, like the ones worn in ancient times by the Ainu of Hokkaido, his bare feet sprinkled in fine golden sand. His balding head was tanned, the nose severe, the forehead overly long, and the cheeks dusted with grey stubble.

'I was on an ocean,' Oliver said distractedly. 'In a frail little dhow, with a triangular sail, and...'

Uncle Sinan smiled.

'And a hull peppered with limpets?'

'Yes.'

'Thought as much.'

'But how did you know?'

'Because I once crossed three worlds in her,' Uncle Sinan said.

Sixteen

A MISERABLE TANGLE of despondency, Nequissimus's whispers were fearful and raw like the death throes of the golden waziz.

Seeping down into Morrock's newly grown ear, up through his spine and into his brain, they breached every synapse and slipped into every cell.

As they did so, they remapped symmetry and order with chaos.

Within fifteen seconds, Morrock had gone insane.

Hands having broken free, he writhed on the ground, his nine eyes rolling, the rows of serrated malbino teeth gnawing at his bristled arms and chest.

On the other side of the glass, Nequissimus took his time to rise. Peering around the cell, his home for centuries, he touched a claw to the corner of an emerald eye.

A moment later, Morrock was standing as well.

Bloodied, panting, his mind fevered and convulsing, he uttered a single word – the secret password to free the locks and cease the Prism's mechanism.

Known only to himself, it was spoken backwards,

inside out, and upside down. So secret was it, no other creature even knew it existed. Passed down through fifty generations of Morrock's line, father to son, the password had been created by the Prism's architect. Hailing from a family of locksmiths in the Dominion of Astrip-Pi, he had believed no lock should be impregnable. So, he built the password into the mechanism, entrusting it to a confidant – Morrock's own ancestor.

Lost in mania, his white bristled torso drenched in his own blood, the veteran guard fell backwards.

As he did so, the password took effect.

The mechanism jammed.

The great iron sails paused for a moment.

The Prism ceased turning – just long enough for the great jinn to mount his long-awaited escape.

A blinding flash.

A flash followed by clamours of horror and resounding joy.

A second flash.

Nequissimus was free.

Seventeen

UNCLE SINAN CROSSED the salon.

Cupped in his hands was a box crafted from aromatic thuya wood from the Moroccan desert... a box dented by hope, fear, and adventure.

Placing it on a carpet, he turned it with care so the clasp faced his nephew.

'What is it?' Oliver asked, the corner of his mouth easing into a smile.

Sinan pressed the tips of his leathery fingers together.

'A surprise,' he whispered in reply.

Oliver's own fingers wrestled with the clasp.

'It's locked.'

Reaching around his neck, the carpet seller tugged out a slender leather cord. Dangling on the end was a miniature silver key.

Uncle Sinan winked.

'One way to find out what's inside.'

The key slipped into the lock, turned clockwise twice, then anticlockwise once, and once again.

Only then did the mechanism click.

Oliver paused before opening the lid.

A moment to imagine and to dream.

Whatever was contained inside was unlikely to be usual – of that he was certain. After all, the unusual was the only currency his uncle valued.

Oliver shuddered as, in his subconscious, the dhow's keel collided with coral. The sun's heat roasted him from beneath his skin, as though cooking him from the inside out.

Breathing in hard, his eyes wide, Oliver jerked back the box's lid.

Inside was a plain lead disc, the size and shape of an ice hockey puck.

Oliver frowned.

'Go on, take it out,' Sinan urged.

His right hand delving into the box, Oliver scooped the object out, sensing the cool weight on his palm.

Turning it into the light, he noticed at once how the sides were adorned in a kind of interwoven frieze. As for the upper surface, it was etched with a curious relief – like the iris of an oversized eye.

A dragon's eye…?

'What is it?' he mumbled, intrigued.

'A paperweight,' replied Uncle Sinan. 'Been in the family for a very long time. Passed down, from father to son. I've looked after it long enough. It's time for me to pass it on.'

'Where's it from?'

Sinan's eyes disappeared in creases, beaming a Cheshire cat smile.

He shrugged.

'From the East,' he said.

'Whereabouts in the East?'

Standing up, the shopkeeper ambled towards the door. Just before he was out of sight, he replied:

'Where an object comes from is not always what matters most.'

Sitting there on the Turcoman rug, Oliver weighed the paperweight in his hand. Although heavy, it was apparently hollow – for solid lead would have been far heavier still.

Holding the upper surface up to his face, he observed the pattern.

The eye.

What he supposed was a dragon's eye.

As he did so, something extraordinary happened.

The paperweight warmed.

Then the eye came alive.

Blinking, it became dull grey lead again.

Eighteen

A FEW MINUTES of silence passed before Uncle Sinan tramped back up from the basement.

Under his left arm was a rolled-up rug, wrapped in brown paper and parcel string. He was dressed in a pea-green safari suit, suede hunting boots on his feet. In his right hand was a walking cane.

Oliver frowned.

He hadn't seen his relative go back downstairs. But his mind wasn't on his uncle, on his costume, or on the package ready for delivery. The front door opened, and the soles of the boots stepped out onto the pavement.

When the Tibetan temple bell was silent, Oliver placed the paperweight on the Turcoman carpet.

He couldn't take his eyes off it.

Both ancient and obscure, there was a supernatural quality about it, as though it was not the work of humankind, but a throwback to another time.

Even though Uncle Sinan was a champion of the fantastic, Oliver decided right there and then not to tell him what he had seen – or rather what he had thought he had seen.

Instinct urged him to keep the secret.

At least for now.

Picking up the paperweight, he got to his feet, his mind willing the dragon's eye to come to life again.

But it did not.

So Oliver turned to place the object on the long table under the shelves, wondering whether he had imagined the eye blink.

As he did so, the ground began to tremor.

Not a distinct vibration like an earthquake, so much as if a tunnelling machine was boring away beneath the carpet shop.

The shaking climaxed.

Then, suddenly…

An explosion!

Hurled across the room, ears ringing, Oliver sensed his bloodstream flood with adrenalin.

Dropping the paperweight as he tumbled, he watched as it flew in slow motion across the shop.

One by one, it bounced down the stone steps, disappearing into the basement's darkness.

Getting to his feet, Oliver rushed to the window and peered out.

A homeless woman had gone nuts. She had purple hair and a supermarket trolley laden with anxious-looking cats. A stray old tom clutched to her chest, she was wielding a butcher's cleaver, with which she was threatening frantic passers-by.

Quickly, Oliver scanned the street.

It wasn't clear what had caused the explosion. Except for the crazy woman, everything else appeared relatively normal. For New York, a crazed woman with a cleaver and a trolley of cats *was* normal.

Oliver's subconscious took over, plotting the pedestrians on a grid, as they would have been half a second before the blast:

Six commuters hurrying home.

A pair of mothers out with their strollers.

A cop on his beat.

A fifth-grader waiting for a friend.

The crazy woman with purple hair.

Determining the angles between each one, as

though they were pins peppering a map, Oliver's mind strained to stay calm.

Then he remembered the paperweight.

It had fallen when he'd tumbled.

Bounced, rolled, and bounced some more.

Even though he hadn't been concentrating, he had seen it arc across the salon, through the hatch, down the stairs, and into the basement's grim underworld.

Quickly, Oliver strode through to the back of the shop, where the hatch framed a rectangle of darkness.

A cold, disturbing rectangle of fear.

Since early childhood he had avoided the hatch, dreading it and what lay beyond.

With good reason.

One summer, his uncle's careless Colombian assistant, Lolita, had locked him down there by mistake. He couldn't have been more than seven, or six. Through an entire August afternoon he had crouched at the foot of the steps – shaking, whimpering, seeking sanctuary in a domain of his own fantasy.

But that was a long time ago.

Oliver was a grown man now, a senior in college, far too mature to be worried by dark basements.

As he took a deep breath, his hand reached in and yanked the chain.

An arc of low-watt light brought life to the

subterranean chamber. Cautiously, Oliver climbed down, grimacing with unease.

As his eyes adjusted, he took in the stock.

Carpets and rugs tied up in hessian sacks.

Hundreds of them.

Silhouettes of woven treasure from all corners of the East.

Treasure thick with roaches, cobwebs, and layered with waxy black dust.

Oliver's mind counted the treads as he went.

Ten... eleven... twelve...

The wooden steps gave way to flagstones.

Cool flagstones on which he had crouched that summer afternoon – voice hoarse from screaming, eyes swollen from tears.

The sharpest detail of memory was the smell.

Not the smell of the basement, but of his own skin. Fortified with adrenalin, his sweat had smelled astringent, like the spray of a tom-cat marking territory.

Hurriedly, Oliver searched the shadows between the bales. He was determined to find the paperweight fast, grab it, and get out as speedily as he could.

But there was no sign of it.

Heaving away random sacks, he hunted behind them. As he did so, the flagstones came alive with roaches, their backs glinting in the creamy yellow light.

Oliver stooped to rearrange another pile of sacks,

when he noticed a little alcove: a recess where the last stair met the base of the wall.

The paperweight was lodged there flat against the stone.

Grooming roaches fretfully from his shirtfront, Oliver leaned down and shoved his hand into the niche. As his fingers jostled about, his thumb pressed down squarely on the pattern etched into the upper surface.

Instantly, the metal warmed.

Tightening his hold, Oliver struggled to jerk the object out.

But, however hard he tried, it wouldn't budge – as though it were rooted to the floor.

Grappling with one hand, then with both, he cupped his fingers around the object. Wrestling with it, he clawed at it, arms heaving, forehead beading with perspiration.

Losing grip, he fell backwards.

As he did so, the dragon's eye came alive again.

Bright and confident, it blinked twice.

Staring down at it, Oliver froze.

For the first time he'd forgotten his fear of the store-room. Terror conjured in childhood was replaced by something else.

By a sense of primitive belief.

The dragon's eye grew more vivid and alert, the iris deepening into golden amber.

Silently, it glanced right.

Left.

Up.

Down.

Spotting Oliver, who was recoiled backwards in a pile of sacks, it observed him with interest.

A full minute passed.

Too alarmed to move, Oliver just lay there, watching the eye watch him. Eventually, he swallowed. Lips parting, he drew in a breath of musty basement air.

As he exhaled, the eye blinked.

From the amber iris a rectangle of uniform blackness was projected. As high as a man is tall, edges blurred, it was blacker than anything existing in nature.

It wasn't two- or even three-dimensional.

Nor was it bound by the limits of anything we are taught to know or understand. Like some newly discovered matter acquired in secrecy from the farthest reaches of science fiction, it was known only to itself.

His breathing shallow, Oliver marvelled at the rectangle, taking in its subtle beauty.

Like a siren bent on seducing him, it seemed to be flirting – not in an obvious or expected way – but through an absence of communication.

Oliver's mind went blank. He couldn't think or feel, hear, taste, or even smell.

All he could do was watch.

Unable to move, he sensed his attention being drawn into the rectangle's spectral depth.

Gradually, images began to appear.

A few at first.

Then, hundreds.

Thousands.

Millions.

Billions.

Randomly, they were projected all at once – together, and each one alone:

An old sea wall, battered and bleak.

A sparrow swooping through a sunset sky.

A pair of lovers standing arm in arm.

A dog with three legs.

A book of poetry, the cover stained blue.

A forest in Finland, low winter sun breaking through the trees.

A falling leaf, the edges tinged with brown.

A box of windproof matches.

An elderly blind man standing amid piles of Spanish books.

Day-old chicks dyed pink.

Weathered prayer flags at a monastery in Tibet.

A washerwoman gossiping to her friend.

A spider.

An ox.

A clock.

A ballerina's shoe.

A limpet shell washed up on the beach.

A carved coco de mer.

A lake, its rippled waters flush with dolphins.

A mutton sausage cut lengthways.

A racing car buried in snow.

The faculty for reasoning suspended, Oliver sensed the images slipping inside him by a primitive osmosis. Soon they were part of him, as though they were his own memories.

Unable to prevent it, his mind sought patterns in the projection. It linked the coconut to the beach, and the beach to the ballet shoe, and the shoe to the woman gossiping, and the woman to the clock.

Each image was linked to every other, set in a grid, and stored away in the depths of Oliver's subconscious mind.

As more and more images were added to the immeasurable catalogue, the more Oliver became a part of the projection.

His back warming, he perceived a stream of extraordinary possibility laid out before him.

Beckoning.

Luring.

Urging him to follow his instinct.

Widened eyes locked on the flow of images, his mouth dry, Oliver reached out a hand.

Seeking information rather than answers, his

fingers moved in slow motion towards the projection. By inches, they drew closer and closer, until the fingertips were actually touching the images...

Images scrolling forward and sideways at lightning speed.

Soaked in detail and colour, Oliver's hand moved into the images and beyond.

Like milk and cookies before bed, they were soothing. Not in an obvious or superficial way, but as an essence.

The essence of a mother's voice lulling her babes to sleep.

Of security.

Destiny.

Hope.

Before he knew it, Oliver's entire hand had disappeared into the projection.

Then his wrist, his arm, and his shoulder.

Face pressed up close to the stream, his eyes strained to focus, his mind lured by the tranquillity.

Without fearing or fighting, Oliver allowed his head to slip through.

A moment of distorted limbo came and went.

Then the rest of him followed...

... into the world beyond.

Nineteen

BLESSED WITH AN imagination more honed than any ever conjured into existence, Nequissimus was capable of conceiving the most outlandish feats of evil and wonder.

In the centuries languishing at the Prism's nadir, he had amused himself by considering all manner of curiosities. Stretching the imagination was a way of passing time, second in interest only to planning the minutiae of revenge.

Now he was free, the great jinn was ready to initiate the total and splendid retribution he had imagined in perfect detail. But before he could unleash unadulterated havoc, he would need to pause.

Three thousand years of confinement had weakened him, and he still needed to be reunited with his soul. Without it, he was in grave danger of being trapped once again.

Having broken free from the Prism, Nequissimus counselled himself to follow the plan he had formulated during his long confinement. All seven of his hearts were coaxing him to strike for immediate vengeance.

But his head shunned them.

In line with plans laid down over millennia, first he would regain his strength. After that he would seek out his soul and free it. Then, and only then, would he be ready to destroy the Realm.

Seething, Nequissimus made a beeline for the Dominion of Farlippia-Ox. Distant from Zonus, the territory was universally considered by all forms – jinn included – as a singularly wretched place. Barren, and yet suffocatingly humid, it was devoid of any vegetation. The only remarkable feature was the colour of the ground – an alluring silvery-blue.

Materializing at a designated spot, Nequissimus closed his eyes. With slow determination, he inhaled. Not the kind of breath one might use to speak. Nor even the gasp a drowning man would take to save his life. But a breath so great as to almost be unending.

His many lungs filled to capacity, Nequissimus opened one eye after another.

And, lowering his head towards the ground, he exhaled.

Supremely powerful, a cascade of freezing wind rained down on a precise spot, stripping away the topsoil and the rocks beneath.

The great jinn blew and blew and, as he did so, a vertical shaft was carved into the ground.

Within minutes it was so deep that it echoed as though it extended to the limits of space and time.

Nequissimus paused.

Stroking a claw to the nape of his neck, he dipped his head into the hole, and descended.

Down through a thousand leagues of rock and compacted bone.

Down until the black was squeezed out, replaced by light.

Down far.

Further.

And further still.

Until he arrived at a cavern.

A cavern where, before being captured by King Solomon, he had concealed something.

A sack.

A sack filled with leaves.

Necromantic leaves to restore his strength.

Twenty

ON THE OTHER side of the projection, the light was dim and subdued, even more so than in the basement.

No sound at all.

The faint scent of lemongrass created a reassuring sense of retreat, like that of a long tepid bath on a Sunday evening.

Oliver stood absolutely still.

Calm yet curious, he found himself standing at the top of a grand spiral staircase. Sweeping round and around, its ornate golden balustrade was adorned with polished gemstones. The steps were crafted from black porphyry, expertly rounded at the edges.

At the bottom of the staircase, in the heart of the spiral, lay a second dragon's eye.

Alert and omnipotent, it was inspecting the intruder.

Overwhelmed with curiosity, Oliver stepped onto the first stair. Glancing down at his feet, he realized they were invisible. He could feel them, but not see them. Instead, his ankles appeared to be hovering above the jet-black steps.

One by one, Oliver descended.

With each step, he found himself reliving memories – memories he had forgotten long before.

The gold molar at the back of his second-grade teacher's mouth.

The day when the fire hydrant on East 8th Street had burst.

The taunts endured for being a geek in physics class.

The strains of a cellist playing Bach in Central Park.

With each step, the memories increased in clarity.

Some were good, others bad.

Each was tethered to emotion.

As Oliver descended, his hand caressing the golden balustrade, his invisible feet taking the steps one by one, he peered down.

The black porphyry was gone – replaced with crushed blue glass.

Then the glass vanished, swapped for a cascade of tiny white daisies.

Undeterred by the changing surroundings, Oliver continued down the spiral.

As he descended, the daisies began to bleed, streaming with droplets of crimson blood.

Scorching brown with heat, they turned to dust.

Creepers and vines flourished over the steps and balustrade, empty space transformed into jungle luxuriance.

Oliver caught a stray thought of Uncle Sinan in his favourite hat.

A grey trilby with a hen's feather tucked under the band.

He remembered the kitten they had saved from drowning.

Uncle Sinan reading to him from the *Arabian Nights*.

Suddenly, Oliver was affected by melancholy.

The hat had blown away in a storm.

The kitten was poisoned.

The book destroyed by fire.

As Oliver's mood grew more sombre, so did the memories.

Mr McGowan accusing him of cheating because no one had ever got full marks on the test.

JINN HUNTER

Oliver's hand was bleeding, slashed with a carving knife.

Worst of all – his parents were gone.

Long faces.

An ocean of tears.

Taking the steps even more slowly, Oliver observed as the jungle matured. It was thick with insects, with animals and birds. As before, it was utterly silent, like a movie played with the sound muted.

Nearing the bottom of the staircase, Oliver sensed a pang of primeval fear.

A few feet away, the eye was feasting on his memories.

The jungle was so dense Oliver wondered how he would ever get back up the stairs. Suddenly, beyond the eye and the seething mass of undergrowth, he spied an outline.

Straight-edged and orderly.

A door.

A door covered in a pattern of repeated scales – like the armoured frame of a prehistoric fish.

Drifting towards it as though in a dream, Oliver felt a blast of searing desert heat on the back of his neck.

He turned fast.

The jungle was burning.

Creepers, vines, succulents, and trees – all ablaze. Shielding his face, he charged back up the staircase, his invisible feet taking the steps three at a time.

Reaching the top of the staircase, he gasped for air. Stooping low so as to stay out of the billowing smoke, he fumbled his way over to the projection.

The images were streaming even faster than before.

All at once and one by one.

Distorted by heat, blurred, shrouded in swirling grey, they were reversed – a mirror image of the other side.

Oliver leapt at the projection.

Slamming at it full tilt, he bounced back into the smoke.

Again, he tried to break through.

And again.

Then a fourth time.

But it was no good.

The projection wouldn't allow him to pass.

Desperate, chest tight, clothing drenched in sweat, Oliver fumbled for a handle, an opening, or a lock.

The projected images seemed more frenzied than before, as if affected by Oliver's own panic.

A war zone with villages burnt out.

A homeless man, his legs covered in sores.

A hurricane making landfall.

An assassin's dagger dripping with blood.

The smoke was getting thicker, easing out the

last strains of soft light. Eyes streaming, his lungs inflamed, Oliver slumped on the ground, his face pressed up into the projection's glow.

There was no hope.

But something inside him was speaking.

A kind of survival mechanism, a machinery that had lain dormant all Oliver's life.

Coaxing him gently, it urged him to think in a new way – to make use of a knowledge hard-wired inside him, a part of every cell.

Search for the pattern... like the patterns you see in everything.

Your life depends on it.

Wiping a blackened shirt-sleeve to his eyes, Oliver strained to focus on the reversed projection. Choking, wheezing, grimacing, he took in the flow of images conjured from the dragon's eye.

For once, there was no pattern.

The objects and the places, the people, emotions, and ideas – each was completely unconnected.

Each was isolated, an island in itself.

Placing his hands on either side of the projection, Oliver absorbed every last detail, every fragment of insignificance. The images washed in and out through his eyes and against his skin, like waves tumbling to the shore.

Oliver saw himself from a distance, crouching there, face pressed up against the stream of life and light. Overwhelming and enveloping, the smoke hung like a veil of death.

Reaching into himself, Oliver struggled to see in a new way.

The images hadn't made sense before. Their randomness was maddening, frustrating to an order-seeking mind. The reverse of what they had been, they were linked in a converse way.

All of a sudden a pattern revealed itself.

A pattern derived from the fact there was no pattern.

Joining the chain links together, Oliver arrived at an answer, although unsure of how he had done so.

The answer made no sense, but he was certain of it.

The image of a sundial covered in dew.

Scanning the projection, he searched for it, drawing the sequence through his skin and into his bones.

Suddenly, he saw it…

A sundial fixed awkwardly to the wall of an English country church, damp with early morning dew.

Thrusting a hand forward, Oliver touched it.

Little by little, his hand, arm, and body followed.

Instantly, he was back in the basement at Ozymandias & Son, the dull lead paperweight resting on his palm.

Twenty-one

THROUGH DAYS AND nights Soulia the aduxa jinn gorged herself on gold.

The more she consumed, the more crazed with greed she became.

On a single morning of feasting she devoured fifty golden lamps crafted in the reign of King Cambyses I, thirty sacks of gold coins pilfered from a wreck off the southern shores of Crete, and two hundred and two bars of bullion so recently acquired from the vaults beneath Threadneedle Street.

Cackling with glee, she stretched out on the magnificent golden chaise longue for a mid-morning siesta. As she drifted towards bloated slumber, an elongated nostril on the right side of her face sounded an alarm.

There was gold nearby.

Soulia scratched a claw down her chin.

Of course there was, she thought. The precious metal surrounded her.

Again, the nostril sniffed – longer and more forcefully than before.

Sitting up, the aduxa jinn concentrated.

As if her life depended on it, she inhaled. In a great twisting stream of sensation, she took in the scent of the cavern and its hoard, the rock walls of the cavern, and the forest above.

Diving into the sea of yellow metal, she materialized herself out of the cavern and up into the forest.

There, beside a boulder and beneath the petrified tree, lay the most perfect object she had ever seen.

A monumental block of pure gold, fashioned in the form of a bull mammoth.

Twenty-two

THE TIBETAN TEMPLE bell chimed as the shop door opened, then again as it snapped shut.

Crossing the salon, Uncle Sinan checked the wall clock against the antique Omega strapped to his wrist. Considering he was the most even-tempered man alive, he seemed unnerved. At such times, the only thing capable of calming him was the uniform *tick-tick-tick* of Swiss clockwork.

While delivering the carpet to a regular customer on the other side of Greenwich Village, the elderly shopkeeper had witnessed something he had hoped never to see.

Proof that the unthinkable had occurred.

Hurrying back to the shop, his nimble feet had paced at double speed, his face drained.

As the Tibetan bell fell silent, Oliver trudged up the stairs, the paperweight in his hand. He may have torn through tangled forests, chased fire, and breathed in plumes of slimy smoke, but there wasn't a mark on him.

Silently, he clambered out through the rectangle framing the darkness.

'You will never believe it, Uncle,' he said, his voice trembling.

'*Believe*? Believe what?'

'Believe what happened down there.'

Uncle Sinan turned towards the hatch. He remembered Oliver's fear.

'Thought you swore you'd never go down there again.'

Oliver held up the paperweight.

'It rolled down. Don't ask me how. There was a blast. And a mad woman with a carving knife and a trolley full of cats.'

'I've lost you,' said Uncle Sinan.

'This isn't a paperweight,' Oliver explained. 'It's anything but that. The eye... the dragon's eye. I'm certain that's what it was... It came alive. I saw everything in the world – all at the same time. A grand phantasmagoria. I slipped through... through the eye.'

'And where did it take you?'

'Into another world.'

Silently, Uncle Sinan filled a porcelain cup with

hot water from the brass samovar in the corner. Holding it up to the light, he looked round at his nephew, and managed half a smile.

'Dragon's eye?' he said. 'Sounds fantastic.'

'That's what it was – *fantastical*!'

'Pleased to hear it,' his uncle mused. 'After all, I've always encouraged you to drink from the cup of fantasy.'

Bristling, Oliver put the paperweight down.

'Indeed you have,' he replied. 'But this time it wasn't fantasy.'

'Not fantasy?'

'No.'

'Then what?'

'It was real. Utterly real.'

'What did you see?'

'A spiral staircase made from stone. Little flowers dripping with blood. A forest grew up as I watched, and…'

'And an ocean of dragon's blood?' Uncle Sinan grinned. 'Told you… I've sailed on it myself. I know it like the back of my hand.'

Oliver slumped onto the Turcoman rug.

His eyes tracing the pattern, he wondered whether it had all been a daydream.

'Must be going crazy,' he whispered. 'Like the woman out there with purple hair.'

Uncle Sinan paced over to the door and bolted it.

He pulled down the shutters, closing up Ozymandias & Son for the day.

'Something's in the air,' he said obliquely. 'Can't tell you what it is, but it's dangerous. You're to stay with me tonight.'

Twenty-three

THE EVENING WAS punctuated with wailing sirens – police cars, and ambulances, fire trucks, and even the bomb squad.

The woman with purple hair, carving knife, and cats, was apparently not the only one on edge.

She was the tip of the iceberg.

An iceberg of lunacy.

All over the city, manifestations of the most bizarre behaviour were taking place.

At Grand Central Station, a businessman ripped off his pinstripe suit in the middle of the evening rush. Pouring a jar of honey over his head, he crawled around on all fours, begging people to lick it off. Instead of avoiding him, the other commuters got down on their hands and knees, and licked him clean.

At the corner of Broadway and West 72nd Street, a hotdog seller held down a passer-by and rammed a bratwurst down his throat, while plucking his eyebrows.

TAHIR SHAH

Six Korean tourists managed to get entry onto the roof of the Flatiron Building. Tied together with canary-yellow cord, they sprayed their heads with shaving cream, and leapt over the edge.

At a gas station in Harlem, an attendant covered himself in premium gasoline and struck a match. Rather than putting out the blaze, his fellow station workers danced around him, applauding.

Teams of news crews criss-crossed Manhattan, their reporters feasting on the oddity, channelling the stories to viewers across the country. An ABC Special was devoted to whether New York had finally lost its marbles. Another, on CNN, considered whether a new and subversive form of terrorism was to blame.

On Central Park West, the celebrated and fearless reporter, Marcie Spark, touched up her makeup and sprayed her hair.

A moment later, the glaring lights were on.

'The Big Apple's rarely known for sanity,' she began, the words slipping out through fire-engine lips. 'But it seems tonight New Yorkers have finally succumbed – and without a full moon in sight!'

Marcie Spark was about to hand back to the studio when, left of field, something caught her eye.

A blur of indistinct shape moving in a beeline towards her.

Dropping the microphone, she swivelled round, and screamed.

As she did so, the mass engulfed her.

From across the street a handful of well-heeled New Yorkers looked on in horror. They watched as a multitude of creatures attacked Marcie Spark and the ABC crew.

Dogs, cats, rats, birds, and insects – each more animated than the last.

With the attack at an end, the food chain turned on itself, halting only when almost every creature had been consumed.

Twenty-four

IN THE APARTMENT above Ozymandias & Son, Oliver and his uncle were glued to the *ABC Special*.

They watched Marcie Spark's signature red lips smudge into the camera lens, before slipping sideways to the ground.

'Bizarre,' said Oliver.

'Not good,' whispered Uncle Sinan.

'Like you said – there must be something in the air.'

The shopkeeper pulled a large handkerchief from his wrist and blew his nose. His compact form rigid as ever, his back ramrod straight, he appeared unusually tense.

'Sometimes we can't understand things,' he said

reflectively, 'especially when we struggle to make sense of them.'

Oliver looked round.

'Meaning what?'

'Meaning there are limits. We think we're masters of the world around us, but we're not. We're just apes who did quite well.'

Oliver got a flash of the afternoon session with Dr Moss. He saw the pattern from the Bank of England vault, and the unsolved mystery of the heist.

'D'you ever get the feeling we're only seeing a fragment?'

'A fragment of what?'

'Of the full picture.'

Uncle Sinan observed his nephew so seriously it seemed as though the room went cold.

'Constantly,' he said.

Twenty-five

HERBERT MORLIB WAS sitting in the front window of his store on West 72nd Street, watching the morning's chaos outside.

A few yards away, New Yorkers were acting most bizarrely, as the lunacy touched the lives of more and more.

Hunched over in an old armchair, his skin silvery-grey, his mouth crooked to the side by a stroke, Herbert let out an unhurried sigh. Too old to be surprised by anything at all, he could remember a time when life was very different.

Business was slower than slow.

Indeed, it was so slow that no one had come in for weeks. A great many shopkeepers might have been bothered at the lack of customers, but it was just as Herbert liked it.

Customers meant unnecessary conversation.

A lack of them gave time for memories.

As the ripened old optician liked to reminisce, at one time the name 'Morlib' was known far and wide. Movie stars and millionaires had been regulars. Droves of well-dressed customers had once queued down the block.

But all that was in the past.

Prising himself out of the chair, the optician shuffled through to the back room. The far wall was covered floor to ceiling in miniature wooden drawers. Each of them contained a set of prosthetic glass eyes. Pulling one out, the optician took in the neat rows, gazing adoringly at the superlative quality. Crafted by his grandfather a century before, they were as old as Morlib's Optical Inc.

Herbert was about to get down to his daily routine, when the shop's door opened and quickly closed. He made out the sound of feet moving between the cabinets. Assuming it was yet another unwelcome representative from the building firm desperate to get their hands on the store, he called out:

'I'm not gonna sell! Told you that a hundred times. Won't sell because I can't sell!'

Shuffling back through to the shop, he saw it wasn't a rep, but an elegant young gentleman whose face was masked in fear.

As soon as Herbert set eyes on the visitor, the sense of trepidation engulfed him, too.

'All correct?' the visitor asked.

The optician nodded.

'Yes. Yes.'

'Nothing untoward?'

'No. Just the state of lunacy out there.'

The visitor rested an attaché case on the top of a cabinet, clicking open the catches. With considerable care, he removed a small silver pill-box, placing it on the floor at the front of the shop.

'Some extra security,' he said ominously.

Herbert Morlib swallowed.

'I'm sure I shall manage,' he replied.

The visitor wiped a handkerchief to his brow.

'Can't take any chances.'

'I told you… they're all correct.'

'Are you certain?'

Herbert nodded.

'Come have a look,' he said.

Twenty-six

THAT NIGHT, WHEN Oliver checked social media, it was swamped with video links gone viral of New Yorkers out of control.

Some were harmless.

Others not.

There was footage of a man trying to peel an onion with his toes.

Another of a little girl doing her best to juggle a pair of calico kittens.

A third video showed a cluster of cops playing Russian roulette with a Glock-19 service revolver.

The most popular of all was of a blindfolded artist tattooing a lion's face onto the belly of his baby son.

Oliver sat on the bed.

Slowly, he took in the attic room – a refuge, and a magical world through his childhood.

The box of soft toys had been generals in his army.

The broken radio, his communication hub.

The mahogany armoire, with its ornate brass handles, a portal to a distant planet.

Leaning back against the pillows, he closed his eyes.

However hard he tried, Oliver couldn't get the basement out of his mind.

Except for patterns, there was nothing he adored more than slipping into fantasy. But the fantasy he had experienced that afternoon wasn't served up by his own consciousness.

Full spectrum and original, it was altogether different.

Reaching over, Oliver picked the paperweight from the nightstand. The lead was cool again. Although a little more dented than when presented to him earlier in the thuya wood box, it was otherwise the same. Switching on the bedside lamp, he examined it, turning it into the shaft of light.

Lifeless, the dragon's eye was once again frozen in relief. The symbols on the band around the edge were orderly, and not especially unusual.

A cross.

A hexagon.

Three diagonal lines.

A cooking pot.

A double spiral.

An egg.

A key.

As he turned the object in his hands, Oliver closed his eyes again. His ears were filled with the cry of gulls overhead, and the noise of breakers colliding with a reef.

His fingertips ran along the band, like those of a blind man reading braille. Uncle Sinan had always claimed the sense of touch was far more revealing than sight.

Caressing the paperweight, Oliver mapped its surfaces with care.

As he did so, he felt a series of hairline grooves on the join where the band and the upper surface met.

Some were close together.

Others further apart.

Almost invisible to the eye, they formed a pattern.

Tracing it by touch, Oliver ran the design through his mind.

It was familiar.

He had seen it recently – of that much he was certain.

Closing his eyes, Oliver leaned back on the bed, his mindscape alive with images from the projection witnessed that very afternoon.

Hundreds of images.

Thousands.

Millions.

Each with its own place on a grid of infinite scope and size.

Scrolling through them, Oliver relived the full stream of emotion.

Elation.

Confusion.

Wonder.

Hopelessness.

Fear.

A pattern revealed itself.

Not the pattern from the paperweight, but one etched into the outer wall of a fortress citadel. No more than a detail glimpsed in a sweeping panorama, it was signalling to him, begging him to take notice.

Returning the paperweight to the nightstand, Oliver switched off the lamp and was soon asleep.

In his dreams, he floated through a kingdom in which the trees were made from smoked glass, the buildings from butterfly wings. The snow was goose feathers, and the wind was walrus breath.

Not far from the attic where Oliver was dreaming, a pool of emerald light hung in the dark sky above the rooftops.

Tumbling and cavorting as it shifted in shape, it was vibrating, moving through geometric symmetries as though preparing itself.

Twenty-seven

IT TOOK A great deal to impress the aduxa jinn.

Having stockpiled such a colossal hoard in the cavern beneath the rock, sheer quantities of gold were no longer as exciting to her as they had once been. Nor was quality, nor beauty. But, as Soulia pondered it, in rare situations one came across a combination of all three:

An abundance of the purest gold, fashioned into an object of extraordinary loveliness.

That was exactly what she found beneath the petrified tree in the forest beyond the gristial rainbow.

Taking her time to examine the details of the golden mammoth, Soulia stepped back, unhinged her jaws, and swallowed the statue whole.

A moment later, she was back in the cavern.

But, as she disgorged the mammoth, something occurred which took her by surprise.

The vast golden statue transformed into a figure dressed in simple blue overalls, a dragon's eye motif embroidered discreetly on its chest. He hurled a net towards the aduxa jinn.

As soon as it touched her, its fibres began constricting their contents, squeezing and clasping until Soulia was squashed into a shape no larger than a bowling ball.

'As a Jinn Hunter sent by Order of Councilus, I have come to take you prisoner,' said the figure. 'You shall return to Zonus with me, where you shall be tried for theft of gold on an immense and disagreeable scale.'

Struggling to move in the confines of the net, Soulia the aduxa jinn voiced a shrill protest.

'Too late for pleas of clemency,' the Jinn Hunter replied curtly. 'To the Prism you go!'

Twenty-eight

AT TEN MINUTES after eight next morning, Uncle Sinan's favourite suede hunting boots shuffled in from the cold.

Trilby and walking cane in hand, a woven vicuña scarf tight around his neck, the shopkeeper had been out to see what was going on.

And what he had seen had filled him with dread.

Every block for miles was marked with carnage. Vehicles smashed into shops. Apartment buildings streaming with smoke and flames. Looters hurrying away with whatever they could carry. Hordes of ragged citizens tearing through the streets on all fours, whooping and hollering as they went.

At breakfast, Oliver crushed the top off a boiled egg.

'My head's aching,' he mumbled. 'Had the strangest dreams.'

His uncle didn't reply at first. After taking a long sip of his tea, he said:

'As I've always told you – where there is good, there is bad.'

'In dreams as well?'

'Everywhere.'

Oliver frowned.

'Even with paperweights?'

Uncle Sinan touched the tip of a thumb to the rim

of the porcelain cup, halting the path of a droplet before it broke free.

'Still thinking about it, are you?'

Oliver blinked.

'I know my own imagination,' he said, 'and that wasn't anything it delivered.'

His uncle tugged out a handkerchief and blew his nose.

'I remember when my father presented it to me,' he murmured, his face hidden in the cloth. 'Said it was given to our ancestor by a farmer on the Mongolian Steppes. He'd dug it up with his plough.'

'Buried treasure?'

'*Buried*, certainly. *Treasure*... perhaps not.'

Oliver probed the tip of a teaspoon down into the egg.

'You've always taught me to embrace fantasy,' he said.

'Yes, I have. After all, the fantastic is a lifeblood – *our* lifeblood.'

'But is it real?'

Uncle Sinan laid down the cup, and looked sharply across at his nephew, his expression souring.

'Fact and fantasy are two halves of the same whole,' he responded. 'Yin and Yang. Opposites and yet equals.'

Stuffing away the handkerchief, he grunted, and said:

'Something can lie dormant for a thousand years and only waken when it meets the conditions. Like a seed finally blown to a distant land awaiting it.'

Oliver looked at the cup resting in his uncle's hand.

'What about lead paperweights?' he asked. 'Can they lie dormant until the right person comes along?'

The elderly shopkeeper sipped his tea, as though refreshed.

'Indeed it is especially true when it comes to lead paperweights,' he said.

Twenty-nine

HERBERT MORLIB LED the visitor into the back chamber which doubled as his bedroom, a hand pressed to his spine so as to ease the pain.

When both men were inside, he shut the door, locked it, and jerked himself upright – his posture perfectly perpendicular.

'Identify yourself,' he said coldly.

Tugging off his horn-rims, the well-dressed visitor wiped a hand over his face. The handsome human features were traded for those of an ogre.

'Operative Zeliak on a mission for the Order of Councilus!' he said. 'Antraxa Code 33/Q!'

Herbert flinched. He had been in the service of

Zonus for decades, having assumed his ancestral role. In all those years, he'd been cautioned time and again about the so-called 'Antraxa Code', but never imagined it would occur on his watch.

Turning to the back wall, the optician withdrew one of the miniature drawers of prosthetic eyes. Selecting a pair of them, he screwed them into his own face. Then, passing the visitor a second pair of the glass eyes, he motioned for him to do the same.

Operative Zeliak nudged the eyes into place as though he had done it a thousand times.

'Ready,' he said.

Herbert Morlib pressed a button on the underside of the drawer. A flywheel spun round fast, and the drawers descended into the ground – revealing an ordinary door.

Leading the way, the optician scurried forwards onto an iron framework, and began climbing down a makeshift network of ladders.

Hurriedly, Operative Zeliak followed.

Within a minute or two, they reached the lowest basement level. Herbert paused, as though whispering a prayer to himself.

Then, intently, he pulled back a reinforced steel door and led the way into Holding Zone J5D/Z.

Thirty

LATE THAT MORNING, the Mayor of New York went on television to make a public address.

Calling for calm, he urged everyone to rally together to heal their community, and overcome the scourge afflicting them. Staff and officers shoulder-to-shoulder squarely behind him, the Mayor pledged to get to the bottom of what was going on, and stamp it out with an iron fist.

Oliver clicked the mute button on the remote.

As he did so, his iPhone rang. He squinted at the display. It was Bill Lewis, his best friend.

'Hey there, Billy. You OK?'

A gruff voice came on the other end, a muffled commotion in the background.

'Hi Ollie, just checking you haven't gone crazy, too!'

Oliver wiped a hand over his eyes.

'Can never be too sure,' he said with a smile.

A raucous grinding noise was followed by screams, and his friend's voice again.

'I'm down in Emergency. Been here all night. Never seen anything like it. The last thirty people I treated were off-the-scale hysterical. Raging. Psycho. Like as though there's been a leak of loony gas or something.'

'Loony gas?'

'They're saying it's a new kind of terrorism.'

'Huh?'

'Psychological warfare. Whatever you do, don't… '

The phone went dead.

Oliver tried calling back, but it didn't go through.

Switching off the TV, he went into the next room, where he found his uncle dozing on the couch.

All of a sudden he caught a flash of early memory, more precious to him than any other.

The edge of a river in late summer, the sun so bright it made him skip and laugh. As he did cartwheels in the long grass, his father called him over to see something in the water. Scurrying down to the riverbank, he followed the end of his father's finger with his own.

'What is it, Daddy?!' he giggled.

'There! Look there!'

'What?'

'*That!*'

Eyes wide, Oliver screamed, and screamed and screamed.

Screams not of fear, but of delight.

Halfway across the river, beside a nest of reeds, was a dolphin. Not any ordinary dolphin. It was coloured in a swirling rainbow pattern.

On its head was a wreath of twisted mistletoe.

Thirty-one

By EARLY AFTERNOON soldiers were filing onto the streets.

The Mayor had called in the National Guard, who were ordered to shoot looters on sight. The entire city was locked down, with a strict dawn-to-dusk curfew in force. All vehicles, except for those of the military and the emergency services, were forbidden.

Anyone displaying symptoms of lunacy was loaded into one of the special trucks, their windows blacked out. Exactly where they were being taken was classified. Word on the street was that it was a secret military unit somewhere in New Jersey.

Like an airborne disease, the lunacy swept through the entire population, irrespective of class, race, gender or profession. And, as the insanity spread, it infected not only humanity, but every living species.

Within hours, the soldiers ordered to arrest the insane were going crazy, too. Some handcuffed themselves to their superiors, or to their vehicles, while others got down and barked like bloodhounds on the scent. Yet more stripped naked and paraded through the streets as living art.

Shortly before lunch, the Mayor was found on the window ledge of his office, a bowling ball super-glued to his hand.

As a throng of assistants pleaded frantically with

90

him to come back inside, he bowled the ball forcefully over the edge.

Immaculate in hand-tailored gabardine, his wrist, arm, and body quickly followed.

Thirty-two

DIMLY LIT, AND deafening with the sound of birds chirruping, Holding Zone J5D/Z was arranged with iron cages.

Tens of thousands of them, rising up innumerable levels, from the floor to the rafters.

In each cage was a bird.

Some were small, others large; some slate-grey or black; more still were blinding in their plumage. Many were recognizable as known species. But yet more were fantastical in their form and colouring – quite different from the birds found in the Dominion of Men.

Cracking his knuckles, Herbert Morlib paced down the main corridor, peering up at the rows of orderly iron cages.

'As I told you,' he said uneasily, 'it's all as it should be.'

Operative Zeliak marched up and down, making the inspection. His breathing was shallow, his concentration absolute.

Suddenly, the optician's tatty old shoes stopped.

Herbert swivelled round to face the visitor, heading back in his direction. His expression had soured, as though he'd solved a puzzle.

'It's here, isn't it?' he asked in terror.

His glass eyes piercing blue, Operative Zeliak looked at Herbert.

'You know I can't answer that question,' he responded sharply.

'I know. I know. But it's true. I can feel it. I can feel it in my bones.'

Thirty-three

NEWS OF THE Mayor's demise hit social media by the time Uncle Sinan went up for his afternoon nap. Climbing the stairs, he renewed the instruction to his nephew – on no account was he to go outside.

The shop's front door was double bolted, but Oliver was curious.

He knew the only cure for his agitation was to take a good long walk, to search for patterns, and to see the mayhem for himself.

Sliding the bolts back, and making sure the Tibetan temple bell didn't chime, Oliver pulled the door open and crept out onto East 8th Street.

A stone's throw from Ozymandias & Son he came across the first evidence of psychosis.

Armed with her own inelegant form of karate, a grandmother was attacking a postman, who had painted his face blue.

A few feet away, an assortment of dogs on their hind legs were pirouetting in a crude ballet.

Across from them, a cyclist had glued his hands to his feet and was foaming at the mouth.

Taking a mental snapshot of the scene, Oliver reflected on it as he walked anxiously towards the park. But before there was time to make conclusions, more examples of lunacy presented themselves:

A woman hacking off her hair with a carving knife.

Honey-bees swarming in the shape of an elephant, above a steam vent.

Six traffic cops lying on their bellies, singing Christmas carols backwards.

Unsure quite why, Oliver overlaid the oddity on the matrix of images he had seen the day before down in the basement.

Fumbling to make connections, he couldn't find any – as though New York's lunacy was somehow separate from the world within the dragon's eye.

Surely nothing wrong with that.

On University Place, a stream of distinct images flashed into his mind.

A scarlet bicycle.

A polar bear with wings.

A bottle labelled 'SECRET'.

A book of folktales without any words.

Romping through reality and into the fantastic, Oliver's mind swept on and on, like a dinghy carried down river and out over a waterfall.

He was in a desert, beneath three suns, the sand made from powdered bones. Burned beyond all recognition, his body was blotched with sores, his face grotesquely deformed.

Staggering forwards, he perceived an ocean of camel's milk, stretching from one horizon to the next.

Oliver stumbled towards it, his tearless eyes almost blind.

As he approached, the milk sea curdled, went hard, and melted into dust.

Oliver heard footsteps rasping over stone.

He turned.

Death was silhouetted against the autumn sun.

Thickset and forbidding, with an athlete's shoulders, he was clutching a meat cleaver. Despite the backlight, the weapon was glinting, ready for use, like an executioner's death blade.

Oliver froze, his mind racing.

Inch by inch the cleaver was raised higher above the figure's head.

Mirages in desert dust.

Waves of curdled camel milk.

Triplicate suns.

Yet, unlike the fantastic backdrop, the executioner was real.

Moving with expertise acquired through great experience, he stepped deftly forward. Knees gently bowed, his shoulders were taut with stored power like a coiled clock-spring.

The weapon plunged, swinging fast in an arc, the blade cleaving the air.

Inches from the target.

Close.

Closer.

Oliver didn't move.

He couldn't.

Lost in detail, his mind was computing.

His nostrils had picked up a scent.

Sulphurous, it was bitter and tempestuous.

A sense of déjà vu, as though he had breathed it in before.

Stealth terror.

Curving as it breached the last few inches of emptiness, the blade's path was lined up perfectly with Oliver's face.

In a moment it would be a part of him, embedded in his face, bisecting right eye and nose.

Time slowing, the point of impact came.

Oliver felt the cold edge of steel make contact with the bridge of his nose. As it did so, his eyes pulled focus – back onto the face of Death – his mind hunting through an endless stream of experience.

Experience locked up in his own DNA.

Facts.

Figures.

Ideas.

Emotions.

Stray thoughts.

Random details.

Trivia.

Nonsense and minutiae.

A positive match.

The same danger had been faced before. Not by him, but by one of his ancestors.

As time faltered, and as his mind raced, Oliver studied the moment in which the very same threat had been evaded.

With absolute precision, he observed how the blow had been previously avoided.

Flipping backwards, Oliver caught Death off balance, thrusting him to the ground.

Chest burning, he sprinted headlong along a side-street. Darting down a narrow alley, awash with rubbish bins and plumes of steam, he played back the impossible somersault responsible for saving his life.

But the silhouette was standing at the end.

Legs splayed wide, waiting.

Spinning round, Oliver sprinted back the other way.

Muscles cramping, he was too drained to think.

Again, he turned.

Looked left.

Right.

Up.

Down.

As before, Death was already there, yards away.

The cleaver had been replaced by a scythe.

Tears streaming down his face, Oliver prepared himself for the inevitable.

The last moment of his life.

With herculean force, the scythe swung towards him. Resigned to defeat, Oliver allowed his body to fold down on itself.

But, as his legs gave way, something unanticipated occurred.

Death vanished.

Inexplicable silence.

Amazed he was still alive, Oliver looked up.

This was no fantasy – no realm of imaginary suns or islands encircled by dragon's blood. It was real.

Sitting up, bewildered, heating vents steaming around him, every cell of Oliver's body was on high alert.

Death had been replaced by an ordinary man. Smaller and far more delicate, he was strangely familiar. Dressed in green tweed, he wore a matching hat, and a pair of sturdy walking boots.

Reaching out, he helped Oliver up.

'The crazy people are everywhere,' he said. 'I told you to stay inside where it's safe.'

Oliver balked.

'*Uncle Sinan*? How... how... how come you're here?'

The shopkeeper scratched a thumbnail to his cheek.

'Happened to be passing,' he said in a cautious tone.

'Down this alley, just when I needed you?'

The shopkeeper smiled through the corner of his mouth.

'Luck,' he shrugged.

Brushing the dirt from his ripped shirt, Oliver pulled a face.

'How did *you* chase *him* away?!'

Uncle Sinan glanced into the steam meekly.

'Never underestimate the strength of an old man,' he said.

Thirty-four

CLOAKED IN MATCHING purple gowns, all fourteen members of the Order sat in silence in the Hall of Sanctity.

Each one was a little older and wiser than the last.

White-haired and wizened, they had a communal

98

age of almost forty centuries. And it was through age they had gained the experience which enabled them to rule over the Realm. No living soul could match their wisdom, or their expertise in the rights and wrongs of jinn.

Seated on cushions stuffed with Arctic lavender, the fourteen elders of the Order of Councilus waited for the head of the penal system to arrive. They had summoned him to explain how Nequissimus could have escaped and, more pertinently, to clarify how he intended to capture the great jinn again.

After an interval of strained silence, the immense doors at the south entrance of the great hall were pulled apart.

A shaft of indigo light broke in, then ebbed away, as the doors snapped shut behind Amalorous.

Gliding forwards with long strides, his elegant form concealed in a black velvet robe, his head was crowned in a matching cap. A profuse white beard tumbled from his face, tapering to a point far below his navel. There was a sense of gravity about him, tinged with distinct sternness, as though he were charged with the most extreme duty imaginable.

And he was.

As head of Zonus, he was in command of the legal system responsible for capturing and sentencing rogue jinn. The entire fraternity of Jinn Hunters was answerable to him, and to him alone.

Regarded as supreme, Amalorous answered only to the Order of Councilus, who ruled over the Realm itself.

In more usual circumstances, the leader was celebrated for his many triumphs – deeds that maintained the balance between good and evil.

But these were anything but usual circumstances.

Striding down the centre of the hall, he made his way to where the members of the Order were seated on benches chiselled from dark petrified wood. All around, marble statues gazed down from the walls, busts of every fellow of the Order since time immemorial.

Although calm on the exterior, inside Amalorous was in turmoil. Taking the last steps more slowly, he bowed in reverence to his superiors, and stood across from them in the dock.

A single droplet of perspiration formed on his brow and rolled down his cheek. As he wiped it away, Morsius, the supreme leader of Councilus, addressed him:

'Grave news has come to our attention,' he began in a voice so frail as to be barely audible. 'News that threatens the entire Realm.'

'Nequissimus,' intoned the robed figure seated beside the supreme leader.

'The escape of the great jinn,' hissed a third.

Amalorous took in the ancients seated before him.

In the two hundred years he had managed the legal system, he had never known such a time of appalling uncertainty, or fear. Never in the wildest reaches of his superior imagination had he foreseen such a calamity.

Only days before, the thought of the Prism being breached, and the most evil of all jinn running free, would have been unthinkable.

'It is with unrivalled regret I stand before you,' Amalorous intoned. 'I appreciate that even the most extreme contrition on my part is not sufficient, and in no way rectifies the loss. Thankfully, I am able to inform you that Nequissimus's soul remains in our safe custody.'

Morsius held up a finger, the bone bent back on itself with arthritis. He was so old he could remember the time when it rained qwagula frogs in the Dominion of Fāā.

'Where is the soul?' he demanded.

'Where it's been for centuries,' the leader of Zonus replied. 'In the holding zone lying in the Dominion of Men.'

'That's not safe!' Morsius riposted.

Amalorous bowed low.

'If I might defend it,' he said clumsily, 'it is far away from the Realm's more tempestuous regions.'

Again, Morsius held up a finger.

'I need not warn you of the danger, Brother

Amalorous,' he wheezed. 'Do not dare to fail, or a second Epoch of Obscurity will befall us.'

The leader of Zonus stood tall.

'Be assured,' he said, 'no Jinn Hunter will rest until Nequissimus is captured and returned to the bleakest, deepest level of the Prism.'

The third member of Councilus craned his neck towards the dock. Compared with Morsius, he was a whippersnapper of a mere three hundred and twenty-three.

'To capture Nequissimus you will need a Jinn Hunter like none other,' he crooned.

His gaze on the flagstones, Amalorous preened a set of ripened fingers through the tangled beard.

'If it pleases the Councilus,' he replied, 'we are to train a Jinn Hunter whose ancestry has prepared him for this task.'

'When will his training begin?' Morsius asked.

Eager to conceal the extent of his anxiety, the leader of Zonus touched his fingertips together.

'He is yet to be initiated into the Cadenta, Your Magnificence,' he explained. 'As you are aware, we cannot begin the training until he has found the skills lying dormant inside him. Only then will he discover the existence of our unseen world.'

Thirty-five

THAT EVENING, ONE news story dominated all the networks: the insanity that had plagued New York was sprouting up elsewhere.

All of a sudden, people across the United States were going crazy – from Oregon to Florida, from Texas to North Dakota. Tens of thousands were now affected by universal lunacy.

Farmers in Nebraska let their livestock out of the pens, and locked themselves inside.

Businessmen leapt from office buildings in Chicago, crowing with laughter as they fell.

Nurses raced hospital beds through Boston's streets.

Firefighters across Montana set tinder-dry meadows ablaze, and danced jigs while the wildfires burned.

As in New York, the human population was not the only one to be affected. Animals, and even insects, were sucked into the lunatic stew.

'Can't watch any more of this,' said Oliver that evening. 'It's as though the natural order has been flipped on its head.'

Sitting in his favourite chair, Uncle Sinan stared into space, his small dark eyes reflecting great fear.

'We're not safe here,' he said, his focus hovering

in mid-air. 'We should go up to the cabin in the Catskills, and wait it out.'

Oliver regarded him quizzically.

'Whatever it is, d'you think it'll just pass?'

'Perhaps not,' Sinan intoned.

'Wish I could say that was comforting.'

Oliver let out a sigh.

'I'm going to bed so I wake up in a normal world.'

Still staring into space, his uncle rolled his eyes.

'I doubt you will ever know normality again,' he replied.

Thirty-six

THE DEPARTMENT OF Caged Souls was one of the most secretive subdivisions operating in Zonus's vast bureaucracy.

Staff employed within its ranks were continually reviewed, checked, and double-checked. For, even greater than the fear of an imprisoned jinn gaining its freedom, was the terror of an escaped jinn being reunited with its soul.

Fortunately, the prison system was so secure that escapes were virtually unknown.

Or rather they had been until now.

The improbability of Nequissimus gaining freedom was matched by the certainty he would mount a bid to be reunited with his soul... a point deliberated over no-end at the Department of Caged Souls.

Experts from all over the Realm were sought to provide opinions on three pressing questions:

1. Whether the great jinn would be able to locate his soul.
2. How he could ever get past the layers of defence.
3. If the soul ought to be moved to an even more secure location.

Days and nights of intensive deliberations ended with the experts deciding that Nequissimus was unlikely to locate his soul or get through the defences. As for relocating it – the unanimous decision was to leave it.

In a terse document accompanying the evaluation, the experts noted that Holding Zone J5D/Z had been operated for millennia. Despite the area having been swamp and jungle since after the last Ice Age, the experts were in agreement. As they saw it, the unlikely development of the island of Manhattan – under which the holding zone was located – was proof of its security.

A second subsidiary panel, established to make sense of this line of thinking, reached no firm conclusions. It was therefore decided to leave the great jinn's soul exactly where it was – beneath the floor of Morlib's Optical Inc., on New York's West 72nd Street.

Thirty-seven

UP IN HIS attic bedroom, Oliver scrolled back and forth through his memory of the combat with Death.

Breaking it down frame by frame, he scanned each one, observing them minutely in his search for details, for clues and, most importantly, for a pattern.

None of it made any sense.

Except for the fact there was no sense.

Uncle Sinan had dismissed Death as just another psycho on the rampage, but Oliver was certain of whom he had been.

The improbability that Uncle Sinan would have been passing right there and then was matched only by the way Oliver had known how to get free.

Leaning over to the nightstand, he stroked a palm over the paperweight and picked it up. Against the day's other drama, he had almost forgotten about it. Cupping it in his hands, he shook it, smelled it, touched it to his ear.

'Tell me your secret,' he said in an unspoken voice.

Turning the object through his fingers, he felt the tiny grooves again, his mind plotting them on a matrix. Then, weighing it in his hand, he wondered whether there could be gas or something else trapped inside.

Slipping off his bed, Oliver paced to his desk, and fished a hand through a cluttered drawer.

Way at the back he found a compass, the kind every school child uses for sketching circles. Taking it out, he placed the paperweight on the desk, pressed the point into the centre of the dragon's eye motif, and began drilling into it with all his strength.

The point slipped easily into the lead.

Just before he broke through into the object's hollow heart, the door swung open fast.

Standing in its frame, his expression fretful, was Uncle Sinan.

'Whatever are you doing?!' he demanded incredulously.

'Just running some quick tests on the... the old paperweight'

'*Tests*?'

'I'm trying to work out what it's for.'

The shopkeeper strode fast over to the desk. Jerking the compass point from the lead, he squinted at the hole. On verifying the paperweight wasn't punctured, he seemed a little calmer.

In silence, he rested the object down on the nightstand beside Oliver's bed.

'Take it from me – there's nothing to test.'

'But there's more to it than meets the eye. I'm sure of it,' said Oliver.

His uncle looked at him reproachfully.

'You are merely its custodian,' he responded. 'Your job is to look after it.'

'Until when?'

'Until you have a son of your own.'

Thirty-eight

ALL NIGHT LONG, Manhattan's streets resounded with the clamour of sirens and screaming.

Oliver lay in bed, his mind racing, his imagination fuelled by the lunacy, the attack, and by the world he had seen projected from the dragon's eye.

However hard he fought to quell it, his attention was drawn back to the kaleidoscope of images he'd witnessed down in the basement. Sitting up, Oliver tried to make sense of what was going on – to find a link between the lead disc and its projections, and the lunacy engulfing New York and beyond.

Uncle Sinan may have frowned on him testing the heirloom, but surely he wouldn't condemn an investigation of another kind.

Climbing out of bed, Oliver pulled on his flannel bathrobe. Paperweight in hand, he crept down to the shop.

Outside on East 8th Street he could hear manic laughter and what sounded like a pack of dogs and cats out hunting.

Through the darkness, he went over to the hatch, leaned in, and jerked on the light.

For the first time in his life he wasn't scared. As though a spell had been broken, he touched the paperweight to his cheek.

Steadying himself against the wall, Oliver counted the steps as he descended.

Ten… eleven… twelve.

Oblivious to the roaches, the spiders, and to the ingrained memories of fear, he got down on his hands and knees and urged the lead disc into the niche, exactly as it had been positioned before.

Still kneeling, he waited for something to happen. But nothing did.

Leaning forward, he turned the paperweight a little to the right, lining up the dragon's eye with the edges of the niche. In the dimness, he relied on the sense of touch.

Still nothing.

Etched into the dark grey metal, the eye was as lifeless as it had been for centuries, since the farmer's plough had supposedly unearthed it half a world away, on the Mongolian Steppes.

Conceding defeat, Oliver assumed he must have imagined the entire thing.

Cursing himself for letting imagination pass itself off as reality yet again, he stooped forward to pick up the disc.

As thumb and index finger grasped the paperweight, he noticed the tiniest trace of wool fluff in the middle of the dragon's eye motif.

Fluff from a tribal rug, coincidentally from the Mongolian Steppes.

Without giving it a thought, the edge of his thumb brushed the fluff away.

In doing so, half a finger touched the centre of the disc, for no more than the briefest fraction of a second.

But long enough…

For the dragon's eye to come alive.

Alert, rational, thoughtful, wise.

Instantly, it began projecting a miscellany of images – one after the next, and all at once.

Microscopic details of intricacy.

Entire solar systems, mazes, and cryptic-looking blueprints.

Stars in distant galaxies.

Ruined desert castles.

Phosphorescent fish.

Arctic tundra.

Tsunamis.

Glass eyes.

Hopscotch.

Billiard balls and chalk.

As Oliver watched, stupefied, one image stuck out from all the rest.

A father, mother, and their little son, on grass at a river's edge.

A hand pointing to the ripples beside a knot of reeds.

A rainbow dolphin dancing in the water, on its head a crown of twisted mistletoe.

Leaning forward, Oliver thrust a hand into the images.

This time there was no hesitation.

As before, his fingers went straight through, his body following.

Once again, he was standing at the top of the grand porphyry staircase, his feet invisible. No longer was there a trace of fire, or forest vines, smoke, or bleeding flowers. It was as though the scene had been reset.

Stepping down to the first tread, he breathed in the scent of lemongrass, his mind struggling to focus. He thought of a library in which all the books were made from stone. Of a flying carpet soaring above a sleeping city, and of a farmstead in the Ozark Mountains fashioned from rose gold.

As his mind scrolled on and on through fantasy, the walls, the ceiling, and the steps themselves, transformed.

One moment they were covered in fragrant grass.

The next, the grass was hidden in snow. But, instead of being cold, the wintry layer was warm to the touch.

The snow, too, vanished, replaced by the sapphire waters of an ocean.

Every detail was in constant flux.

Textures and temperature.

Levels of illumination.

Colours.

His senses stimulated, Oliver felt a vitality he had not experienced until then.

As before, he descended in absolute silence.

Spiralling down fast, he was at ease. Instead of questioning the surroundings, he found himself wondering why his world was so rigid.

At the bottom of the staircase, the great dragon's eye dilated as Oliver approached, as if welcoming him.

Staring deep into it, he took in the vast iris, bloodshot capillaries radiating out through a surrounding expanse of amber.

All encompassing, the eye was somehow detached and alone.

Oliver suspected its purpose was to shelter him and that, in return, it was extracting memories as a toll.

Memories both real and imaginary.

The more he cleared his mind, the more it was entertained by recollections and ideas.

He thought of a shipwrecked sailor clinging to the hull of his upturned craft.

A log cabin in Appalachia.

A box containing a pair of dried lizard's feet.

A fox cub hatching from an egg.

Fireflies trapped in a screw-topped jar.

An Indian maharajah perched on a crystal throne.

A buzzard circling roadkill.

Six comets racing across a winter sky.

Moving away from the staircase, Oliver came to the door that was festooned in a pattern resembling the oversized scales of a primitive fish. He had caught a glimpse of it the time before, while tearing through the creepers and the vines.

As he neared it, a bell chimed, and an invisible mechanism shuddered into life.

The door swung inwards.

Cautiously, Oliver stepped through into an immense space.

A void, it was absolutely black, utterly empty of light or sound, temperature or smell.

As Oliver stood there, his feet visible once again, the door slammed, its mechanism locking.

Fearful at being trapped beyond the projection a second time, Oliver's dread was tempered by curiosity.

The void seemed to lure him into it.

Hesitantly, his feet treading in nothingness, he

moved forward. As one foot paced in front of the last, his imagination sparked with fantastical images.

He imagined fabulous creatures with forked tongues, fish scales, and armoured hooves.

Little imp-like figures, shackled together in chain gangs.

Reptiles poised on two feet, their bloated bellies strewn with barnacles.

Human-like forms standing as tall as ships' masts.

Glass bottles dangling from a line – a miniature organism ensnared in each one.

Ape-like animals inside out.

Monsters so terrifying the emptiness beneath them had turned to stone.

Oliver imagined legions of officials in matching uniforms all around him. Hurrying about with brusque authority, they were apparently in charge – making sure the creatures were kept in line.

Yet again, Oliver wondered what was going on. He half-expected to wake up in his own bed, the recent events nothing more than part of his richly elaborate dreamscape.

By closing his eyes he chased the illusion away.

But when a moment later he opened them, Oliver grasped that what he had imagined to be illusion was not.

It was reality. Or, rather, it was a mundus imaginalis, a form of reality more real than reality itself.

As the details of each creature slipped crisply into view, the void transformed into a vast space with blurred and indistinct boundaries. The size of a thousand aircraft hangars, it was so large that it almost defied any sense of scale.

Every inch of it seemed to be teeming with life.

Fantastical creatures everywhere.

A few were assisting the guards in uniforms. But most were being admonished, examined, measured, interrogated, or hosed down with an oily pink liquid propelled by turbines made from brass. A great many more were waiting their turn, trussed up in cages, in nets, in chains, or herded into pens, circled by what appeared to be a form of living razor-wire.

Some of the creatures were protesting in outlandish languages, pleading for freedom. Others were brawling with each other, attacking the guards, or doing anything they could to mount an escape.

Intrigued, Oliver strolled through the lines of creatures, taking care not to get too close. Despite possessing a first-rate imagination, he had never dreamed of anything like it.

Snaking his way through a corner of the colossal hall, he was struck by something: no one was taking any notice of him.

It was as though he were invisible.

On the far edge of the hall, Oliver paused to marvel at a massive grizzled foot, armoured with triple rows of claws. The size of a city bus, it was shaking, the body towering above begging for mercy.

As he leaned back to get a view of the creature's head, a figure hurried toward him.

Tall, dignified, and yet anxious, he was dressed in a black velvet robe and matching cap. His face greatly aged and bearded, the brow lost in wrinkles. He seemed ecstatic at setting eyes on the visitor.

'Welcome! Welcome!' he exclaimed, pushing fast through the throng of creatures and guards. 'Words cannot express my delight in welcoming you among us at long last!'

The elderly figure reached out for Oliver's hand, shaking it forcefully in both of his.

'What joy! What elation!'

'I'm sorry,' Oliver said. 'I don't know what's going on.'

'We've been waiting for you,' replied the man in black velvet. 'Waiting for so long, but now you're here.'

'Waiting... for *me*?'

'Oh yes, yes, yes... for YOU!'

'For how long?'

'Oh, my oh my... for an eternity and three quarters at the very least.'

Oliver balked.

'Haven't got a clue what you mean,' he replied. 'I don't know where I am, or who you are.'

116

Taking a step backwards, Amalorous bowed deeply in reverence, and introduced himself.

Once vertical again, he thrust his wizened arms up into the air above like the branches of a leafless tree.

'Welcome to Zonus!' he exclaimed.

Thirty-nine

WITH THE EDGE of a claw, Nequissimus sliced the sack open and caught a first scent of the dried leaves contained inside.

Even though King Solomon had been hot on his trail, he had taken the time to conceal the precious hoard. A life dedicated to wickedness had taught the great jinn to always prepare.

Spilling out of the sack, the leaves were khaki in colour, and so dry they turned into dust at the touch. His eyes blinking as he brooded, Nequissimus caught a momentary flash of how the sack and its contents came into his possession.

A kingdom of uncertain name, discovered on a journey of routine destruction, had been inhabited by a life-prolonging race of ifrits. Kindly by nature, the creatures had welcomed the jinn with pomp and ceremony as on the rare occasions that a stranger arrived.

But, unlike other visitors to that land, Nequissimus refrained from giving thanks. Instead, when his hosts were sound asleep, he whispered a small but effective incantation.

Within a moment, the assembly of ifrits had been transformed into identical khaki-coloured leaves. Gathering them up in a sack, the great jinn secreted it away in a fold of scaly skin.

Blinking broodingly once again, Nequissimus coughed over the leaves.

Instantly, they were transformed into the very same ifrits that had welcomed him so long before. Bewildered at finding themselves alive, the creatures rejoiced and embraced.

It was then that one of them, an ifrit child, spied the gargantuan and demonic form of the great jinn looming over them like a death-cloud.

Known for bravery in times of adversity, the ifrits may have mounted an attack.

But the odds were against them.

His mouth opening no more than a fraction, Nequissimus exhaled gently in the direction of the ifrits.

Before they could react in any way, they were turned into a powder, the hue and consistency of talc.

Head lowered and eyes closed, the jinn breathed in.

Every single grain of ivory dust was sucked in over

his interminable rows of triangular teeth.

Once digested in his stomachs, the powdered ifrits were absorbed into the bloodstream.

Transported to every cell, the tonic began to work on restoring the great jinn's strength.

Forty

AMALOROUS GRASPED BOTH Oliver's hands and shook them hard in his.

Feverish with excitement, laughing maniacally, he danced a jig, swirling the visitor around with him.

'Can't tell you what it means to have you here!' he yelled out against the backdrop of commotion and noise. 'A dream of dreams! A miracle come true!'

'Think I'm missing something,' Oliver said, perplexed. 'It's *me* who's in a dream. Any minute now, I'll wake up in bed.'

Cupping an arm around his guest's shoulder, Amalorous guided him towards the middle of the hall, zigzagging expertly through the slipstreams of chaotic activity.

'Oh no. Oh no, no, no!' he huffed uneasily. 'Please understand something… this is no dream.'

Oliver grinned.

'You're passing *this* off as reality?'

'*Reality*?' Amalorous chuckled at the notion. 'A

little word with big meaning,' he said. 'A hybrid of fact and fantasy rolled into one. Reality is never what we imagine it to be.'

'I know what it is,' said Oliver. 'And it's got precious little to do with any of this.'

Amalorous held up an index finger. Casually, he jabbed it towards a pair of frostbite jinn trudging by in chains, then at a throng of half-pygmy jinn and, lastly, at a waxed jinn from the Dominion of Spoo, approaching lugubriously on all fours.

'Make no mistake about it,' he said solemnly, '*this* is the real world.'

The spiked tail of an immense dinosaur-like fiend swung past. Oliver managed to leap out of the way in the nick of time.

'What the hell was that?!'

'A crestula jinn,' Amalorous said disapprovingly. 'They've got a lot to answer for. Entire kingdoms have been trampled beneath them, all because they won't show a little common courtesy.'

Oliver held out a hand, motioning for Amalorous to wait.

'Where exactly are we?' he asked.

'I told you. In Zonus.'

'And what – or where – is that?'

'It's at the heart of everything. The place from which the Realm is managed and administered, and from where rogue jinn are kept in line.'

Just then, a creature resembling a fluorescent pink werewolf scampered past at double speed.

'Is that one of them?'

Amalorous squealed in laughter.

'No, no, no! He's not a jinn,' he said. 'He's one of the guards. A particularly gifted one as a matter of fact.'

Oliver paused at what looked like a pool of sticky black treacle, hovering a foot and a quarter above the floor. The surface appeared rippled, as though touched by a breeze. All the other creatures kept well away. Even the guards assigned to it maintained a safe distance.

'Don't get too close to him,' warned Amalorous, his eyes wide with alarm. 'He'll swallow you up and spit out your bones!'

'What is he?'

'A snark jinn who's in a lot of trouble.'

'What's he done?'

'He devoured the royal family of Masticula-Plik. A terrible matter as you can imagine. But, to tell you the truth, in all my years I've never encountered a snark jinn with good manners.'

Oliver's gaze panned up from the treacle-like liquid, and onto the ancient's face, his own expression mirroring bewilderment.

'By jinn you mean *genies*?' he said softly. 'Like Robin Williams in *Aladdin*? The loveable blue ones that grant three wishes and get trapped in lamps?'

As leader of Zonus, master of the legal system, Amalorous was not unused to explaining the truth.

'We don't call them "genies" here,' he said. 'We know them as "jinn". As for Hollywood, it's got a lot to answer for – always promoting the absurd idea they're affable and meek. There's a good reason for it of course. I'll tell you about it another time.'

Amalorous let out a grunt.

'In reality – a word I use with circumspection – there's nothing in the entire Realm quite so malevolent as a rogue jinn.'

'What's a rogue jinn?'

The leader of Zonus sighed despondently.

'Jinn who have strayed from the path of rectitude,' he rejoined. 'Using their powers to cause turmoil and disturb the peace.'

'Why do they go rogue?'

'For a million and three reasons,' Amalorous mumbled. 'None of which is very important now.'

Oliver glanced at a fluffy bear-like creature trussed up in an iron cage, conveyed through the throng by a team of guards.

'Some of them look anything but dangerous,' he said.

Amalorous slapped his hands together hard.

'Never be fooled!' he cried. 'When it comes to jinn, the most harmless-looking species can do the worst damage. They can shape-shift into any form they choose. Not all of them of course, but most. Jinn can make themselves look like you, or I, or transform into trees or buildings, into insects, or seductive women. They can even turn into a glass of cool water on a roasting summer's day.'

'Are they all bad?'

'No, no… of course not,' Amalorous said. 'A great many jinn are pillars of society. But when they go rogue, they tend to raise terror on an unspeakable scale.'

Signalling towards a low doorway on the other side of the hall, Amalorous led the way to his private study. With so many creatures to dodge, and such a distance to cover, it took an age to reach it.

As they neared, the door opened automatically, swinging shut as soon as they were safely inside.

The octagonal study's walls were lined in books – each one bound in identical leaf-green leather. The ceiling was hung with oil portraits.

Framed squarely in each was the sombre image of an elderly bearded figure in black velvet robes. Twelve generations of Amalorous's line had held the post to which he himself had been elected, a little more than two centuries before.

The leader of Zonus invited his guest to sit on a sofa, upholstered in an elaborate peacock feather design.

As Oliver sat down and leaned back, he sensed something odd.

The furniture was breathing.

Amalorous clicked his fingers.

Sculpted from aged walnut, a large armchair glided across the parquet to where he was standing.

'Shape-shifting jinn have their uses,' he said, 'especially those jinn who pledge to serve.'

Oliver stroked a hand over the peacock upholstery.

'This is a jinn?' he whispered in disbelief.

'Of course it is,' Amalorous replied. 'All the furniture's jinn. Means I can change it whenever I like.'

He slapped his hands together.

The peacock pattern turned into leopard skin, the walnut chair to brass, and the leaf-green bindings to a sharp shade of crimson.

The elderly leader of Zonus gazed up at his great-great-great-grandfather, a facsimile of himself. Intently, he looked down across the crimson spines, and onto Oliver's youthful face.

'I can imagine some of this may seem a little far-fetched.'

Oliver winced.

'You mean the genies?'

'*Jinn*,' Amalorous corrected. 'As I told you we call them "jinn".'

'Hardly noticed them,' said Oliver with a shrug.

The sofa on which he was sitting let out a cough, politely excusing itself.

'I'm pleased to hear it,' the leader replied. 'The Dominion of Men... the mortal world you've always known... it does exist,' he said.

'The Dominion of Men? You mean *my* world?' Oliver asked.

'Yes. That's how it's generally known by the few who care about it.'

'Is it at the centre of it all?'

Amalorous guffawed.

'Oh no, no, no,' he gasped. 'Of course not! It's nothing more than a trifling backwater – a backwater at the furthest reaches of direst insignificance.'

Distracted, his mind hunting for patterns in the leopard spots, Oliver turned to Amalorous.

'What exactly *is* the Realm?' he asked.

Before the leader could provide an answer, the door swung open and a creature entered, a silver tea tray balanced nimbly on an upturned palm. Seven foot three, he resembled a grizzly bear crossed with a king penguin.

Crossing the study with giant strides, he placed the tray on a small round table, bowed deeply, and slunk away.

Amalorous poured the tea, offered Oliver a cup, and breathed in the steam from his own.

'Imagine if there was a library of a hundred billion

books,' he said, taking a sip. 'And that every letter, in every word, in every sentence, on every page, in every book, was linked directly to every other letter. And, imagine if the way we thought the universe was arranged was just plain wrong. That our inability to perceive all dimensions meant we never did more than scratch the surface.'

Again, the leader sipped his tea.

Peering deep into Oliver's eyes, he said:

'Like the letters in the books, everything in the Realm is connected with everything else by invisible conduits, in a vast and interwoven labyrinth. Learn to navigate the conduits, and there's no end to the possibility.'

A white-gloved hand materialized from nowhere and poured more tea. Amalorous, who seemed very thirsty indeed, drained a full cup in a single gulp.

Leaning forward, he placed a set of wrinkled fingers over Oliver's eyes.

All of a sudden, the conduits were visible.

Millions upon billions of them in the study alone.

Just as Amalorous had said, everything was joined to everything else in an interconnected matrix, infinite in complexity and scale.

The letters and the words in all the books were connected.

The furniture was connected to the letters and the

words, and to the portraits, and to every individual dab of paint within them.

The portraits were connected to the papers on the desk, and to each hair in the leader's beard, and to the threads in Oliver's bathrobe.

In turn they were all connected to every inch of yarn in the rug on the floor, and to every other fragment of the whole.

As if the connections were not enough, every molecule of everything was connected to every other molecule in straight lines and zigzag ones as well.

The leader's hand returned to his lap, and the conduits vanished.

'How can there be so many connections?' Oliver whispered.

Amalorous downed a third cup of tea, which had appeared as if by magic.

'Most people don't know how Google can search all the knowledge in existence in the blink of an eye,' he said, 'but yet it does. As with the Internet, it's not important how it works, but the fact it does.'

'Don't understand,' said Oliver. 'Can you explain it again?'

'This is not the time,' Amalorous replied pensively. 'Everything you need to know will be clarified in due course.'

His mind having taken a mental snapshot of the

room, Oliver began counting the leather books at lightning speed. As he counted, they turned from crimson to fuchsia, and back to green.

'Still don't understand why I'm here,' he said. 'Or, even how I got here.'

'You found your way,' Amalorous answered. 'That's all that matters. You must understand we have no power over you. We can't tell you when to come or leave. All we can do is to be thankful you're here, and hope that you will stay.'

'Why?'

Restlessly, the leader of Zonus shifted in his chair, as if the pleasantries were over.

'A terrible thing has taken place,' he explained, his face gaunt and strained. 'A jinn has escaped from the Prism – the penitentiary in which rogue jinn serve out their time. No ordinary inmate, he is the most wicked jinn in existence. Every moment he remains at large, he doubles in strength. If we don't catch him soon, it'll be too late.'

Amalorous whistled.

Instantly, a book flapped down from the highest shelf, and swooped into the leader's hand. Opening it apparently at random, he found himself on the desired page.

As Oliver would learn, almost nothing in the Realm was ever random.

'Nequissimus,' he read with loathing, 'a jinn hell-bent on destruction, and on grim adversity of the most heinous and despicable nature. Captured by King Solomon and incarcerated in the ultimate cell at the Prism.'

The leader tossed the book over his shoulder, and it flapped back up onto the shelf.

'*Nequissimus*?' crowed Oliver, barely able to pronounce it.

'Evil incarnate. That's what he is. He won't stop until the Realm is destroyed and every living creature has been driven insane.'

'The lunacy?' said Oliver.

'Yes. Precisely. Even your little backwater has felt its effects, but they stretch far beyond.'

'How does he drive people mad?'

'Simple… by whispering. It's how jinn wreak havoc. Like poison gas, it can turn the most even-tempered life form insane. With Nequissimus free, no living thing is safe.'

'How will you catch him?' asked Oliver.

'Won't be easy,' Amalorous retorted.

'Can't you use some of those guards out there? Looks like you've got plenty of them.'

The leader of Zonus frowned, his forehead craggy and bleak like the end of the world.

He observed Oliver hard, his face a mask of desperation.

'To catch Nequissimus we need your help,' he said.

129

Forty-one

HOUR AFTER HOUR, the insanity spread.

Having crossed mountain ranges and oceans, spanned deserts, seas, and national boundaries, it became a world-wide phenomenon. Within a day and a half of Nequissimus's escape, the entire world was gripped by lunacy.

In each country the insane were dealt with differently, depending on political systems, beliefs and superstitions.

As in the United States, northern European nations did their best to maintain order and control. Victims were isolated and taken away to secure units. The system worked until the guards themselves went mad. A full breakdown in law and order quickly followed, and all Hell was unleashed.

In the wilderness of the African Congo, the lunacy was regarded as a manifestation of the ancestors' wrath. Fires were kindled, flames licking the night, sacrifices were made – both animal and human.

Far away, in the Himalayan stronghold of Bhutan, sequestered in their cliff-top monasteries, Buddhist monks turned to the scriptures to explain the scourge. Instead of regarding it as divine retribution, they regarded the insanity as a plague that could heal as well as bring pain.

In Australia's Outback, the leaders of an

Aboriginal tribe gathered together and listened to the earth. Walking the songlines across the baked desert plains, they sang to their forefathers who they believed held all the answers to salvation.

And, lost in the jungles of the Upper Amazon, the Shuar turned to a narcotic beverage to give them answers. Former head-shrinking warriors, they brewed the lining of the caapi vine in an ancient ritual, as they did in times of terrible uncertainty.

After days and nights of preparation, they sat in a circle, kindled a sacred fire, and consumed the concoction known as the 'Vine of the Dead'.

For the Shuar, reality was illusion, and illusion was reality.

Only by imbibing the potion did they believe they could reach the real world – and bring back answers to restore the balance in the illusionary world in which they lived.

Forty-two

EXCUSING HIMSELF FOR a moment, Amalorous paced through to an anteroom, where another figure was waiting.

Subdued, lean, and with a ramrod-straight back, he was Annis. The most celebrated Jinn Hunter of his generation, he had trapped and imprisoned hundreds of rogue jinn, before eventually retiring owing to injury. His old friend, Amalorous, had then asked him to head the Cadenta, the training academy of Jinn Hunters.

The anteroom was designed in such a way that its occupants were overlaid invisibly in the study next door. The feature allowed the two men to observe Oliver at close quarters, as though they were actually right there beside him.

Still unnerved by the living furniture, he got up, walked over to one of the shelves, and pulled down a book at random. Flicking through it, he found the pages filled with a mass of handwritten scribble. The script and the language unfamiliar, Oliver wasn't even sure whether he had it the right way up. Holding it into the light, he tried to make sense of it.

As he did so, he noticed the script changing. It was as though the page was being written and rewritten as he watched.

Sensing the preferred language of its reader, the text translated itself into English.

A particular paragraph caught Oliver's eye:

To trap a wayward jinn one must first gain its soul. This is done by summoning the soul, which is most usually contained in the form of a bird. Trap the bird and the jinn will be disarmed. Disarm it, and there is a hope it can be contained. Like other creatures, jinn are born, have offspring, and die. They may be slain, but only in certain circumstances, once the soul has been contained.

Reading the passage, Oliver wondered how to summon the jinn soul. Before the question was fully formed in his mind, the answer was scribbled on the page in English:

Whistle the correct notes and the jinn's soul will be revealed.

As Oliver turned to the next page, Amalorous stepped into the middle of the room, the head of the Cadenta Academy beside him.

Both men remained invisible to Oliver.

'Look! He's inquisitive!' the leader of Zonus said. 'A fine quality for a Jinn Hunter.'

'You know as well as I, curiosity alone won't be enough,' Annis responded icily. 'Look at him! He wouldn't last a minute out there with Nequissimus hunting him!'

'I remind you he already survived an attack.'

Annis groaned.

'He was under our protection.'

Leaving the book, Oliver inspected the objects on the desk. He was drawn to the paperweight. A glass tube, it was filled with blue liquid, in which a minuscule female jinn was trapped. She had three heads, tentacles, and eyes embedded into all nine of her feet. Holding the object up to his face, Oliver turned it on its end, and watched as the jinn slipped gracefully down the tube.

Inches away from him, Annis shook his head despondently.

'We face a predicament perilous beyond words,' he said. 'The entire Realm is threatened. Unless we do something, and do it fast, annihilation is the only certainty.'

Amalorous peered up at the ceiling.

The portraits were a comforting reminder of successes in times past.

'Our ancestors faced terrible ordeals of their own,' he said.

'As terrible as Nequissimus?' Annis spat indignantly.

'Yes! I need not remind you that he was once free.'

'Caught by King Solomon!' snapped the head of the Cadenta Academy.

Amalorous squirmed.

'Well, what about the sabatine jinn?'

'Caught not by a Jinn Hunter, but by a humble fisherman!' quipped Annis.

The leader of Zonus smoothed a hand down his beard.

'Let's not waste time on details,' he said, 'when we could be devoting our full attention to that boy.'

Both Annis and Amalorous turned to the far end of the study, where Oliver was toying with an antique brass telescope on a stand. Putting an eye to the viewing lens, he found himself peering into the furthest regions of the Realm.

A dominion beneath a sky blackened with fear.

Fields lined with rows of human heads, not lost in battle but grown from seeds.

Fodder for a cannibal king.

The leader of the Cadenta shook his head again.

'He doesn't have any idea about anything,' he said. 'There's no way he'll ever make a Jinn Hunter.'

Approaching the telescope, Amalorous observed Oliver, as a father might do his son.

'You know it as well as I – his ancestry is grounding enough,' he said. 'It's inside him, in every cell, ready to work for the good of us all. If nothing else protects him, the ancestry will. It's an instruction manual to the ways of jinn.'

Annis rolled his eyes.

'What good is pedigree when pitted against a foe like Nequissimus?'

'It will help,' Amalorous intoned feebly.

His face flushed with emotion, Annis looked hard at his old friend.

'I need not remind you of the secrets,' he said.

'*Secrets?*'

'What happened to his parents for a start... and...' Annis coughed into his fist. 'And the other matters.'

'Trust me,' whispered Amalorous, 'I would never break my word.'

Forty-three

ONCE AMALOROUS HAD returned to the study, and the tea tray had been cleared away, Oliver let out a chuckle.

'Since I was a kid everyone's poked fun at me,' he said. 'They claimed I was a dreamer... a fantasist... a guy who lived in a world of his own. I pretended they were wrong, that I was just like one of them. But being here with you, the flying books, the outrageous furniture, and all of *that* stuff out there, I have to admit they may have been right all along. My reality is the fantastic – but it's a fantasy all the same.'

Amalorous glanced down at the floor sternly. Without looking up, he said:

'Step forward and hold the corner of my robe.'

'What for?'

'So that I might show you something.'

'What?'

'Something you need to see.'

Hesitantly, Oliver did as the leader of Zonus asked of him, grasping the corner of black velvet.

As soon as the cloth touched his fingers, it seemed to furl around them, holding Oliver rather than him holding it.

'Ready?'

Oliver shrugged.

'Sure.'

The parquet began to quiver, and the oils on the ceiling did the same. His hand curled up in the folds of cloth, Oliver felt it warm.

Then the journey began.

Rising effortlessly into the air, Amalorous soared out into the colossal hall, where newly caught jinn were being registered and prepared for trial. Oliver trailed beside him as they rose upwards. Soon, even the greatest of the rogue jinn were no more than pinpricks far below.

Ascending higher and higher, the leader soared out of the hall, to where the legions of archivists toiled.

A moment later, he was hovering above a marvellous library.

Hanging in emptiness, it was circular in shape, rising hundreds of feet into the void. The volumes were in identical blood-red bindings, the shelving containing them curved round and round, stretching up until it reached the blackness beyond.

Without warning, Amalorous plunged downwards through the stacks, falling for what seemed to Oliver like an eternity.

Falling until they reached the Abyss.

As he plunged downwards, Amalorous dodged a multitude of ladders criss-crossing the stacks.

Some were vertical, others at acute angles, rolling backwards and forwards on brass castors.

Clutching hold of the ladders was a race of diminutive creatures, known as 'maestros', the ancestral archivists of Zonus. It fell to them to recall every detail of every trial that had ever taken place, and to supply the information to the courts.

Furled up in coarse black capes, embroidered with feathers from the aromatic qavak bird, they hailed from a desert island in the Dominion of Xoliam, three and a third zorl lifetimes away.

Maestros may have been diminutive in stature, but their eyes were very large indeed, and their memories were exceptionally well-honed. It was said they could remember everything they ever read, or heard – every idea, smell, sound, taste, and sight, and every whisper that ever touched the wind.

Nearing the lowest limit of the library, Amalorous arced steeply round to the left, and out into the Abyss.

His hand furled tight in the black velvet robe, Oliver caught his first sight of the Prism – where the rogue jinn languished, and from where Nequissimus had so recently escaped.

The immense iron sails clattered around through the void, turning the Prism slowly. As Amalorous banked obliquely to the right, Oliver set eyes on the pair of bottle jinn responsible for the fugian wind. Enslaved for eternity, for truly dreadful crimes, they took it in turns to blow into the great iron sails.

Below the bottle jinn, the mechanism, and the sails, lay the Prism.

The triangular sheets of impenetrable glass, which formed the inverted pyramid, dazzled Oliver as he passed. Like a brilliantly cut diamond revolving in a jeweller's window, it was spectral, almost as though it didn't exist at all.

As Amalorous swept on, Oliver made out assorted teams of technicians dwarfed by machinery. Some were lubricating the gears, tightening the bearings, or polishing the clockwork mechanism of the great escapement. Like the archivists in the library, or the malbino guards who patrolled the Prism itself, they too had been selected for their ancestral professions in antiquitas.

Soaring between the sails, Amalorous pitched abruptly, and descended onto the Prism's upper surface.

There the malbinos would cluster around the campfires by night, to gorge themselves on ghost venison stew, and swap tales of their forefathers. It was there, too, the guards had congregated so recently in panic, as news of escape spread through Zonus and out into the Realm.

As Oliver's subconscious caught patterns in the stray venison bones, counting them, Amalorous plunged down through the Prism itself.

A creature languished in every cell, each one

different in size and shape from the last. Some were so bulky they had little or no space to move. Others were dwarfed by the vast emptiness.

There were jinn with fifteen hooves, and others resembling fish. Some had horns, or beaks, or armoured scales, or mouths filled with interwoven rows of serrated teeth. Yet more were brooding silently, while others screeched in tortured rage. More still were covered from head to toe in slimy green mucus, secreted by jinn in times of distress.

As the leader dived down through the alleys and lanes backing onto the individual cells, Oliver felt elated and shocked. The Prism was like something from the furthest limits of his own imagination, the scale defying description.

Down, down, down they went.

Tearing along the twisting tunnels in which malbinos stood guard.

All of a sudden, Amalorous came to a halt.

'We are at the Prism's deepest point,' he said, in the only line of explanation offered during the flight. 'These quarters are reserved for evil personified. It was here Nequissimus lived, and where he shall be returned.'

Peering down through the cell's octagonal floor, Oliver felt the cold blackness of the Abyss below. His line of sight ranging upwards, he looked up – towards the ceiling.

By a state of unexplained refraction, he found he could see up through every level, and into every cell.

All at once, he viewed the wretched lives of every jinn incarcerated there, in a patchwork of imprisonment. Like the projection of the dragon's eye, it was impossible to understand.

Grimacing, the leader of Zonus breathed in hard.

'Can you smell that?' he said.

Oliver sniffed the bitter, pungent stench.

'Sulphur?'

Amalorous nodded.

'Nequissimus,' he said.

Forty-four

THE NEXT THING Oliver knew, he was back in the empty void, the legions of jinn prisoners vanished from sight.

Cold and alone, he wondered again whether the entire experience had been a figment of imagination.

As in a dream, his mind filled in the details, allowing him to see it all, as though it were a woven tapestry laid out across the floor.

He thought of the maestros on their perilous ladders, criss-crossing the stacks. Of the venison bones strewn over the Prism's upper surface. Of the jinn in the great hall, and of those already paying the price for their misdeeds. He thought of the living furniture, the portraits of wizened old men, and of Amalorous as well.

As if having been wished into existence, the leader of Zonus appeared.

'We are not accustomed to begging,' he mumbled.

'For what?'

'For help when it's needed most of all.'

'Help with Nequissimus?'

Amalorous moved closer.

'I cannot tell you why or even how,' he said. 'But you have the ability to assist us in a singular way. You are not normal.'

Oliver almost smiled.

'Do *you* have any idea what normal is?'

'Perhaps not,' Amalorous said. 'At least not when compared to what you regard as ordinary.'

'Normality's an overrated idea,' countered Oliver.

The leader of Zonus pinched the end of his nose in thought.

'Just as there are varying degrees of normality, there are different versions of reality as well,' he said.

'What do you want of me?' Oliver asked suddenly.

'For you to join our ranks.'

'As a piece of living furniture?'

Amalorous failed to get the joke.

'To join us as a Jinn Hunter,' he said.

Oliver choked.

'I couldn't hunt a dead chicken around a farm yard,' he grinned, 'let alone catch the most wicked creature in existence.'

The leader of Zonus seemed despairing.

'You are our only hope,' he replied, his expression bleak.

'That's absurd,' Oliver replied with a sigh. 'If the Realm is as infinite as you claim it to be, then there must be plenty of brawny, quick-witted warriors ready to step up to the plate.'

The leader of Zonus shook his head.

'Believe me, we've searched.'

'*Everywhere?*'

'In every dominion and in every kingdom, in every layer and sub-layer, in every cleft and conduit,' Amalorous said. 'In all those places, across the entire Realm, yours is the only name spoken. You are the only living creature with a chance of defeating Nequissimus.'

Oliver sighed again.

'So tell me, what exactly are my odds of survival?'

Amalorous winced. It was a question he had hoped not to hear.

'Fair,' he countered.

'And how exactly "fair" would fair be?'

The leader of Zonus gulped.

'There is a chance,' he said.

'A chance…?'

'A chance you will survive.'

'Are we talking single, or plural?'

Amalorous winced again.

'*Single.*'

'A single chance I won't be evaporated, ripped limb from limb, or that I don't go whacko like all the rest?'

Amalorous blinked.

'A chance is a chance,' he offered optimistically.

'Well, I'd say they're delightful odds,' quipped Oliver. 'Tell me, what are the chances against – that I perish in the line of duty as a Jinn Hunter?'

The leader of Zonus twisted the bezel of his ring awkwardly. He had never been good at hiding apprehension.

'We have a department devoted to calculating the odds of all possibilities,' he replied.

'Have they crunched the numbers on my odds at survival?'

'Indeed they have.'

'And they are?'

Amalorous eased his shoulders back.

'A little under four billion, six hundred million and two to one – *against.*'

Oliver might have glowered, but instead he laughed.

'I'm going back to my ordinary life,' he cried. 'To

my uncle and his carpets, to my math class, my dorm room, and to the tiny world that's my home – a world currently drowning in madness. *Who knows*? I might even get used to that as well.'

A second time the leader of Zonus implored. But no amount of pleading or flattery would change Oliver's mind.

'You are in astonishing danger!' Amalorous exclaimed in an outburst of last resort.

'Aren't we all?'

'Perhaps, but none more than you.'

'And why would that be?'

'Because Nequissimus is hunting you.'

'*Me*?'

The leader nodded.

'That was him out there… the one you assumed was Death.'

Oliver frowned.

'How did you know?'

'What?'

'That I was attacked… that I thought it was Death…'

'He's planning to get you even before you start hunting him,' the leader countered, without answering the question.

'We're going round in circles, aren't we?' Oliver said, rolling his eyes.

'But, it's the truth.'

145

'Why would Nequissimus bother to single me out?'

Amalorous took a step forwards, his face inches from Oliver's own.

'Because he knows that, in the entire Realm, you're the only person capable of capturing him.'

Wiping a hand down over his face, Oliver regarded the wizened figure before him.

'And, why would that be?'

'Because you are descended from the most celebrated line of Jinn Hunters – *the Jinnslayers*.'

Oliver balked.

'Thought your business was trapping jinn, not killing them.'

'You're right, it is. But in certain circumstances there's no other choice.'

'Then why not slay Nequissimus, rather than send him back to the Prism?'

The leader of Zonus took half a step back, as though the question had caught him off-guard.

'For all sorts of reasons,' he replied, ambiguously.

Oliver recoiled.

'Don't take it personally,' he said coldly, 'but my answer is still – *NO*!'

His face ashen, the leader looked out into the Abyss.

'So be it,' he said mournfully.

Easing the gold ring off the finger on his right hand, he presented it to Oliver.

'What's this for?'

Amalorous smiled.

'Something to remember us by,' he said.

Forty-five

THE POWDERED IFRITS circulated through the great jinn's corporal form, renewing strength to every strand of sinew, every organ and cell.

Within moments of ingesting the potent tonic, Nequissimus felt stronger than he had since the cursed afternoon on which Solomon had trapped him.

Lids blinking slowly over his eyes, he caught a snatch of memory... humiliation... the shame of capture, the wretchedness of a show trial, and the life sentence at the lowest depths of the Prism.

The memory haunted the jinn like nothing else. The subjection to ridicule was his reason for exacting total revenge.

On the brotherhood of the Jinn Hunters who ensnared him.

On the clerks, the legal counsel, and the witnesses.

On the maragor judges who sentenced him.

On the Order of Councilus who imprisoned him.

But most of all, on the Realm itself for waging war against him.

His mind clearing from the fog of incarceration, Nequissimus gathered his thoughts.

Where to begin?

With a flutter of disorder and fun?

Yes. Yes.

Pondering the question, the great jinn noted the single prey that would ensure his liberty.

The Jinnslayer.

Or rather, the only man alive ever likely to be worthy of the name.

Forty-six

CLIMBING THE STEPS from the basement, the paperweight warm in his hand, Oliver sensed something different at Ozymandias & Son.

Sublimely still, it was almost as though the carpet shop had been ripped from its foundations on East 8th Street.

Oliver called out for Uncle Sinan, but there was no sign of him.

The old shopkeeper's boots were missing from where they were usually squared beside his favourite chair.

Oliver assumed that his uncle had ventured outside.

Going upstairs, he changed, came back down,

and slumped in a chair. In his own time he pondered what he had seen in the basement… or rather what he imagined he had seen.

Leaning back, he reflected on the Prism.

The more he considered it, the more Oliver realized he could think in an unconventional way.

Like a key turned in a lock, thinking of the Prism seemed to allow his consciousness to roam free. Oliver concluded that it was somehow linked to the fact the prison prevented the rogue jinn from free thought.

Gradually, his ponderings turned to his uncle's lifelong obsession.

The obsession for Oriental rugs.

As he had been told time and again since early childhood, carpets were in the family blood – a secret knowledge with the power to inspire dreams.

Moving slowly through the shop, Oliver took in the patterns woven from coloured thread.

Kilims crafted in Cappadocia centuries before.

Ikat robes from Uzbekistan.

Heriz prayer rugs in raw silk.

And, Saliani runners from Azerbaijan.

Raised in the tradition of carpet lore, Oliver knew the subtleties of each style, the techniques, and the secrets. Uncle Sinan had schooled his nephew in the alchemy of carpets, passing on a kind of inner appreciation.

An appreciation based on patterns.

As the old shopkeeper would say, patterns – and the knowhow to create them – were guarded as treasure by carpet-weaving tribes. A delight to the eye observing them, or to the hand brushing over them, their magic ran far deeper.

Uncle Sinan swore the carpets he sold had talismanic properties. They kept them safe, he said, just as they did anyone wise enough to purchase them. 'Look beyond the obvious,' he would say, 'and you will perceive other dimensions – dimensions that will turn what you think you see upside down and inside out.'

His mind wandering, Oliver thought of the riverbank in the late summer sun, of his mother and father, and of the dancing dolphin in the mistletoe crown.

The small of his back warming at the memory, he heard something out on the street.

Footsteps... and a voice.

A voice he recognized at once.

'Hey Ollie! You in there?'

Springing up, Oliver fumbled with the locks.

'Am I glad to see you?!' he yelled, jerking the door back.

The Tibetan bell swinging wildly on its chain, Oliver's best friend slipped into the shop. Dressed in hospital scrubs, a trench coat pulled over them, his dark curly hair was matted and unwashed, his eyes rimmed in circles of fear and fatigue.

'Been on patrol with the medical unit,' he said. 'Jesus! It's a frigging mess out there! Never seen anything like it. Just can't understand how so many people could have gone nuts all at once.'

'Well you've found the one oasis of calm left in town,' Oliver said.

Bill hovered near the doorway. He seemed jittery, almost as though he were fearful – not of what was waiting in the streets, but of the carpet shop itself.

'Gotta get back out,' he grunted. 'Left my team down at the park.'

Oliver held up a hand.

'Hold on,' he said, running to get his coat, 'I'm coming with you!'

Forty-seven

MORTIMER BASKART WAS sitting in front of the TV, watching a documentary about koi carp – a can of extra-strength cider in one hand, and a packet of salted peanuts in the other.

Given the widespread state of lunacy, it seemed remarkable the television station was still broadcasting.

His phone had been tapped, as well of those of

his family and close friends. A pair of officers were staked outside his flat in an unmarked car, and a team of detectives were sifting through every facet of Baskart's life. As with all other professions, the police force was functioning in a fragmentary way, dozens of officers having succumbed to madness.

Like all the guards on duty on the night of the heist, Mortimer Baskart was a prime suspect. With pressure mounting from the very top of government, every line of enquiry was under investigation. Every sane officer on the case had the same gut feeling – that the guards were in on it.

It was just a matter of time before one of them slipped up.

The documentary ended and the credits rolled. Gripping the can of cider between his knees, Mortimer fumbled for the remote. As he did so, the vaults beneath Threadneedle Street were targeted a second time.

In an event witnessed not only by the duty guards and the CCTV, but by the special staff combing the vaults for clues, five thousand tonnes of bullion rematerialized on the uniform blue shelving.

The gold bars were not in order, and a few were missing – having been consumed. But, other than that, they were much as they had been before the heist.

Word of the mysterious reappearance spread. As

champagne corks popped across London and far beyond, Soulia the aduxa jinn was dragged away for trial. The judge sentenced her to one hundred and thirty years' incarceration – a reduced term in light of the fact she had assisted in helping the hoard to be returned.

In cases where the original owners were not contactable, or were long since dead, the golden objects were sold, the funds used to cover the enormous costs incurred by the TRD, the Treasure Repatriation Department.

As for Mortimer Baskart, he was pardoned, retired early on full pension, and presented with a wristwatch. Bought in bulk by the Bank of England direct from a dealer in Beijing, the supply of watches were fake gold-plate.

Forty-eight

OLIVER BENT DOWN to tie his shoelace outside the carpet shop.

As his fingers shaped the bow, his mind on autopilot, his eyes took in the patch of paving stone beside his shoe.

Nothing unusual about it.

A uniform slab of pressed concrete like any other.

But, his knee clenching to stand, Oliver noticed something bizarre.

He was watching the paving slab at a micro level, his attention trained on the hairline cracks, as though viewed through a microscope.

Rubbing his eyes, he looked up at the sky, then back down at the concrete.

A solitary ant was marching across the top edge of the paving stone, a grain of dirt clutched in its mandible. Absorbed, Oliver viewed it up close, as though he were shrunk to its size, or it enlarged to his.

'Something wrong?' Bill asked, waiting for his friend to get up.

'Huh? Oh, nothing. My mind's playing tricks on me… again.'

They walked east, taking a left on Greene.

Signs of insanity were evident all around.

Mangled remains of people driven to jump.

Cars smashed head-on.

Burnt-out buildings.

Strangers jousting with scaffolding poles.

Oliver caught a flash of the Prism, then of the dragon's eye. Without thinking, he looked down at his hand.

The ring Amalorous had given him.

Until that moment he had quite forgotten about it and, for the first time, he observed it with care.

As with the ant on the paving stone, he found he could make out the smallest detail of pattern as if it were under a microscope.

One side of the ring was gold; the other, silver.

The bezel was set with a triangle of rust-red cornelian. Holding it close to his face as he walked, Oliver studied the pattern. Like the grid of an electronic circuit-board, it was imprinted with straight lines.

Criss-crossing lines forming a kind of angular maze.

Drawn into it, Oliver found he could make sense of the detail – detail that was surely invisible before.

'D'you feel the same?' he said, looking over at his friend.

'What d'you mean?'

'Dunno really. Just... the same... the same as you always have?'

Bill shrugged.

'Guess so.'

'No weird insights?'

'No.'

'Glad to hear it.'

Oliver thought of telling Bill about the dragon's eye, and the world he had spied beyond it. But his best friend had no interest in fantasy. He regarded it, along with imagination, as a refuge for weak minds.

Walking in time with one another, they turned left onto Washington Place, the park now only a block away.

The body of a man was dangling from a lamppost outside NYU, suspended by his feet. Tied around his neck, a sign was flapping to and fro. Daubed in silver paint, the script read:

'ONLY THE BLIND SEE'

Oliver got a flash of a tree deep in a forest, the boughs contorted, as if writhing in terrible pain. Hanging from them like fruit, were dozens of hornets' nests, as large as watermelons. As he watched, the hornets swarmed, attacking each other. One by one, they fell to the ground dead, their miniature bodies piling up until the forest floor was carpeted in them.

Bill grimaced at the hanged man.

'There has to be a scientific explanation to all of this,' he said.

Oliver focussed on the trees ahead, their leaves golden.

'Not sure if science has the answers this time,' he replied.

Bill was about to respond, when he stopped in his tracks.

Recoiling, he slammed a hand to the side of his head, his face screwed up. He clicked his neck left, then right, mumbling something over and over.

A single word:

'Calimaster... Calimaster.'

Hands shaking, it looked as if he was going to pass out.

'Bill! Bill! What's wrong?!' Oliver shouted.

His friend's face and fingers were swelling, his body shuddering and juddering as if frozen to the bone.

In a frantic movement, he lurched forward and grabbed Oliver by the neck, strangling him.

Eyes bulging in a face turning ruby-red, Oliver floundered about like a sailor drowning at sea.

Swollen to ten times their normal size, Bill's hands clamped down all the harder, throttling his friend.

His grip tightening all the more, he broke into hysterical laughter.

Laughter punctuated by the single word bellowed over and over:

'Calimaster! Calimaster! Calimaster!'

Losing consciousness, Oliver glided low over the forest. Calmed, his mind drank in the colours, cacophony, and smells. Far below, the hornets had become flowers, the ground beneath them an ocean of white fire.

Pulled back to the present, Oliver slumped down onto the pavement. One of his fingers was tingling, the finger with the ring.

A reflection of no concern, his mind blocked it. After all, a tingling finger was of no consequence when survival was at stake.

But the tingling grew stronger.

Turning from the faintest trace of vibration, it swelled into a shuddering wave of bone-numbing force.

All of a sudden he was standing upright, as though nothing had happened.

On the ground, lying on his side, blood streaming from his ears, was Bill.

Doubling over in horror, Oliver shook his friend.

But there was no reply.

Bill Lewis was dead.

Forty-nine

PANICKED, OLIVER STRUGGLED to think straight.

Throat burning, eyes streaming, all he could think of was to get back to Ozymandias & Son, and to lie low there until his uncle's return.

Hands clenching into fists, he breathed in deep, and began sprinting in the direction of East 8th Street.

The clamour of rushing water filled his ears, like the swirling roar of waves echoed in a seashell abandoned on a deserted shore.

All of a sudden, it was replaced by a tremendous grinding noise.

The noise of steel rasping over stone.

Twenty feet away, rearing up on its fender, a UPS delivery van shot forward, propelled by immense force.

Oliver leapt out of the way.

A second truck rose up, hurtling towards him like a missile.

Again, Oliver dodged it just in time.

As soon as it was gone, another vehicle shot forward.

Then another.

And another.

And, six more after that.

As though an exterior force was controlling him, Oliver managed to avoid the missiles by fractions of an inch. Assuming good fortune was his protector, he had no idea the jinn in the cornelian ring had been assigned to protect him.

Picking himself up, Oliver kept going, until he reached the door of Ozymandias & Son.

With still no trace of Uncle Sinan, he hurried down to the basement, the paperweight in his hand.

Fifty

IN THE WAKE of the great jinn's escape, the celebrated malbino guard, Morrock, was relieved of his duties.

His foot, and the ear sprouting from it, was examined by a committee of more than six hundred experts. Hailing from a wide range of specialized fields, they made all manner of examinations, and dictated their diagnoses to a blind mole scribe. With great care, for which mole scribes were known, he recorded the comments in a ledger bound in charred mortle bark.

The first, a surgeon, claimed Morrock had been contaminated by breathing in his own perspiration.

The second, a psychologist, explained the ear was the result of despair in childhood.

The third, who was not a physician, but a sculptor, suggested the foot be amputated, and pickled in the juice of fermented figglewist fruit.

One by one, the experts stepped forward, gave their opinions, basked in the limelight, and sauntered away. Their egos bloated at having been called upon, most were interested only in being regarded as important. None of them was sensible to the woes of the veteran guard, or to his injured foot.

With a service record unequalled by any other living malbino, Morrock was more expert in the ways of rogue jinn than any other. Amalorous had considered him the most trustworthy malbino alive. Never for a moment had he imagined the veteran guard could have colluded with Nequissimus.

But, someone had to be blamed.

By the strict code of Zonus, the fact the great jinn had escaped through Morrock's failing was unforgivable. Respect for unblemished service was set aside.

Crouching in the corner of his meagre lodgings, Morrock waited for his fate. Constructed from jade-green marble, the room was empty – except for a heap of stale old straw, and a stone box.

A box which housed the guard's worldly possessions:

A battered tin containing the back tooth of a popofof fish.

A dried red flower without smell.

A blunt drawing pencil given to him as a child.

And, a spoon made from carved alabaster – a spoon considered by dwarf geese to be the most powerful amulet in existence.

In the hours after the jinn's escape, the ear on Morrock's foot turned black, and began to rot. Most of the experts had suggested cutting it away.

When the idea was voiced, the disgraced guard pleaded for it to be left just where it was…

An unsightly and cautionary reminder to malbinos and others, that danger was ever-present and near.

Fifty-one

HAVING PASSED THROUGH the projection once again, Oliver found himself at the top of the spiral staircase.

On the right of it was standing an exquisite grandfather clock, which he had not observed before.

Rather than made from metal and wood, it appeared to be living, shaped in the form of an elderly gentleman. The clock's hands were centred on the tip of his nose, the arms swaying back and forth as twin pendulums. Free from limitation, the single pair of hands appeared to tell the time in every place all at once.

In Zonus and throughout the Realm.

Across every dominion and kingdom.

On distant planets.

Beneath the seas.

In the heavens.

The clock's hands even told the time in the Vanished Empire of Trystia – a land where there was no such thing as time.

Intrigued, Oliver examined it.

As he did so, the clock morphed into the shape of a sleigh, and the staircase into a spiralling piste of compacted ice.

Climbing aboard, Oliver lay flat on the sleigh's length.

Before he could take a breath, the vehicle plunged headlong into the spiral.

Twisting down.

It corkscrewed round and round.

Racing at breakneck speed, until the track was no more than a smudged blur.

A blurred helix of candescent ice.

As Oliver descended, the ring on his finger tingled once again. Seeping from the cornelian triangle, the jinn protector slipped through the pores of his hand, into his bloodstream.

Once inside Oliver, it swam into his mind, where it planted something incapable of ever being removed.

The seed of a Jinn Hunter.

Fifty-two

AT THE END of the spiral, the sleigh whooshed past the dragon's eye, and flew through the fish-scale door, which opened in the nick of time.

Down the tapered corridor it careened, before hurtling into the great hall, where newly captured jinn were being processed.

Slaloming through the tumultuous mass of life, the sleigh swept into the leader's study, before screeching to a halt.

As Oliver recovered from whiplash, the sleigh melded silently into the shape of a leopard-skin couch.

Seated opposite, Amalorous pressed his fingertips together reflectively.

Befuddled, Oliver stood up.

He collapsed on the floor with a *thud.*

'Take your time,' said the leader of Zonus.

'Must have got on the wrong ride,' Oliver spluttered.

'Speed sometimes has its uses.'

'Does it?'

'Oh yes, the faster you go, the more you can pack in,' Amalorous said.

He clicked his fingers.

Instantly, the leopard-skin couch melted beneath Oliver and scooped him up.

Only when Oliver was sitting back comfortably, and a white-gloved jinn had served tea, did the leader of Zonus speak again.

'Happy to see you home,' he said.

'*Home?*'

Amalorous touched the edge of a thumb to his lips.

'Oh, I should assure you he's safe,' he said.

'Excuse me?'

The leader smiled.

'The answer to your question.'

'Which question?'

'The one you are about to think of.'

His brow knotting in a frown, Oliver thought of his uncle.

'He's safe.'

Glancing at the leader, Oliver tapped his temple.

'Are you in there?' he asked.

'I'm everywhere,' Amalorous replied, the words attended by the faintest hint of a chuckle. 'Well, almost everywhere.'

Silence prevailed for a good while.

Not a sound, except for the rustle of the furniture rearranging itself from time to time.

Oliver took in the shelves, the books' spines now bound in ivory white.

'I've decided to help you,' he stated, without looking at the leader. 'Because, the way I see it, I hardly have a choice.'

Amalorous smoothed a hand down his beard. Beneath the veneer of decorum, he was gloating.

'I hoped you would see sense,' he responded.

Peering at the floor, Oliver's eyes traced the parquet's grain.

Unsure how, he knew the source of the wood.

A lone tree in an endless expanse of jungle.

A vine twisting up through the forest.

Winding round and round, snaking upwards through branches.

High into the canopy.

Oliver had never been to a jungle, but he knew right there and then the vine had dreamlike powers – that a single drop of its sap could restore the life of a dying man.

Tapping a fingertip to his head a second time, he wondered what was going on.

'Still in there?' he whispered.

Amalorous wagged an index finger left, then right.

'Not this time.'

Another silence.

The leader of Zonus clapped his hands together.

'It's time to begin!' he exclaimed. 'There's not a moment to waste!'

Fifty-three

WITH EVERY PASSING hour, the world order collapsed a little more, as the lunacy sunk deeper into the fabric of nature and society.

Driven to breaking point, civilizations resorted to anything but civilized means.

In some dictatorships, people showing signs of insanity were rounded up and cast into the ocean, shot by firing squad, or gassed.

Struggling to remain impartial, the Occidental world did its best not to rush to judgement. Working in secret laboratories, its best scientists examined the brains of the living and of the dead.

Meanwhile, conspiracy theories raged.

From Argentina to Armenia, and from Stockholm to Shanghai, troops massed on national borders. Across the world, long-range missiles were made ready in their silos, as propaganda units churned out a tidal wave of disinformation and vitriol.

In a top-secret bunker south of the White House, the President and his senior staff were briefed. The room in which the meeting was taking place had been swept for every conceivable kind of listening device.

Once the President and his top officials were seated, the US Army's Chief of Staff, General 'Mad' Max Brockmill, got to his feet. The chest of his immaculate dark-blue uniform was adorned with medals gained in the line of duty.

With a shaven head, he was neckless, his face as savage as it was cold.

'Mr President,' he said, his features snarling, 'as you know, we have monitored all the usual suspects. The Russians, the Chinese, and the full deck of tin-pot dictators. If it's a consolation, we can say with certainty that what we're experiencing wasn't cooked up by any of them.'

Known for his composure in hard situations, just as he was for not mincing his words, the President waited for the Chief of Staff to finish.

'What are our choices, General?'

The right side of his face clenched in nervous spasm, Mad Max Brockmill barked:

'I say we nuke 'em, sir!'

The President held up a hand.

'Nuke *who*?'

'All of 'em, dammit! Let's nuke 'em all!'

Fifty-four

BEFORE OLIVER HAD time to change his mind, Amalorous escorted him to the offices of the legal department – a subdivision of a subdivision of a subdivision.

Although he might normally have gone through the great hall, the leader of Zonus was in a hurry.

Haste called for tunnels.

Tugging away a square of carpet in the corner of his study, he pulled back a trapdoor, and led the way down steep steps into an underground passage.

The walls and ceiling radiated an unearthly light, emitted by a pinkish-blue slime secreted onto the backs of the beetles living there.

Zigzagging along, the tunnel went up, then down, down further, and around, doubling back on itself.

Unspeakably damp, it smelled of hosolica lizards.

'Can I ask where we're going?' Oliver asked, hurrying to keep up.

'Told you... to the legal department.'

'Why?'

'Because the paperwork has to be completed before we can get started.'

'What paperwork?'

'You'll see,' mumbled Amalorous under his breath.

'This may sound crazy,' Oliver said, shuffling forwards, 'but all the blood's rushing to my head.'

'Quite normal.'

'Is it?'

'Oh yes. Of course it is.'

'Why's that?'

'Because we are upside down.'

Amalorous was struck his visitor would have questioned such an obvious and insignificant matter.

'You must remember something,' he said, shuffling faster, the tunnel meandering ahead.

'What?'

'That in the Realm the improbable is probable.'

Before Oliver could voice a reply, a door slid back, and Amalorous stepped out into the offices of the legal department.

Beneath dozens of candle-lit chandeliers, wax dripping like winter rain, were hundreds of low wooden desks. Piled with heaps of dusty papers, each desk was attended by a team of ghoul-like creatures. Their feet were small and rather dainty, their ears elongated, and they smelled of overripe prunes.

They rushed about, jabbering to one another in a guttural language articulated not by their mouths but by their ears.

As soon as they saw the leader of Zonus, they fell into orderly rows, stood to attention, and saluted with all five of their hands.

The only one who did not salute was a little girl.

Unlike the rank-and-file clerks, she didn't have petite feet, five hands, or extra-long ears. Nor did she smell of prunes.

Reserved and delightfully soft-spoken, with an enchanting face framed by pigtails, she was wearing a flower print dress.

Oliver ran a hand towards the ghouls.

'Who are they?' he whispered.

'Forlocks,' said Amalorous.

'*Forlocks*?'

'High-speed legal conveyancers. The backbone of Zonus if ever there was one.'

The leader strode up to the child and explained what was needed. Even before he was finished, the girl – whose name was Tameleth – spat out a set of orders in the raucous language of the forlocks.

Scurrying about with papers, quills, and

dictionaries, the clerks got down to drafting the document. The faster they worked, the larger their ears appeared to grow, and the more pungently they smelled of prunes.

'What are they doing?' Oliver questioned.

'Drawing up the standard contract.'

'What contract?'

'Nothing more than a formality. Think of it as an insurance policy if you will.'

Oliver appeared anxious.

'Don't follow,' he said.

The leader of Zonus slipped him half a smile.

'I wouldn't waste your time worrying about it.'

A minute passed.

A minute in which the sound of scurrying feet and the scent of prunes grew far more pronounced.

The forlocks lined up and saluted again.

Standing before them, like an officer at the head of an army, was Tameleth.

Poised between her and the forlocks stood a low wooden table.

On the table was a document, a soaring hymn to small-print legalese.

Tameleth nodded to Amalorous, who held up a quill.

'It's customary to sign such documents in the blood of a jusiack fish,' he said. 'But sincere apologies, for the fish are rare nowadays, and we are in a tremendous rush. Would you mind signing it in blue-black ink instead?'

Oliver took a step back.

'What exactly am I signing?' he asked. 'It looks very long and detailed... *Very very* detailed.'

Taking a page at random, he tilted it into the candlelight. Inscribed in an unintelligible script, the text was so small it was close to microscopic.

Amalorous brushed a hand at the papers, ducking his head to the side as though hinting at an explanation.

'The Realm is so vast even the most elementary legal document tends to get out of hand.'

'Does it?'

'Oh yes,' the leader responded distantly. 'You have no idea. This one's stripped down – no more than bare bones. You should see the divorce contracts they have in the Dominion of Lû. Takes an entire forest of trees in paper to print one out.'

Oliver nudged a hand at the document before him.

'Can it hold me to anything?' he asked.

Amalorous held up a scented qavak feather.

'Trust me,' he replied.

'Are you absolutely sure I can?'

The leader of Zonus nodded meekly.

With Tameleth and the throng of forlocks gazing on in witness, Oliver took the qavak-feather quill and signed his name neatly in blue-black ink.

Even before the ink was dry, the contract had been stamped and stamped again, and bound in the blood-red bark of an afafula tree.

Thicker than Oliver was tall, it smelled of roasted almonds, was magnetic to metal objects, and seemed to possess an energy of its own.

Donning their qavak-feather capes, a pair of forlocks set off to heave the document to the great archive, where the maestros would be waiting for it.

Thanking Tameleth, Amalorous led the way down another tunnel – one that would have been off limits to Oliver only moments before.

'You're in the system now,' he said, passing back a burning torch.

'I don't understand.'

'Well, now you've signed the standard contract,' Amalorous explained, 'it's unlikely you will ever breathe a word.'

'A word… about what?'

'About what you have seen here in Zonus, or indeed, anywhere else in the Realm.'

The tunnel spiralling and zigzagging ahead, Oliver held the torch up high as he hurried to keep up with the leader.

'And why's that?' he asked.

'Would have thought it obvious,' Amalorous riposted.

'Why?'

'Because you signed a legal document and, by doing so, you've accepted a sacred oath. Break it and you'll be in forfeit.'

'*Forfeit?*'

'Yes. Forfeit.'

'And the penalty for forfeiture is?'

'The usual stuff,' said the leader, his pace quickening as the tunnel sloped sharply downhill.

'By "usual", you mean…?'

'You know…'

'Er, no… can't say I do.'

Amalorous shrugged.

'That your blood will be drained and fed to phosphorescent swine. That your teeth will be extracted and ground into dust. That your muscles and sinews will be pickled in marsimus juice. And, that once removed through your eye sockets, your brain will be blended with wild herbs and…'

'*And?*'

'It's best for me not to say.'

'Why not?' Oliver asked intently.

'Because, believe me, there are some images you just don't want going in your head.'

Fifty-five

An outpost in the Great Emerald Desert, the Caravanserai of Mishmak was a refuge to a full gamut of wretched and degenerate jinn.

Gamblers, fugitives, and wrongdoers of the highest order, all of them were lying low in what was regarded as one of the most inaccessible corners of the Realm.

A few of the clientele taking refuge there spent their time plotting how to wreak destruction on all life forms except for their own. But most had no clear master plan. Instead, they whiled away the centuries in splendid and uproarious debauchery, until their funds or their luck ran out.

One thing united all the jinn who took sanctuary at Mishmak: their communal appreciation for the ripe fruit of the smorop tree.

The plant's precise botany had never been properly studied, nor had its effect on the jinn psychology. All that was known was that its fruit – a firm, fungal-like pod – drove every species of jinn wild with desire.

At certain times in history, entire religions had grown up, venerating the smorop fruit. Wars had been fought over it, too. In academic circles across the Realm, the plant was discussed, debated, and deliberated upon. Throughout antiquitas, jinn youngsters had been put to sleep at bedtime with far-fetched tales of treasure, adventure, and smorop pods.

Just as the jinn at the Caravanserai of Mishmak passed the days thinking of the smorop fruit, so did the legions of jinn languishing at Zonus, in the depths of the Prism. It was said the only way to endure an eternity of incarceration was by fantasizing about smorop pods.

So universally adored was the fruit, that gangsters and racketeers far and wide made fortunes for themselves by supplying it. In some kingdoms, the smorop seeds were used as currency. In others, bribes paid in the fruit bought political favour and fuelled the underworld.

Fearing a descent into lawlessness, as had happened throughout history, the administrators in Zonus set out to put an end to the obsession with smorop pods. They did all they could to adulterate the fruit, so the taste was no longer favoured, and to destroy plantations with blight.

For sixty-six seasons, smorop crops failed.

Then a few of the seeds were smuggled across the Great Emerald Desert by a secretive and subversive character named Mr Ot.

Far from the prying eyes of the administration, he began full-scale production, while ensuring that he – and he alone – held the monopoly on smorop pods.

JINN HUNTER

Few at the Caravanserai of Mishmak had ever seen the elusive figure. All they knew were the rumours:

That he lived in a palace under the ground.

That he was attended by otter-like servants, called locāxula.

That he hoarded a vast supply of dried smorop pods in a treasure vault fashioned from the stomach of a starved wasp jinn.

The secret of Mr Ot's success lay in the ruthless and extreme way he controlled the smorop trade. Hardly a tree, seed, or even a pod existed that he had not bought or sold.

There was not a jinn at Mishmak who would not have swapped his avian soul for the chance to feast in Mr Ot's treasure vault.

Except one.

His name was Borbor.

Hulking, meek, and covered in shaggy yellow fur, he was lugubrious, kind-hearted, and not overly bright. He hailed from a species of lemon-yellow jinn called 'clusots', who were universally liked because of their willingness to help others in need.

Borbor was the only jinn dwelling on the far side of the Great Emerald Desert known to dislike smorop pods.

For this reason, he had found work at the Mishmak Lodge – the one licensed establishment in existence at which smorop pods were regularly served.

Abhorring the fruit as he did, Borbor was trusted, for he had no interest in gorging himself on the stock.

For more than a century, he had been in the employment of the mysterious Mr Ot, the proprietor of the Mishmak Lodge and the man with a monopoly on the smorop pod trade.

In that time, Borbor had become known to and liked by the jinn who patronized the Mishmak Lodge. Courteous, and not easily angered, he could stand up to even the most unruly patrons. In the rare cases when he was riled, he reacted with swift and immediate determination – by writing the names of offenders on the back wall behind the bar.

A name inscribed there meant no smorop pods and no excuses – no matter what.

At the same moment Oliver was signing the contract drawn up by the forlocks, a messenger was arriving at the Caravanserai of Mishmak. Having crossed the Great Emerald Desert in a whirlwind, he appeared to be in a hurry.

A destination that took considerable time to reach, Mishmak was rarely associated with haste of any kind.

Dressed in a purple cape, with shoes carved from solid brolloc bone, the messenger strode up to the Mishmak Lodge, and pushed open the doors.

The saloon was packed, as it was on most evenings, with depraved examples of jinn. In high spirits, they were gambling, cheating, lying, boasting, and gorging themselves on their prized smorop pod ration.

The messenger pushed through the swing doors.

All eyes turned.

At Mishmak, strangers were judged with intense suspicion. Strangers in the livery of Councilus were universally regarded with suspicion and disdain.

Word of Nequissimus's escape had spread throughout the Realm faster than any news in the history of communication. Although there had been some merriment, the information was complemented by a great deal of anxiety.

Nequissimus on the loose meant Jinn Hunters hunting him, and that meant trouble for everyone else lying low at the far side of the Great Emerald Desert.

In the middle of the saloon, a pair of identical tortoise jinn engrossed in vosssuk, paused from their game. The one on the right armed himself with spikes. As he did so, the one on the left cheated, by twisting a stone piece three degrees towards the wall. The subtle move instantly transformed what may have been the worst position in the history of vosssuk, to a spectacular victory.

Across from the tortoise jinn, a group of marmot jinn secreted unctuous poison over their scales.

Lost in shadows near the back, a bottle-nosed

jinn transformed himself into a pea, and rolled into a crack in the floor.

The messenger strode into the middle of the saloon, doors flapping behind him.

Without trepidation, he sidled up to the bar.

'I have an urgent communiqué for Borbor, the son of Torbor, grandson of Vorbor,' he announced.

Borbor put down the smorop pod he was peeling, and blinked.

'I am he,' he replied.

Without delay, the envoy extracted a scroll from the velvet pouch dangling at his waist. Untying a rubicund ribbon, he opened out the document, cleared his throat, and read:

'Borbor, the son of Torbor, grandson of Vorbor, you have been summoned by the Order of Councilus.'

The lemon-yellow jinn appeared fretful.

After all, a summons from Councilus tended to mean one thing and one thing alone:

A trial, followed swiftly by imprisonment in the Prism.

But, as Borbor pondered it, the envoy had not been accompanied by Jinn Hunters.

'Am I in trouble?' he queried uneasily.

Clicking the heels of his brolloc-bone shoes together, the envoy bowed, passing Borbor the scroll.

'Your instructions are contained in this,' he said.

Fifty-six

THE TUNNEL ENDED in a doorway so low Amalorous and Oliver had to crawl through on their hands and knees.

Carved from rock crystal, yet another stretch of tunnel spanned out. It was followed by a ladder, stone steps and, finally, by an iron trap door.

The leader of Zonus heaved it back.

Having clambered through and dusted himself off, he held a finger to his lips.

'Quiet as you can,' he muttered.

'Where are we?'

'In the High Court.'

Making his way to the back, Amalorous ushered Oliver to one of the benches, carved from petrified wood. Spectators from across the Realm were in attendance, some of them travelling for months, or even years.

Few trials in recent memory had attracted as much attention as the prosecution of the midian jinn. Having tormented the Blackened Islands for decades, he had been trapped by the skill of Epsilius.

The courtroom was octagonal, a shape reviled by jinn. It was known to instil fear in them, although the exact reason why was a matter of heated debate.

Arranged on seven sides of the courtroom, the benches were packed with relatives of the rogue jinn's victims. A great many others were only there because of the media frenzy accompanying the trial.

At the front of the court, a stenographer, bred specially for the task, stood astride an outsized mechanical machine. Like all stenographers working in Zonus, she was a phynx. Feathered on one side and bald on the other, she had a funnel-shaped ear on the top of her head, two-dozen hands, with more than a hundred fingers on each. Recording the proceedings verbatim, she typed simultaneously in six hundred and twelve languages.

Behind the phynx stenographer sat three orlibs, the judges as impartial as they were unbribable. Although not human, they resembled toddlers, and were dressed in robes made from waxed pink taffeta and mealy grub silk.

Two of them were girls. The third was a boy.

Trussed up in the dock, sentries standing either side, was the midian jinn. His head slung low, he was hunched over, all three paws twisted together at his chest.

The chief orlib hammered a gavel down hard.

'In the case of Zonus versus defendant No. Z876T/T5161,' he began, reading a document typed sideways in single space legal gobbledygook. 'It has been determined by experts that the crimes committed by the defendant are genuine and beyond bona fide. For terrorizing the Blackened Islands, and dominions too numerous to mention here, the defendant shall be incarcerated in the Prism for one hundred and twenty-three years, sixteen days, three hours, and eight minutes.

'When he has served this sentence without parole, he shall be banished to the Island of Aoldrœm, in the Archipelago of Trill, to live out his days.'

Once again, the gavel slammed down.

The midian jinn was led from the dock, the courtroom buzzing with gossip, applause, and with the rumpus of spectators shuffling away.

Amalorous motioned to a side door, the one usually reserved for court staff.

'The judge seemed very heavy handed,' said Oliver as they went out.

'On the contrary,' replied the leader of Zonus. 'Thought it was a rather lenient sentence.'

'*Lenient*? He was given a hundred and twenty-three years!'

'I'd have given him twice as long,' Amalorous grunted.

'Why?'

'Because it takes time to punish a rogue jinn.'

'Does it?' asked Oliver.

'Oh, yes. You see, when jinn go rogue certain characteristics change inside them,' the leader explained.

'Like what?'

'One might call it internal wiring.'

'You mean, the way they think?'

'More than that. It affects their gamma-alpha-omega-beta pathways.'

'What are they?'

'All in good time,' said the leader of Zonus, shepherding his guest through yet another tunnel.

'I still don't get it. Are all jinn wicked?' Oliver asked.

Amalorous balked at the question.

'I told you before... of course not!' he exclaimed. 'There are a great many kind-hearted jinn.'

'Like the furniture in your study?'

'Indeed.'

Turning to Oliver, Amalorous touched a bony hand to his shoulder, as though he had something important to impart.

'When jinn are good, they are very good,' he said. 'But when they are bad, they tend to be wicked beyond belief. Unlike other species, most jinn don't have halfway settings. They're either black or white.'

'Can you ever make a bad jinn good?' Oliver asked.

The leader thought hard for a moment or two.

'There's always hope,' he replied.

'Even for Nequissimus?'

Amalorous sighed.

'Alas,' he said, 'the great jinn is the one exception to the rule.'

Fifty-seven

BACK IN THE colossal hall, a goose-footed jinn was being led through in chains.

Whimpering, moaning, and pleading for its life, the voluminous creature had been trapped in the Slaked Slew Forest. The order for capture was made because the jinn had been tormenting a community of silitia worms residing there, under a slimy grey rock.

Goose-footed jinn were not usually hunted as rogue. Generally agreeable, well liked, and little bigger than thimbles, they kept to themselves most of the time. The only problem was when they got it into their heads that a calamitous occasion was about to occur.

For them, imagined events involved interminable fear.

Fear the sky was about to become the ground.

And, the ground, the sky.

When terror of the calamitous occasion befell them, goose-footed jinn mushroomed in size.

One minute they were no larger than a thimble.

The next, they were the size of an apartment building, the stupendous bulk tottering above tiny webbed feet.

Leading the way past, Amalorous tut-tutted at the commotion.

A pace behind, Oliver was about to shoot out a volley of questions, when he made out part of a very familiar face.

'I don't believe it!' he huffed. 'How could it be?!'

Amalorous didn't hear. He was busy inspecting a fossil jinn from Speeg.

Craning his neck to the left, Oliver tried to get a better view.

Fifty feet from him, hidden behind an oversized warthog-like creature with a serpentine tail, was Bill Lewis.

Oliver rushed forward into the fray.

Circumventing a scorched mound of festering filth with a single bloodshot eye at the front, he worked on passing a huge shackled jinn with a pair of elephant heads.

The more he attempted to reach the spot where he was certain he had seen his best friend, the more he was prevented by the swathes of hunters and their captives.

Scurrying under the legs of the double-headed elephant jinn, Oliver shoved the warthog away, and found himself face-to-face with Bill.

He might have wondered how his best friend since fifth grade could have been there in the great hall, having so recently been a bloated, lifeless mess.

But it wasn't the question that posed itself.

Even though Bill's face was recognizable, the body to which it was attached was certainly not.

Every inch of the hall was heaving with oddity. For Oliver none of it compared in sheer shock value with his friend... or rather the permutation standing six feet away.

Bill's face was mounted on a narrow head with horns and spear-shaped ears. An elongated neck connected it to an alpaca's body below... a body dressed in the overalls of the Cadenta.

Unable to say anything, Oliver just stood there, gawking.

'*Bill?*' he moaned after a tortured pause.

His neck swivelling round, the alpaca looked at him.

'Hello,' he replied cheerily.

'Bill... that you?'

His friend's face squinted.

'Excuse me?'

'Bill! What's going on?!'

The alpaca struggled to deliver a smile.

'Think you're confusing me with someone else.'

'Aren't you Bill... Bill Lewis?'

'No. Afraid I'm not.'

'Then... who are you?'

'I'm Zelgar.'

'*Zelgar?* What are you doing with my friend's face?!'

Bill's cheeks blushed.

At that moment, Amalorous strode up.

'Thought I'd lost you!' he cried out, panting.

'I've found my best friend,' Oliver replied.

'*Really*?'

'Well, not exactly. He's a cross between my pal Bill, and a llama.'

'An *alpaca*,' Zelgar corrected.

'What's the difference? The fact is that you've got Bill's face strapped onto the front of your head!'

Known for good manners, Zelgar was clearly piqued.

'We must be going!' Amalorous said.

Oliver exhaled.

'Can I have a minute to get to the bottom of this?'

'You're sure to be seeing more of each other,' the leader replied. 'That reminds me, your training is about to begin at the Cadenta.'

'The what?'

'The Cadenta… Academy of Jinn Hunters.'

'Where's that?'

The leader of Zonus pointed to the floor.

'Down there,' he said.

'Underground?'

Amalorous didn't answer.

Instead, he touched the tip of a finger to his lips.

'There's not much time, but before we get started,

188

I should like to make an introduction,' he said. 'To someone who can fill you in with the nitty-gritty.'

'Nitty-gritty?'

'The nitty-gritty about jinn. He knows more about them than anyone else alive.'

'Who does?'

'Morrock.'

Making use of a particularly efficient shortcut – reserved for top officials – Amalorous led Oliver up, along, and down, until they reached a slender tunnel carved through bedrock.

Set in the middle of it was a triangular door, fashioned from fish bones and splinters of jade-green marble.

'These are the lodgings of a malbino guard... the one who let Nequissimus escape,' the leader whispered, as his knuckle rapped on the door.

'Is it he who knows about the nitty-gritty?' Oliver asked.

Amalorous nodded quickly.

'Before you go in, I should explain something.'

'What?'

'That malbinos don't have ears.'

'So how's he going to hear me?'

'Through telepathy.'

'I see,' said Oliver, even though he did not.

A fumbling, mumbling sound came from inside.

It was followed by banging, crashing, some cursing and, eventually, by the sound of hinges creaking.

The door opened wide enough for Morrock to peer out.

Startled at seeing the leader of Zonus on his doorstep, he jerked the door open, apologized, cursed, and apologized again.

Finding himself in the presence of such high authority, the disgraced guard was filled from the tip of his toes to his temples with indescribable dread.

The visit could only mean one thing: punishment and public ridicule for allowing the great jinn to escape.

But Amalorous didn't seem angry. Quite the opposite in fact. Having greeted Morrock warmly, he made the introductions.

Oliver and the malbino shook hands.

'I'd be grateful if you would fill in some of the gaps,' Amalorous said. 'You see he doesn't know the first thing about jinn.'

The veteran guard promised to reveal everything he knew. Bowing his head in thanks, the leader of Zonus let out a snort of approval, and vanished.

Oliver found himself alone with the guard in the tiny cubicle, his subconscious mind finding patterns in the marble, his nose on edge at the smell.

Plumping up a pile of sour old straw, Morrock invited his guest to sit. In his own time, he set about brewing up a pot of drem-drem tea. Malbinos regarded preparing the beverage as a sacred act. No member of the clan worth his salt would not have the constituents needed for drem-drem tea at hand.

A single pot of it required a variety of ingredients, which included:

A spoonful of ear wax from a spatula whale.

A jar of fermented pioaha cream.

Six leaves plucked at night from a marmary bush.

A sprig of lavender grown secretly on the southern slopes of Mount Zylovos.

And, most importantly of all, a wart from the left cheek of a souloulou bear.

Turquoise in colour, drem-drem tea was oily, inky, and had an aroma not dissimilar to festering parsilimus pods.

When the beverage was brewed, Morrock poured three cups.

A first for Oliver.

A second for himself.

A third for the spirit of his ancestors – guardians to the guardians of the Prism.

Timidly, Oliver took a sip, his lips and mouth instantly turning numb.

'Delicious,' he lied.

Sipping from his own cup, Morrock exhaled blissfully.

'Perfect,' he said.

'Delicious,' Oliver mumbled, a second time.

'So…?' the veteran guard asked. 'What can I tell you?'

'About jinn,' Oliver answered. 'And about Nequissimus.'

Morrock's head jerked up, his multiple eyes narrowing at the name. Nudging all four thumbs down at his foot, he let out a squeal of anguish.

'He did *that*!'

Oliver took in the spiral of rotting flesh and did his best not to flinch.

'What is it?'

'An ear.'

'I thought malbinos don't have ears.'

'They don't.'

Explaining how Nequissimus had foiled him, and how he had been relieved of his duties in disgrace, Morrock wiped a hand to his eyes.

'Rogue jinn get up to all sorts of misdemeanours,' he said. 'They give in to temptation, and I don't blame them. After all, if I could summon a treasure vault by clicking my fingers I suppose I would, too. But Nequissimus is different.'

'How so?'

'Because he can harness ultimate power.'

'If he's so sly, how was he ever caught in the first place?' Oliver asked.

Morrock poured a little more drem-drem tea.

'King Solomon possessed a seal with the power of controlling all jinn,' he explained. 'It allowed him to speak the language of animals, as well, and gave him a thousand other powers. Through the Seal of Solomon, Nequissimus was captured and incarcerated.'

'Where's the seal now?'

Morrock shrugged.

'Buried or lost in some distant kingdom or dominion I should imagine.'

'What's the difference?'

'Between being buried or lost?'

Oliver blinked a 'no'.

'Between a dominion and a kingdom.'

'Simple,' Morrock said. 'Dominions are clusters of kingdoms.'

'Which one is Nequissimus from?'

The veteran guard probed a thumb to the rotting black mess on his foot.

'From Grarpï.'

'Where's that?'

'In the Dominion of Paradisiacal Joy.'

'Sounds nice.'

'Well, it isn't. It's the most wretched hellhole of a place. Nothing but fever swamp and xirid plague.'

Oliver rearranged himself. The straw on which

he was sitting was so old it turned to dust when he moved.

'Had Nequissimus ever tried to escape before?' he asked.

'No, never,' Morrock replied. 'He was waiting for the perfect moment... for the conditions to be just right. You see, Nequissimus is different from all other jinn.'

'How?'

'Because nothing is quite so important to him as perfection.'

Oliver frowned.

'But, surely, there were systems to prevent him from getting free?'

'Of course there were,' the guard replied. 'But there was a flaw – a password built into the system... a password bequeathed to me, as it was to every member of my ancestral line.'

'D'you think he'll ever be captured?' Oliver asked.

'Hope so, and I hope soon. Because with every moment of freedom he gets stronger.'

Sighing, Morrock poured himself and his guest more tea. Out of courtesy, Oliver downed his second cup. His eyes were throbbing, as if they were being sucked from their sockets.

Morrock held up the pot.

'How do you like it?'

'It's very... er... unusual,' Oliver replied.

'It's the ear wax which is hard to come by these days,' the old guard clarified. 'Used to be available just about anywhere... but these days there's a shortage.'

'Where do you get the wax from?' Oliver asked.

'From my sister who lives in the Dominion of Lapopopo. The spatula whales grow legs in winter and roam the Fazzisti Mountains. They like the soil, you see – because it's mossy and zarid, and tinged with patrax dust.'

'Don't know what that is,' Oliver said, taking another sip.

'Patrax dust?'

'All of it,' he said.

Digging his rump deep into the straw, Morrock grinned, his nine eyes blinking long and hard in mellifluous satisfaction.

'Which kingdom are you from?' he asked.

Oliver shrugged.

'From New York, I guess. Except it's not exactly a kingdom.'

The disgraced guard mumbled something.

'Do you know it?'

'Only by reputation.'

'And what do people down here say about the Big Apple?'

'The Big?'

'*Apple*. The Big Apple. It's what we call it.'

'They say it's full of the craziest people in all the Realm. That they are even madder than the barking Moots of Listermot.'

Unaware his hair had turned turquoise, a short-term effect of the drem-drem tea, Oliver broke into a grin.

'And how are the barking Moots of Listermot?' he asked.

Morrock looked askance.

'Fluted to the gumbles,' he replied.

'Is that crazy?'

'Oh, yes. Really crazy,' he said, earnestly.

'How crazy?'

'As crazy as jostixill fish.'

PART TWO

MAZUMAGAT

One

ONCE THE POT of drem-drem tea was drained, Oliver was escorted by a marmut to Dream Room No. 6½.

His hair still tinged turquoise and his mouth still numb, he caught an alarmed glimpse of himself in a mirror hanging at an angle above the bed.

Compared to the modest quarters where the malbinos lived, the dream room was luxurious. Windowless and soft, the room's walls were padded in a profuse layer of taupe-coloured felt. The floor and ceiling were studded with miniature red beads. As for the bed, it was fashioned from an enormous seashell.

Although he hadn't been drowsy when he got there, Oliver felt overcome with fatigue as soon as he set eyes on the bedstead. Stretching out upon it, he fell at once into a deep, childlike sleep.

In his dreams, he was transported to the Dominion of the Serpent Queen: a land where snakes were the masters, and all other forms of life their slaves.

As Oliver slept, his eyes twitching fitfully beneath their lids, Amalorous entered. Within a short while, he was joined by Annis, head of the Cadenta. He was the first to speak:

'The Order of Councilus would be displeased were they to know you planted a jinn seed.'

The leader of Zonus smoothed a hand down through his beard.

'What was I to do?' he replied.

'How about allowing him to make choices for himself?'

'You saw it as clearly as I – he had no intention of joining us.'

Annis walked around the bed.

'You know that a Jinn Hunter can't hope to survive if he hasn't made the decision for himself,' he remarked brusquely. 'The seed you have planted will linger inside him, forever an Achilles' heel.'

'Nonsense!' Amalorous thundered. 'It'll lie dormant, protecting him like an amulet.'

Annis was unable to control his rage.

'No amount of training will ever turn Oliver Quinn into a Jinn Hunter!' he yelled. 'Least of all one capable of combating Nequissimus!'

The leader of Zonus turned despairingly to his friend.

'You are the wrong man to judge, and you know it,' he replied, his expression sullen. 'In any case, what other hope do we have? There's no choice but to place all our faith in this boy. The future of the Realm itself rides on his life and on his name.'

Two

THROUGH MONTHS OF scorching heat, Oliver criss-crossed the Dominion of the Serpent Queen, on a secret expedition.

Forbidden to disclose the details to anyone, he was subjected to constant attack.

In the swamps of Slōnt, he battled an army of black-tongued mambas. In the Forest of Gryn, he slayed the last known hollow-tooth python. After that, donning crampons, and with ice picks, he scaled the oiled cliff-face leading up to the Serpent Queen's palace.

Overpowering the guards, Oliver crept silently into the private chambers, where the queen was reclining on a dais in the dimming light of dusk.

Taking a phial from his waist belt, he gripped the queen's head in a morsolog neck hold. As she writhed about, coiling around him, he succeeded in milking her venom, before escaping the way he had come.

All of a sudden, Oliver was awake.

Eyes opening, he drank in an endless breath.

Fitfully, he took in his surroundings, easing a hand to his head, which felt as though it had been smashed against rocks.

Oliver could have sworn the bed in which he was sleeping was shaped like a giant shell, that the walls were taupe felt, or that the ceiling and floor were studded in blood-red beads.

Squinting, his head throbbing, he wondered how his memory could have been so faulty.

For the bed on which he lay was fashioned from a plank of driftwood, withered and worn by a hundred million tides.

The walls, ceiling, and floor were coarse, undressed stone.

As for tranquillity, it was gone – replaced by a sense of abysmal doubt.

Oliver listened.

A sound was echoing in the distance.

A muffled sound like the pounding of pickaxes on rock.

Jumping up from the bed, Oliver searched for a way out.

But there wasn't one.

The door had vanished. Now completely sealed, the chamber had no exit to the world beyond.

Oliver's ears reported a faint murmuring breaking over the rhythmic pounding of the picks.

Straining to listen, he focussed on it.

Little by little, it grew louder.

And louder still.

Desperate for the throbbing to end, Oliver rubbed his head. But something was ordering him to forget about the pain and to concentrate.

To calm down and to prepare.

The murmuring turned to gushing – amplified as though the volume had been turned up full blast.

Dead still, Oliver concentrated, his ears reporting impending danger.

A tidal wave.

The chamber began to tremor.

A moment later it was shuddering and shaking, infused with a rush of cold air and dust.

Oliver scanned the room for the hundredth time.

Impregnable...

No door or windows.

No escape.

The shuddering knocked him to the ground.

Clambering to his feet, he glanced at the rock-hewn floor.

Then up at the ceiling, and down the walls.

Freezing water was thundering in.

Rushing.

Surging.

Gushing.

In panic, Oliver scrambled onto the wooden plank.

The water was rising fast.

Up to his knees.

A moment after that, it was above his chest.

Throwing back his head, he took in the ceiling again.

No longer studded in beads, it was now paved with eyes.

Thousands of living, lilac eyes – each one watching him.

The water was high now, the driftwood bobbing up and down on its surface.

Something was poking out in the corner, where the ceiling met the wall.

A rusted iron lever.

Unsure of exactly what he was doing, Oliver paddled over.

Hands scooping the freezing water as it churned around him, he grabbed the lever.

With all his might he tried to wrench it down.

But it was jammed.

Again, he jerked it downwards.

Then up, and down.

Over and over.

The water now no more than six inches from the ceiling, the last of the air was being forced out.

Still bobbing up and down on the plank, Oliver's face was pressed up right against the eyes, his body stretched out along the plank.

The more frantic he became, the more eagerly they seemed to watch him.

Clearing his mind, Oliver struggled to think in a different way, as the last snatch of air departed.

His head plunging below the surface, he writhed in slow motion, peering up through the water.

Serene and silent, the lilac eyes observed him from their magnificent constellation.

A blurred pattern.

A pattern in the eyes.

Like the seedpods of a sunflower, they swirled out in multiple synchronized spirals.

Spirals of eyes, increasing in size as they grew farther from the centre, with the one in the middle the very smallest of all.

Fibonacci's sequence.

Muscles cramped, lungs drowning, Oliver sensed his mind working double speed, as though time itself had slowed.

The eye in the middle was not like the others.

Not lilac, but a shade of green.

In an act of profound certainty, as though he knew exactly what he was doing, Oliver thrust a hand up through the water.

The pad of his thumb jabbed hard into the eye.

A wailing pitch of excruciating pain.

A clicking sound.

The iron lever swung down in a perfect arc.

Instantly, the flooded chamber drained.

Three

NEQUISSIMUS MAY HAVE been free, but he was unable to quell the memories plaguing him.

The more pronounced the lunacy became that he exacted on the Realm, the more the recollections haunted him. Long before Solomon had sprung his trap, the great jinn roamed the Realm's innumerable permutations, in a desperate and diabolical attempt to revise the course of history.

As he soon found, however, a rogue jinn's fate was unlike other creatures' timelines – which are infinite. No amount of recalibrating configurations of possibility allowed certain events to take place.

Events such as the capture, sentencing, and the imprisonment of insubordinate jinn.

Established at the moment of creation, the fixed state ensured wayward jinn did not tamper with their own destiny.

Delighting in the lunacy that had spread like a tempest through kingdoms and dominions, the great jinn brooded once again on the day he had lost his liberty.

Having paused on his travels to exact a little mischief at a far-flung caravanserai, he roasted a wedding party, before turning an entire generation of ghoul infants inside out. Delighted with himself,

Nequissimus then spied a beggar hobbling out towards the desert.

Almost lame, the figure was furled in sackcloth up against the wind. His feet were bare, and his movements forlorn.

Rather than providing salvation, as a kindly jinn may have done, Nequissimus winked an eye in the direction of the pitiful traveller.

A bolt of lightning ranged down from a clear blue sky, striking the man full force.

To the great jinn's amazement, the traveller was not evaporated as he had expected. So, Nequissimus sent a second lightning bolt, then a third.

The figure remained unharmed, his sackcloth robe barely even singed.

Gliding over from his vantage point, the great jinn descended a few feet beyond where the figure was standing.

'What manner of sorcerer are you that you go unharmed?' he asked, his tone piqued and intrigued.

Lowering the sackcloth hood that concealed his head, the traveller regarded the jinn. Tranquil, his aged face was swarthy and sincere.

'I am flattered that such a mighty jinn as you would waste his time with an adventurer as humble as I.'

Nequissimus cackled.

'Fruit hanging closest to the ground is as worthy as that on high branches,' he replied.

The traveller grinned.

'I assure you, O great jinn, I am a wretched piece of fruit that will give you no satisfaction. My skin is weathered and worn, and the flesh beneath it is equally unsightly.'

Stooping, until his grotesque scaled head was inches away from the traveller, Nequissimus snarled.

'I shall decide whether you are eaten, or merely slaughtered as a passing pleasure!' he boomed.

The traveller pulled the folds of his tunic apart, bearing his chest. So emaciated was he that his ribs were sticking out beneath the taut, leathery skin.

'I hope you find some nourishment in me,' he responded, 'but apologize in advance for wasting your time.'

Narrowing his eyes, Nequissimus ground his rows of back teeth together in irritation.

'It's no wonder fate has sought to cast you in the role of a beggar, tramping from kingdom to kingdom. The same fate which created me in the form of the preeminent jinn in all existence!'

Again, the traveller grinned.

'How right you are, O mighty creature,' he said, bowing in reverence. 'Now, if you please, dispatch me.'

Nequissimus had almost considered letting the wretched adventurer go free – but doing so would suggest he was softening. As he pondered it, in his line of work reputation was everything.

So, arching his back, he considered quickly how best to transform the traveller into dust.

But, before the incantation left his head, the traveller held up a hand.

'A small and insignificant query,' he said.

'What?!' bayed Nequissimus, looming to full height for maximum effect.

'You really must forgive me,' the forlorn figure intoned, 'but I am curious by nature. As such I am intrigued to know how exactly you are planning on ending my life. You see, as I will be slain in the process, I won't ever get to know how exactly I came to die.'

The great jinn frowned, confounded at the question.

'I'm going to turn you into dust,' he said. 'That's all. Fine white dust.'

The traveller's head seemed to droop.

'Oh, I see,' he said ruefully. 'What a shame.'

'*Shame*?! How could it be a shame?!'

'Well, if I am honest, I was hoping for something a little more... you know... extravagant.'

Nequissimus, whose patience was wearing thin, flexed his talons and spat:

'How dare such a miserable wretch expect an ending more glorious than he deserves?!'

'I do apologize!'

Nequissimus balked.

'Very well. If you are ready, I will dispatch you now.'

'Of course. My sincere apologies.'

Looming even taller than before, Nequissimus was about to release the spell, when the forlorn figure before him held up his hand again.

'Forgive me for mentioning it, Your Magnificence – especially at such an inconvenient time – but I just noticed a little spot of dried blood to the right of your nose.'

Once again, the scales of the great jinn's brow rippled in a frown.

'What of it?!' he snarled furiously.

'You're right,' the traveller replied. 'It's of no consequence, and is certainly not something that ought to concern a jinn as great as you. But...'

'*But*...?'

'But since it looks a little silly, I would be happy to brush it off.'

Nequissimus rolled his eyes in rage.

'Once I have ground you into dust,' he scowled, 'I'm going to curse every grain!'

'Very well,' said the traveller. 'Even though they may laugh at you in the next kingdom you come to.'

The great jinn gnashed his teeth and breathed fire out to the horizon.

Then, in a move that even surprised himself, he

turned back to the traveller and lowered his head to the ground.

'All right!' he bellowed. 'Wipe the dried blood off quickly and we shall get on with the business at hand!'

Within a heartbeat, the adventurer pulled a tiny flask of fluorescent green was-swas from the folds of his robe. Without delay he dabbed a little of the ointment to the left of the great jinn's left nostril: the one patch of unprotected skin on a jinn.

Telescoping down to miniature size, the great jinn was knocked out cold. Casting off his sackcloth robe, the traveller revealed himself as none other than King Solomon, the Jinnslayer.

Five minutes later, Nequissimus's soul had been extracted and caged, and the wickedest jinn in history was on his way for the trial at Zonus.

Four

THROUGH SEVEN DAYS and nights, Oliver's adventures continued.

In that time he found himself in ever more perilous situations, pitted against all manner of foes.

He tramped across deserts of iron filings, and trekked through canyons carved from prehistoric bone. He glimpsed his own reflection in a pool of singing water, and camped in a copse of fabled bobastia trees. He fought sabre-toothed tigers and three-eyed ogres, staved off swarms of red ghouls, and waded across rivers infested with syfetic leeches.

One week, one hour, and one minute since entering the chamber, Oliver awoke with a start. Amalorous was standing at the end of the seashell bed. His wizened hands were holding a set of dark-blue overalls – uniform of the Cadenta.

'How were your dreams?' the leader asked tenderly.

Oliver wiped the sleep from his eyes.

'I was in a distant kingdom,' he said. 'It was…'

'A dream,' Amalorous whispered.

'No, no… It wasn't! It was real.'

The leader of Zonus managed a smile.

'As I have told you, reality and fantasy are one and the same,' he said. 'They coexist as two halves of the same thing. But in this case they took place within a realm known as "dreamtime".'

Sitting up, Oliver wiped his eyes again.

'Was I really asleep?'

'Yes.'

'How long?'

'For days.'

'What a waste of time!'

Amalorous tossed the overalls down onto the bed.

'From now on you'll wear these,' he said.

'Does the training start now?'

'It's already begun. Dreamtime was the first part of the training.'

Oliver seemed dubious.

'When is sleep good for anything?'

The leader of Zonus regarded him, his eyes tired and wise.

'On the contrary,' he replied, 'sleep is good for everything. Learning through dreams is the key to understanding the Realm.'

'How so?'

'Because when you dream, you free your mind.'

Five

A DRAGON'S EYE motif was etched into the doors of the Cadenta hall, the iris amber-yellow, the symbol framed in a band of chiselled gold.

Looming a hundred and fifty feet high, both portals were festooned with incantations and with cowrie shells. Standing to attention on either side was a uniformed guard, the dragon's eye insignia emblazoned prominently on their chests.

'Can't take you inside,' Amalorous said to Oliver, as they slipped into the entrance's shadow.

'Why not?'

'Because, when you enter the Cadenta Academy for the first time, you must do so alone.'

'Another tradition?'

The leader of Zonus bowed towards the great dragon's eye, and hurried away.

Oliver paused at the entrance as if rooted to the spot. He caught a series of memories, none more than a splinter of detail from dreamtime.

A blind white fish swallowed by another twice its size.

A kingdom defeated by a sense of guilt.

A little pink berry growing from a feather.

A single page of text, rumoured to contain more wisdom than all the knowledge in the Realm.

Examining the giant doors and the insignia that was now familiar, Oliver felt a pang of trepidation welling in the pit of his stomach.

It was replaced with elation, and by a sense he was capable of absolutely anything.

Stepping forward to the threshold, he took a deep breath.

The guards stooped low in deference.

With all their strength, they pulled the portals open wide, welcoming Oliver Quinn inside.

Six

A VAST CIRCULAR space, the Cadenta hall smelled faintly of overripe sardines.

The floor was marked out in an intricate black and white design – what looked like a kind of labyrinth. All around, candelabra hung down from chains, the candles set into iron holders cast in the dragon's eye motif.

Stepping inside, Oliver was excited, desolate, and confused.

But, most of all, he was curious.

Curious to know the secrets of jinn and of hunting them.

The hall was empty, except for a single plastic garden chair.

Walking towards it, Oliver was overcome with emotion.

He felt like weeping, laughing, singing, screaming.

As the waves of sensation dissipated, he heard a voice – a solemn, spiteful voice.

'Blood, and blood alone, binds the Brotherhood of the Cadenta!' it boomed. 'To break the code is to face the ultimate retribution. To question it, is to doubt the premise of life itself. To shirk from the line of duty is to fail… and failure of any kind will be punished. Punished in blood!'

The voice fell silent.

Oliver glanced down at his feet, his mind locking onto the labyrinth traced over the floor.

'Sit down!' the voice commanded.

As instructed, Oliver sat, his eyes on the maze.

He sensed a shadow falling over him. Cool, and strangely alluring, as though more than the absence of light in the outline of a man.

Slowly, Oliver's line of sight rose from the floor and, as it did so, he set eyes on Annis for the first time.

'I am the chief instructor,' he said. 'That means I am the sun above you and the moon below you. I am the conscience in your head, the pulse in your veins, and the ambition in your heart.'

'Am I the only person training here?' Oliver asked, surprising himself for daring to speak.

The instructor held out his left hand, the palm upwards.

The hall was instantly packed with people and with creatures, all dressed in uniform blue overalls. Some were ancient, while others were children. They came in every imaginable shape and form.

Many were engaged in unarmed combat. Others were hunched over leather-bound tomes, or were piecing clockwork machinery together. More still were giving demonstrations on specialized entrapment techniques, or reciting long texts committed to memory. A few were simply sitting on green plastic chairs, eyes closed, apparently asleep.

Annis let his left hand fall to his waist. Except for he and Oliver everyone else disappeared from sight.

'You must learn the ropes like all the others,' he said, caustically.

'Like a sailor?'

The chief instructor grimaced.

'Yes, like a sailor. But our ropes aren't made from hemp, but of empathy.'

Oliver smiled cheekily.

'The Ropes of Empathy?' he asked.

Annis scowled.

'The Ropes of Mazumagat,' he said.

The sardine stench seemed to disperse, replaced by a more pleasant aroma of melted caramel.

Oliver was prepared for the first lecture on jinn hunting.

But the chief instructor ambled away to the far end of the hall, where he chatted to someone who was not visible. Puzzled, Oliver felt uneasy, as though Annis reminded him of someone – someone he had always known.

Peering up at the candelabrum hanging above him, he glimpsed a memory. A dream. Or rather a mixture of both.

A fantasy from the City of Imaginary Minds.

A dungeon, dismal and candlelit.

The clanking of rusting chains.

The pervading stench of fear.

Prisoners bleeding from torture, united in despair.

All except a young man with a tattoo the size of a postage stamp on his chest. While the other inmates were resigned to their demise, he – and he alone –

was sanguine, in what was surely the face of certain death.

His secret was simple.

Each night, when the other prisoners slept, he would slip out of the dungeon, and embark on a fantastic adventure. Through lands summoned from the farthest reaches of possibility, he would live the fantasy within the infinity of his mind.

Oliver blinked.

Annis was standing over him again.

'You will not breathe unless I give you permission to do so,' he said. 'Neither will you rest, or think, or pause, unless the command comes from me, and me alone. Do you understand?'

Wondering what kind of a maniac was in charge of the Cadenta Academy, Oliver tasted acid in his mouth. Straining for a wisecrack to lighten the mood, he froze.

The instructor raised his hand a second time.

Maintaining eye contact with his pupil, he let it fall.

The Cadenta hall was not a hall any longer.

It was a desert.

A blazing, fiery desert of interminable blood-red dunes.

Stretching out in all directions, they only ended where the landscape curved into the horizon.

The chief instructor was poised in the same

position, his shadow shortened, a yak-leather riding crop clenched in his right hand.

'Get up!' he barked.

Oliver obeyed, his feet bare, his toes sinking into the dry sand.

'I'll kill you if I have to,' Annis said bitterly. 'For death is a small price to pay, if it makes you learn correctly.'

Oliver cleared his throat.

'Why exactly are we here?' he asked, bewildered. 'Where is *here*?'

The riding crop swished, left then right.

'*Silence*! You may only speak when I permit it!' Annis broke into a grin. 'You'll soon be incapable of conversation.'

Again, the riding crop swished.

As though it controlled an invisible temperature gauge, the sun's heat increased tenfold.

Oliver's clothing was drenched in sweat, his head peppered with blisters.

'Water,' he slurred, his voice almost inaudible.

Annis tossed a metal object down onto the sand.

A soup spoon.

Reaching down incredulously, Oliver picked it up.

'Water,' he repeated, softer than before.

'Dig a hole!' the instructor ordered. 'Make it as deep… as deep as…' he paused to think for a moment, 'as deep as the wisdom of a fool.'

'A what…?'

Swishing the riding crop yet again, Annis leaned back on the green plastic chair, now shaded by a lofty coconut palm.

The chief instructor took out a goliath-sized pocket watch.

'Get on with it,' he said. 'If you dilly-dally, I shall lose what little patience I have left.'

Seven

THE DAY AFTER the messenger had come and gone, a lone figure pushed out from the baked clay walls of the Caravanserai of Mishmak.

Over his right shoulder rested a slender cane. A plaid cloth tied at the end. Packed in straw, an underripe smorop pod was bundled up inside.

The fruit was not for the traveller himself, as he detested the taste of smorop pods. Rather, it was destined as a gift to the Order of Councilus. They may not have been jinn, but it was the thought that mattered, and lemon-yellow jinn were renowned for their thoughtfulness.

Plodding with deliberate steps, Borbor made a beeline towards the Great Emerald Desert, in the direction in which he imagined Zonus to lie.

Most mild-mannered jinn like he might have

materialized themselves instantly at the destination, but Borbor believed in doing things the right way.

And, as far as he was concerned, the only right way to travel between two fixed points was to do so on foot.

Besides, he regarded walking as massage for the mind.

Taking his bearings from Jistipimas, a constellation favoured by clusots like he, Borbor allowed his worries to well up, mature, and evaporate in time with his strides. Other than his expertise in preparing smorop pods, worrying was something in which he excelled.

First, he worried how long it would be before his sadistic employer, Mr Ot, found someone or something to replace him. He often hinted that a clockwork machine could prepare smorop pods. Unlike his devoted lemon-yellow employee, it would require no holidays, or payment.

Next, Borbor worried the Mishmak Lodge would be attacked, burned to the ground, or turned to fala-fala stone. Or, even worse, that a grangulus would burrow up through the deepest reaches of the desert, and swallow the entire caravanserai in a single dislocation of its mandible.

Most of all, Borbor worried whether the Order of Counculus would punish him when he eventually reached Zonus.

Every jinn alive had heard of the penalties meted out by the Order. Their methods were a communal obsession in dominions and kingdoms far and wide.

Lying low in debauched drinking dens, fugitives discussed little else.

Aboard frail dhows plying serpentine seas, weathered mariners droned on and on about the barbaric cruelty of the Order's wrath. Reclining in their jewelled palaces, princes and kings listened as their viziers cautioned about the Order. Even smox fleas on the backs of vermilion jinn were not immune. Those who understood their language maintained they rarely conversed about anything else.

When no more than a bundle of matted brown fur, Borbor had been coaxed to sleep each night by the threat of the Order.

'They'll shave you with a sharpened trowel,' his grandmother had crooned, looming like a death shadow over his bed. 'They'll pin you out with iron stakes in the Desert of Secret Wishes.'

'What will happen to me there?' the little Borbor had asked, pulling the covers up to his chin.

'The great wind will grind over you for eternity, like a baker's millstone, turning you from a nice little clusot boy into dust.'

Borbor had never quite believed his grandmother.

But, as one foot plodded in front of the last towards

the first horizon, the lemon-yellow jinn turned the matter over in his mind.

As he puzzled it, there could be no good reason why the Order of Councilus might want a jinn so insignificant as he.

No good reason, except to grind him up into dust, just like his grandmother had said.

Eight

WITH EVERY SQUARE inch it excavated, the soup spoon grew hotter and hotter, the sun searing down.

Having lost sense of time, all Oliver could think about was refreshment.

A glass of chilled water, droplets condensing on the side.

Nearby, Annis was reclining, his pocket watch in one hand, a tall cool drink in the other.

Unimpressed, he was keeping an eagle eye on the progress, or rather the lack of it.

From time to time he would mumble something to an invisible life form, motion as though signing a document mid-air, or would growl an order at Oliver.

'You're slacking!' he yelled, taking a sip of his cocktail. 'I've seen zothula fish doing a better job, and they don't even have fins, let alone hands and feet!'

'Can't go on,' Oliver moaned, collapsing into the brick-red sand.

He lay there, waiting for compassion.

For the order to stop.

For a swig of cold, clear liquid.

Or, at least for a moment's rest in the shade.

Annis was seething.

Regarding weakness as a cancer, he considered it the ultimate danger. Nothing disgusted him more than a student unwilling to defy barriers of exhaustion and pain.

Sliding the riding crop from under his arm, he swished it far more ferociously than before.

Instantly, the sun's strength doubled, then tripled.

Face streaming with sweat, eyes blinded, Oliver peered upwards.

Until then, a single sun had roasted him.

But now there were three of them.

'If you don't dig much faster,' Annis snarled, 'you'll be the laughing stock of the Academy.'

The last thing on Oliver's mind was what others thought of him, but he kept digging nonetheless.

The hole inched deeper.

At last, Oliver felt the delicious sensation of cool sand below the baked surface.

Gradually, he perfected a digging technique. Streamlining it, he found he could move larger amounts of sand swiftly, and with relatively little effort.

Cackling with pleasure, he dug faster and faster.

But something was wrong.

He looked up.

The chief instructor had disappeared.

Sighing, Oliver tossed the spoon down. With Annis gone, he could rest. He was about to relax in the shade, when his gut told him to keep going.

It was surely a test.

Picking up the spoon once again, he dug away double speed, until the hole was two feet deep. Face burned, arms and hands aching, he wondered whether he had reached the required depth – equal to the wisdom of a wise fool.

Annis reappeared.

Raising the riding crop high, he swished it down like an executioner removing a head.

The desert vanished.

There was not a single grain of sand.

Nor a hole.

Nor a soup spoon.

Nor a sun, let alone a pair of them.

Oliver found himself seated on the green plastic chair again. Above, were the candelabra. Below, the black and white labyrinth spanned out beneath his feet as before. He was no longer tired, or thirsty, and his overalls were clean.

Opposite, feet splayed apart, stood Annis.

Without a word, he tossed the oversized pocket watch up into the air. The front glass caught the candlelight as it whirled round and round.

A moment or two later the silver case was back in the instructor's hand. His eyes panning out from the watch, Oliver realized the training hall had changed again.

The chief instructor and he were in a far smaller room.

Panelled in antique oak, its mullion windows gave out to a perfectly manicured lawn. Halfway down the far wall was a grand fireplace, a medieval tapestry above it.

In the middle of the room stood a teak dining table.

At an angle on the right edge was a book of poetry, bound in the skin of a dok-kod calf.

'Close your eyes and tell me the story!' Annis demanded.

'What story?'

'The story of the room in which we find ourselves.'

Oliver cleared his throat.

'Well, there's a fireplace and a table, and a nice garden out there…'

Annis slapped his hands together hard.

'I don't want details!' he cried. 'I want a story!'

'Don't know what you mean,' Oliver said.

'Think about it,' said Annis. 'Think hard and think fast. I shall give you one minute. If you can't tell me the story by then, I will punish you.'

His eyes still closed, Oliver scanned his memory, his mind searching for patterns, and for the story.

'I can smell beeswax,' he said. 'It suggests the room was recently cleaned. There's a half-burned wooden bucket on the fire, and a broken wine glass on the shelf near the window...'

Glowering, the chief instructor swished his riding crop.

Oliver's hands began to tingle, then to burn. Opening his eyes, he looked at them, mystified as to how they could be in such indescribable pain. As he held them to his face, the skin turned leathery brown, cracking and festering.

'Give me another chance!' he pleaded. 'I beg you!'

The riding crop swished from left to right.

Oliver's hands were soft and pink again.

His eyes closed.

A second time he scanned the memory of the room, taking in the details. His mind made out patterns in the tapestry, and in the carpet on the floor, in the grain of the wooden table, in the book's binding, and even in the sunlight streaming through the windows.

Oliver forced himself to see deeper.

To descend down through the layers.

'This is the private study of a jealous and conniving

prince,' he said. 'He spends all his time plotting against his father, the king, and against his older brother, who is in line for the throne. This morning, the prince, whose name is Marcillus, couldn't stand it any longer. Having heard his father was about to name his brother as successor, he dreamt up a plan. Smashing a wine glass, he slashed his arm in zigzag lines – the symbol of his brother's...'

Right, left, right, the riding crop swished fast, silencing Oliver midstream.

'I've heard enough,' said the chief instructor. 'You will go to your lodgings now, and speak to no one on the way. We will reconvene tomorrow morning, at six. Do you understand?'

Oliver opened his eyes.

'How have I done?' he asked, a smile traced on his lips.

Annis appeared gravely displeased.

'You want praise, don't you?' he spat accusingly.

'Um, er. No, not really.'

'Yes you do!'

Taking a step forward, the leader of the Cadenta regarded Oliver in a way in which he had not observed him before. Eyes glinting like black opals, they hinted of awful terror.

Overcome with panic, Oliver wanted to look away. But, however hard he tried, he could not.

As though he were being hypnotized from back to

front, his mind's eye filled with images.

Not of objects or places, but of emotions.

He saw raw anguish, bloodcurdling and cold.

Hopelessness.

Trepidation and dread.

Heartbreak.

Torment.

Sorrow and woe.

'Abandon the need for the praise of others,' growled Annis. 'And learn to find acceptance in your own ability.'

Nine

As OLIVER LAY on the seashell bed, turning the day's events over in his mind, the lunacy continued to wreak havoc in the Dominion of Men.

In a new progression, those who had already gone insane began losing their sight. The first cases were recorded in New York. Within hours, people across the world were going blind.

At the same time, scientists in the US military discovered a correlation between sanity and blood sugar levels. The less sugar ingested, the less likely an individual was to go insane.

Through an administrative error, news of the link was leaked.

Overnight, sales of chocolate, processed sugar, honey, sweets, and even artificial sweeteners, nosedived.

Hours later, a secret government department in France discovered the insanity could be treated in certain patients by using an experimental compound called XYP-55. The drawback was that the drug led to total memory loss as well.

At a private research unit north of Beijing, a team of molecular biologists discovered a protein that appeared to alleviate the symptoms. Hailing it as a miracle cure, they were about to go public, when Party officials shut them down.

The research and equipment was seized, and the scientists were rushed away to an undisclosed military installation.

As the party officials saw it – why make money with a cure, when you have a chance to control the entire world?

Ten

WHILE OLIVER SLEPT, a handful of high-ranking administrators visited his bedside.

They included Morsius, supreme leader of Councilus, as well as Amalorous.

Watching their newest pupil as he tossed and

turned, they considered his progress and the task ahead.

It was the leader of the Cadenta Academy who spoke most forcefully:

'By sending this boy to war against Nequissimus, we are leading a day-old lamb to slaughter,' he said.

The supreme leader balked.

'Surely a small price to pay if it provides the required result.'

'Forgive me, Your Eminence,' said Annis, 'but I can hardly think of a single Jinn Hunter who could stand up to Nequissimus.'

'So...?'

'So do you really think this boy has a hope of capturing the great jinn, and returning him to the Prism?'

Hands clasped together at the waist of his long robe, Morsius sighed dismally.

'We can only try,' he intoned. 'If we do not, the Realm and everything within it will be annihilated.'

Eleven

OLIVER DREAMT HIS way through trials and tribulations.

He faced birds with tigers' heads, and dragons disguised as unicorns, strode through forests in which trees were armed with swords, and crossed deserts over which black wind raged.

As dawn approached, he found himself at the edge of a river. His mother and father were close, the warm sunlight playing over his skin. Following the line of his father's finger, he saw it for the thousandth time.

The dancing dolphin in the mistletoe crown.

Waking in the seashell bedstead, Oliver's adventures melted away.

Soon afterwards, he was standing in overalls at the great doors to the Cadenta hall, guards at attention on either side.

Fatigued from his night wanderings, Oliver thought of Uncle Sinan. Where was he? Would he go mad like everyone else? But, as he mused about it, his uncle was the one man who could pit himself against anything – even Nequissimus.

Bowing, the guards pulled back the mammoth doors, the dragon's eye dividing down the middle.

As before, the circular hall was bathed in yellow light from the candelabra, the floor concealed in the black and white labyrinth.

This time he was not the only student.

More than a hundred cadets were in training. Some appeared human; others were certainly not. Dressed in the same dark-blue overalls as he, each was preoccupied with specific activities.

On one side of the hall, a cluster of trainees were

climbing over each other, somersaulting down.

Across from them, a lone cadet was reading a thick treatise on clockwork brass machines. Oliver recognized him as the alpaca with Bill Lewis's face. Standing on his back hooves, he was turning the pages fast while reciting a mantra over and over.

In the middle of the hall, a slender straight-backed young woman was staring into the distance. A thick mane of blond hair flowing down her back, her hands were clasped as in prayer, her face rigid, eyes unflinching. She was gripped by tautness, as though desperately willing something to happen.

Taken by her loveliness, Oliver approached half a stride at a time.

Even when he was up close, the woman didn't move a muscle or flinch.

All of a sudden, snarling, her hands flopped down.

'To hell with you!' she bayed.

'*Me*?'

'Yes, you!'

'What did *I* do?'

'You broke my concentration! I was in Klozross! It'll take me hours to get back there!'

The woman ran a hand through her hair. Unable to help itself, Oliver's mind counted six fingers.

'*Kloz*...?'

'...Klozross!'

'Where's that?'

'In the Kingdom of Gròósol,' she said, baffled at being asked such an elementary question.

The alpaca with Bill Lewis's face strolled up.

'I'm guessing you're new here.'

Oliver nodded.

'Started yesterday.'

'What are you?' the alpaca asked.

'What do you mean – *what am I*? I'm called Oliver. Oliver Quinn. I'm studying at the Courant Institute. Feel as though you'd know that.'

'I told you, you've confused me with someone else.'

Oliver's line of sight panned from Bill's face down over the alpaca body.

'I'd say that's an understatement.'

The blond woman rolled her eyes.

'Zelgar asked *what* you are, not *who* you are!'

'I'm… er… *human*,' Oliver said.

'Human… *and*…?'

'*And*…?'

'And what else?'

Oliver shrugged.

'Just human.'

'You're not half-and-half, like us?'

'Half-and-half-*what*?'

'Half-jinn. Half-something-else.'

'No.'

'Oh,' said Zelgar, disappointed.

Oliver cast an eye around the hall.

Like the alpaca, the majority were definitely from the non-human side of the fence. But some, like the young woman with six fingers on either hand, appeared human.

At least on the face of it.

On noticing the newcomer, another cadet sauntered over to him. He looked at least a thousand years old, was missing an eye, and both his thumbs.

'What's your reason?' he probed inquisitively.

'My reason…?'

'Your reason for being here,' said the woman.

Oliver traced a hand down over his chin.

'Don't really have one,' he said.

'Oh,' retorted the ancient figure.

'What's *your* reason?' Oliver asked.

'His village was destroyed by pygmy jinn.'

'And my family were buried alive by vermilion jinn,' the alpaca explained.

Oliver turned to the woman.

'What about you?'

Even frostier than before, she spun round and walked away.

'You've insulted her,' said the ancient.

'What did I say wrong?'

'No one ever asks Amarath about her family.'

'But I didn't. Don't even know who she is.'

'By asking what she's doing here at the Cadenta,' the alpaca said, 'you're inferring.'

'Inferring *what*?'

'Inferring she must have come from somewhere else.'

'But I wasn't.'

'Yes you were,' the alpaca replied. 'And you know it.'

'This is ridiculous,' Oliver quipped defensively. 'You're nuts.'

Twelve

THROUGH THREE DAYS and nights, Borbor the son of Torbor traipsed in a dead straight line across the surface of the Great Emerald Desert.

Not once did he stop.

Not even when his stomach growled from hunger, which was all the time. With each step, he struggled to forget about food, and to think moral thoughts.

The reason was the legends.

No wilderness was so steeped in folklore as the Great Emerald Desert. Over the years he had worked at the Mishmak Lodge, not a single tale of it had escaped Borbor's ears.

The nightly feastings on smorop pods were accompanied by an endless stream of stories.

Stories devoted to the bizarre underbelly of the desolate expanse that was not green but brown.

They differed depending on whose mouth was doing the telling, and on whose ears were listening. On occasion they were embellished to the point of absurdity. But, most of the time, there was no need to exaggerate.

Because the truth was strange enough to satisfy anyone at all.

The legends always included similar ingredients:

A traveller disorientated and lost.

An insatiable greed.

A terrible fear.

A gruesome and perplexing end.

One version had become embedded in Borbor's mind, drilling in deep like a taproot. It had been told to him long before, when he first arrived at the caravanserai.

The story featured the ill-fated journey of a klunial.

Employed by the Realm's administrators, the raven-black creatures were charged with making sure jinn did not abuse their powers, or gain wealth for themselves in fraudulent ways.

The klunial in question had arrived at Mishmak on an especially dark night, having crossed the Great Emerald Desert from west to east.

His fur had turned ivory white from fear.

All the more remarkable because, as everyone knew, klunials are not easily alarmed. Indeed, almost nothing ever frightened them at all.

Slipping in through Borbor's ears, the wayfarer's tale had taken a firm hold in the depths of his imagination.

It had involved a maraxa, a bottle snake, and a tempest as tall as the Realm itself was wide.

After three days of trudging, and of trying to keep the stories out of reach, Borbor allowed a stray thought into his mind.

A single dried seed sitting on a saucer.

In turn, the thought made him think of a field planted with melons.

The melons led him to imagine large green stones.

And, the green stones led to a thought of the Great Emerald Desert not brown, but green.

Until that moment, the surface of the desert hadn't seemed especially abnormal. It had been barren and brown, like almost any other desert. But, as soon as Borbor's mind thought of emeralds, what he saw began to change.

All of a sudden, there were emeralds everywhere.

Some no bigger than blueberries.

Others the size of footballs.

A few of them were larger than houses.

Fearfully, Borbor struggled to put the emeralds out of his head. The more he thought of them, the more they were there – clear as crystal.

Stepping up his pace, he hurried on to the horizon, doing all he could not to pay attention to the stones.

But, as everyone who'd heard the legends knew, if you thought of emeralds, they appeared and, if you looked at what appeared, you descended down the slippery slope.

The Slippery Slope of Cursed Imagination.

Borbor marched dead straight. The cane slung over his shoulder, the smorop fruit tied up in a cloth at the end, his mind forgot about the emeralds. Instead, it thought about rain.

Not any normal rain.

Rain falling from the ground, up to the sky.

Before he had a chance to exchange the thought for another, it began to rain – droplets forming in the emerald dust, and rising upwards into the heavens.

It began as a light sprinkle.

The more the lemon-yellow traveller struggled to purge the thought, the harder it poured.

Soon, it was torrential.

Taking on a life of its own, the rain began to freeze, turning to hail, and the hail to snow.

Suddenly, Borbor was staggering forward in a blizzard, desperately fighting to put one foot ahead of the other.

It was then he heard the muffled sound of a child's voice.

'Fall on your hands and knees and climb down into my hole,' the voice said, no more than a whisper on the wind. 'It's snug and warm down here, and you'll be safe.'

Jabbing fingers in his ears, Borbor refused to listen.

But the voice came again, louder than before.

'I can save you,' it insisted. 'Trust me!'

'No! No! No!' Borbor exclaimed. 'I know what you are! Away with you!'

'But I am a little girl. My name is "Bellissima",' the voice purred. 'I want to be your friend.'

'*Nooooooo*!' the jinn cried yet again, struggling against the snowstorm. 'I've heard the stories and know who you are!'

Again, the angelic voice came.

All the more enchanting than even moments before, it charmed Borbor, as the wind and the snow froze him to the bone.

Five seconds later, the blizzard was a distant memory.

Borbor was sitting in an onion-shaped hole beside a log fire deep underground.

Across from him sat a mixture of a parrot and a dog, who answered to the name 'Bellissima'.

'You're a maraxa, aren't you?' said Borbor accusingly.

Preening a wing down her long drooping ear, the creature looked at its guest sideways.

'And why do you think that?'

'Because I've heard of maraxas, and of what you…'

The creature tilted her head a fraction, so she might hear a little better.

'Of what we…?'

Having remembered what maraxas were known for doing, Borbor froze.

'Of what you do,' he said, finishing his sentence.

'And what exactly do we do?'

'You lure lost travellers into your holes, make them powerless, and then you devour them. But first, you show them something. Something truly wondrous.'

The creature preened herself.

'Look into the fire,' she urged. 'It will help you forget the cold.'

Borbor was about to protest. Instead of doing so, he gazed into the flames.

But he didn't see fire. He saw treasure instead.

A cavern filled from stone floor to vaulted ceiling with immense riches.

Blocks of gold the size of chariots.

Magnificent urns studded in precious gems.

Chests brimming with glittering jewels.

Sacks overflowing with silks, spices, and rare perfumes.

'Take anything you like,' offered Bellissima affectionately.

The lemon-yellow jinn forced a paw over his eyes.

'Shan't!' he cried.

'Why not?'

'Because I know what will happen if I even look at it!'

'How is it you know so much?'

'I've heard the legends – that's how!'

Lids slipping down over her eyes, as though drifting into sleep, Bellissima sighed.

'Pray tell… what will happen if you look at the treasure?'

'I'll become greedy and unhinged, and will foam at the mouth, and then…'

'And then?'

'Then you will turn me into a maraxa just like you!'

'Nonsense,' smiled the maraxa drowsily.

'I know it's true. But… but… but…'

'*But*…?'

'But that little chest over there full of pearls looks so pretty. I would like to have it very much.'

Lustfully, his lips white with foam, Borbor reached out a paw.

Unable to control himself, he imagined fondling the pearls.

Eyes glazing over, his mouth foaming all the more, he felt peculiar.

Not the kind of peculiar he felt when embarrassed, or shy.

But odd in a new way.

Squinting at the treasure, rocking back and forth, he slipped into the hurly-burly of paranoia, the secret weapon of the maraxa race.

As he did so, he sensed something happening.

His lemon-yellow fur was changing into feathers, and his nose was transforming into a canine snout.

Stoking the fire, the maraxa remained calm, as she bided her time. Ensnared almost beyond the point of redemption, the prey was within her grasp.

Seconds passing like hours, Borbor made out a rustling noise.

A noise that sounded to him like the last strains of a lemon-yellow jinn's sanity seeping out into the wind.

Although far larger, his body was identical to the maraxa seated opposite, preening her feathers in the flames' warm glow.

Resigning himself to his fate, Borbor apologized.

Firstly, to his parents for being such a disappointment.

Next, to Mr Ot for being devoured.

And, to the Order, for failing them.

As the last wing feathers fell neatly into place, the lemon-yellow jinn thought of his beloved home – the Caravanserai of Mishmak.

He thought of a line of glum faces, united in disappointment.

His family.

His employer.

The Order of Councilus.

He thought of smorop pods and of how he disliked their taste very much indeed.

Lastly, he thought of the unripe fruit packed up in straw, tied to the end of his cane.

In a dexterous movement, Borbor snatched the cane in his beak.

Thrusting it towards the fire, he plunged the prized smorop pod into the flames.

A flash of blinding light.

A flash followed by squawking cries of lament.

The emeralds, the blizzard, and the maraxa were gone.

Instantly, Borbor was back in the desert. Over his right shoulder was the cane, the smorop pod hanging heavy at the end.

Forcing his mind to stay trained on the horizon, Borbor pushed on, one giant foot pacing after the last.

As he did so, he congratulated himself for remembering the secret.

The secret of a fruit adored by all jinn except for himself.

That, when plunged into fire, a smorop pod rewinds time.

Thirteen

SHORTLY AFTER SIX a.m., the great doors of the Cadenta hall swung open, and a pair of figures went in.

Familiar to every cadet, both were feared.

On the left was Annis. Beside him, Amalorous.

Taking their positions at the midpoint of the hall, they stood in silence as, pausing from their training, the cadets gathered around.

The chief instructor of the Cadenta Academy raised a hand.

'We have this morning received news,' he said. 'News that the reign of terror has reached a fresh extreme.'

Annis paused, so as to look into the eyes of every student. His expression frozen, as though all were doomed, he went on:

'Our most courageous Jinn Hunters are out there now, doing all they can to capture Nequissimus, and put him back where he belongs.'

Amalorous stepped forward.

'Nequissimus will be returned to the ultimate cell,' he declared. 'You may balk at my confidence. After all, as I speak, the great jinn is terrorizing every layer and sub-layer of the Realm, tormenting every permutation of possibility. But...' the leader of Zonus continued, his oyster-grey complexion flushed pink, 'we will vanquish him, and he will languish for an eternity in the wretched depths of the Prism!'

Resounding through the hall, a cheer wafted up into the darkness above the candelabra.

When silence had returned, a cadet at the back called something out.

Amalorous beckoned him forward.

'What is it?' he asked sternly.

Fearful and stooping, the trainee cleared his throat.

'What if there is no way to capture Nequissimus, sir?'

The leader of Zonus smoothed a hand down his long beard.

He did not reply, not at first.

Only after a full minute of silent reflection, he said:

'It is our universal hope that among you all there is a Jinn Hunter in waiting – one who will defeat our terrible adversary.'

Annis held up a hand.

'Always remember something,' he said, his voice sour. 'For it may save your life, or even the future of the Realm itself. It is this:

'The ability to defeat evil does not come in the form of great physical strength, or even a dazzling mind. It occurs not from the outside, but from the inside. An inner strength... a fortitude... it lies in a way of thought... in the reverse of everything you have ever known to be true.'

246

Fourteen

DEEP IN THE Forest of Silent Fear, beyond the Mountains of Kastilash, stood a magnificent hardwood tree.

The trunk was criss-crossed with lianas and vines, the upper branches bathed in a ghostly platinum light. A sea of identical trees stretched out in every direction. Each one as unyielding as the ground beneath and as limitless as the heavens above.

The only difference was that this particular tree had a growth swelling out of its leeward side.

A gnarled and twisted russet-brown growth, shrivelled and chapped by the elements and by time.

Not a single creature in the forest had ever noticed the tuberous swelling or, for that matter, the hardwood tree. No more than a sliver in the backdrop of existence, it was unremarkable, and so was overlooked.

Home to many kinds of colourful birds, singing melodies from dawn until dusk, the upper branches were mottled with slink moss. In the crevices and cracks along the tall proud trunk, lizards and beetles took refuge through the long, uneventful days.

But the birds, the lizards, and the beetles were not the only creatures living on the hardwood tree.

High up on an unusually broad branch, entwined with coiling vines, a horned possum jinn was basking in the balmy sunlight of late afternoon. He was brawny and blubbery, his red eyes overly large, and his mouth framed by razor-sharp teeth.

On his lap were strewn the remains of the most recent feast – a family of golden marshmak birds, snatched from a nearby nest an hour or so before. Around his left ankle was an iron clasp, bearing a code in precise lettering – 87492226518/PO/L/KM.

Gradually, the possum jinn succumbed to laziness as possum jinn are known to do. Slouching back drowsily against the mottled tree trunk, his red eyes closed.

Soon he was snoring, shuddering in repetitive waves of sound.

As he slipped into a fantastical dreamscape, the tuberous growth at the base of the hardwood tree began to move.

Inch by inch, it crept up the trunk, ascending so stealthily that nothing in the Forest of Silent Fear noticed.

Not even the tree itself.

Reaching the upper branches, the growth glided to the left, slipping along in silence to where the possum jinn was fast asleep.

All of a sudden, the lump halted five yards from the jinn.

A little time passed.

The gnarled russet-brown growth transformed in colour and shape.

The camouflage gone, a figure was revealed.

Epsilius, most celebrated Jinn Hunter of all.

Swarthy and big-boned, his face was a picture of grim determination. He might have passed as a wicilian, from the southern shores of the Terranean Sea. But, although his face and form appeared vaguely human, his hair was certainly not.

It was made from flames.

Stealthily, the figure pulled a net of silver mesh from his waist belt.

Taking careful aim, he hurled it at the possum jinn, which was still lost in childlike slumber.

Instantly, the net made landfall against the creature's skin. As soon as it did so, it began to envelop it, trussing the prey up in the silky gossamer of interwoven mesh.

Screeching, squealing, howling and gnashing, the possum jinn lurched to life, bracing itself for attack.

But, the more it struggled and writhed, the more the silver mesh constricted, until the jinn was bound up in a package no larger than a bowling ball.

'I curse you from the furthest reaches of the most putrid hell!' shrieked the trapped jinn. 'I'll suck out your innards and swallow them whole! I'll dissect your...'

Snapping his fingers, the Jinn Hunter silenced his foe.

'Hush, you wretched creature!' he yelled. 'By the Order of Councilus, I have been sent to capture you. You will be tried, sentenced, and dispatched to the Prism, where you shall live out your days.'

'*Sentenced?!*' squealed the jinn, its voice compressed into little more than a squeak. 'Sentenced for what?!'

The Jinn Hunter referred to a scroll, kept in a canister at his waist.

'For the destruction of the Dominion of Sacred Glass, and the enslavement of its king,' he said, the flames on his head licking the approaching dusk.

'Let me go!' cried the possum jinn. 'I'll give you half of all the wealth I have amassed. You will be richer than the King of Frastilas! Imagine it! Such wealth, merely in return for setting me free!'

Epsilius slipped the scroll away.

Shimmying down the branch, he grabbed the prisoner. Then, with it squealing offers of wealth and words of flattery, he climbed down to the forest floor.

The possum jinn tucked under his arm, he began the long journey back to Zonus.

Fifteen

WHEN AMALOROUS AND Annis had finished their address, a shrill whistle sounded, and the training resumed.

Awkwardly, Oliver waited for orders. He was about to approach the chief instructor when he and Amalorous strode out of the Cadenta hall.

'Best get on with your training,' said the alpaca, who was close by.

'But I don't know what kind of training I should be doing.'

The blond woman with six fingers thrust a hand towards the far end of the Cadenta hall.

'Go down there and get on with it!'

'But…'

'Get the hint and leave us alone!' Amarath snapped.

His head low, Oliver didn't reply.

Ambling away across the hall, his eyes were on the labyrinth etched into the floor. As he wove through the throng of cadets, each of them engrossed in their training, his concentration waned.

Oliver floundered across a plain strewn with bleached bones, hands tied behind his back. Feet bare, toes bloodied, his body was naked except for a pair of ragged shorts.

As though the situation were not wretched enough, he was forced to move fast in zigzag motion.

For, hanging down from the heavens on great iron chains, were hundreds of steel scythes. Arcing to and fro, they sliced through anything in their path.

Oliver's mind found patterns in the bones and in the chains. It even found patterns in the arrangement of the scythes – executioners of a great many travellers like he.

As in a dream, the predicament had no beginning or end.

A middle ground, it just hung there, suspended in limbo, in nothingness.

Zigzagging across the plain, scythes sweeping back and forth like vengeful pendulums, Oliver questioned where the fantasy was leading.

Much of the time his fictions were detached from reality, or what he assumed reality to be.

But, unlike most of the others, this one was shockingly authentic.

There was not a sensation he couldn't actually feel.

Terror.

Exhaustion.

Anguish.

Pain.

Most of all, he felt a sense of abandonment, as though the world had turned its back on him.

That was the moment Oliver understood.

This was not a fantasy, but cast iron reality.

A reality fabricated by the labyrinth beneath his feet.

Sixteen

ZEBRA STRIPES TINGED in electric blue, the furniture and walls of the leader's study camouflaged into one another.

Sitting at his desk, eyes closed tight, Amalorous was imagining a time of glory yet to come.

A time in which every single member of the Brotherhood of Invincible Jinn had been returned to the cells in the lowest depths of the Prism.

A time when the Realm was once again free from the name currently shrouding it like a plague cloud.

Nequissimus.

The leader's thoughts turned to Oliver, to the dim hope that he – and only he – would save the day and, in doing so, might save the Realm.

Like almost everyone in Zonus, the leader had been raised with the myth of the bloodline. An ancestry with influence and power, one which had never been properly described.

Until Oliver had first passed through the dragon's eye, Amalorous had high hopes. He had expected a warrior, a leader both of jinn and of men. A champion worthy of the title bestowed on those of his line.

The Jinnslayer.

The leader's mind was filled with Oliver's innocent face. He sighed. How could such a great and noble bloodline have spawned such a frail and pathetic example of humanity?

Grooming a hand down through his ample snow-white beard, Amalorous chastised himself for not taking care. Nequissimus had been his responsibility. He, and he alone, was accountable for the Prism's security.

The leader of Zonus sighed again.

As he did so, he prayed that the scion of the proudest lineage of all would metamorphose...

Transforming from a feeble excuse for humanity into the greatest Jinn Hunter since King Solomon himself.

Seventeen

GLINTING AS THEY swung through blazing sunlight, the scythes cleaved the stifling air.

Bewildered, Oliver hobbled between them, his mouth parched, his skin covered in welts and sores.

Time and again, he collapsed, his bloodied knees digging down into the bleached bones stretching from one horizon to the next.

Despite fatigue he managed to pull himself clear in the nick of time, before the great scythes arced towards him, slicing him clean in two.

As he stumbled on, snaking between the blades, an image came into his mind.

The image of a soldier slumped on the ground, a bandage coiled tight around his eyes.

Oliver's feet staggered on in a faulty rhythm.

Left.

Right.

Left.

Right.

His concentration shifted from the scythes to the bones, and on to the soldier. The more he focussed, the more detail Oliver observed.

Filthy and wretched, the soldier was dressed in the khaki uniform of the Welsh Infantry, a blackened tin helmet clutched between his hands. Shell-shocked, blinded by shrapnel, he was waiting to be evacuated from the trenches at the front.

Huddled all around him were injured men from Kitchener's shattered army, the gaunt face of each hung with fear and fatigue.

In the distance the *Boom! Boom! Boom!* of heavy guns resounded, the barrage pounding the blood-drenched ground.

The more Oliver concentrated, the more detail he made out. The stench of death. The scent of

Woodbines hanging from soldiers' lips. The infernal buzz of the flies swarming over the living and the dead.

But, it was the sense of futility that caught Oliver's attention most keenly of all, as though everyone there was trapped in limbo, just like himself on the desert plain.

As he drank in the details, Oliver realized he was no longer on the bone-strewn wasteland, scythes sweeping to and fro from chains. Instead, he was actually there in the trench with the blinded soldiers, the rats, the flies, and the filth.

He was clothed like any other corporal, his feet bandaged, the right side of his jacket covered in blood.

Crouching low in the trench, the explosions close and getting closer, he tried to piece together what was going on. Like the desert and the scythes, it was too real to be a figment of imagination.

All of a sudden, Oliver heard his name spoken.

Swivelling round, he saw a face – a face that he recognized.

Annis.

Like he, the chief instructor was dressed in the uniform of the Welsh Infantry of a century ago. He was about to say something when a shell exploded in No Man's Land.

Deafened, they were both flung to the ground.

'What... what... what the hell's going on?' Oliver stammered.

'The Kaiser's ordered an onslaught,' the leader of the Cadenta quickly replied. 'Get down, or you'll get your head blown off!'

'I don't understand... What are we doing here?'

'Observing.'

'Observing, what?!'

'Life... and death.'

The chief instructor smiled – a rare example of pleasure exhibited on his lips.

'Will you explain something to me?' Oliver asked.

Annis jerked back his head, as though waiting.

'Why aren't rogue jinn simply disposed of instead of being locked away in the Prism?'

'*Disposed of?*'

'You know...'

'No,' Annis asserted. 'I do not.'

Oliver cleared his throat.

'Why don't you just kill them?'

'Because we're not murderers,' Annis replied.

'Not even in the case of Nequissimus?'

The chief instructor clicked his tongue, signifying the negative and, at the same time, he clapped his hands, twice.

The trench vanished, along with the soldiers, and the stench of war. The clamour was replaced by the graceful melody of a harpsichord.

In disbelief, Oliver wiped a hand over his eyes.

Now dressed in the livery of the majestic House of Hesse, he was standing in a long sunlit corridor, the walls hung with splendid portraits of nobility.

Beside him, equally immaculate in court attire, was the chief instructor.

'Where are we?' Oliver asked, disoriented.

'In a European palace.'

'Because...?'

'Because we are observing,' said Annis, pointedly.

'I'm impressed,' Oliver grinned, taking in his costume. 'This is first-rate fantasy. There's not a detail I can't see.'

'That's because we're not in the preserve of the imagination,' Annis responded.

'*Huh*?'

'This isn't a fantasy.'

Oliver peered along the corridor, admiring the suits of armour, the portraits, and the silken walls.

'So, you're telling me we're actually at the court of... let me guess, Louis XIV?'

'Not exactly.'

'*Ha*! I knew it was a fantasy!'

'But it isn't a fantasy... nor is it the court of Louis XIV.'

'So whose palace is this?'

'King Frederick's, of course.'

'*Frederick*...?'

'Frederick I of Sweden.'

'Where are we?'

'At Drottningholm Palace, a little west of Stockholm.'

'And, er... *when* are we?'

'The year is 1745.'

'*1745?*'

The left side of his face catching the summer sunlight, Annis nodded.

'Wednesday, 16th June 1745, to be exact,' he said.

Eighteen

BY THE TIME Epsilius arrived with the captured possum jinn, still compacted into the size and shape of a bowling ball, the processing hall at Zonus was thronging with activity.

Day and night, hunters returned with rogue jinn from all corners of the Realm. The busiest periods were early morning and the middle of the night. This was because the conduits into Zonus swelled at these times – a result of the Realm's exterior magnetism.

Weaving through the multitude of hunters and their captured jinn, and the legions of officials and auxiliary staff, Epsilius strode up to one of the processing desks.

Without looking up, a clerk counted out three-dozen forms. She possessed a wide flat head, bottle-green skin, six arms and hands, and half as many lips, forming a curious triangular mouth. Her name was Mimi-Mo.

'Species?' she grunted, her voice husky.

'Possum jinn.'

'Previously registered?'

'Yes.'

'Number?'

'T807P5221.'

'Hunter's number?'

'Eight. Seven. Four. Seven. Seven. Three. Two.'

Mimi-Mo paused, grunted again, all six of her hands recoiling.

In a movement of considerable agitation, she looked up from the paperwork and onto the face of the figure standing before her – the figure whose head was crowned in flames.

Mimi-Mo's triangular mouth pouted, spluttered, and pouted some more.

Every clerk in the processing hall knew that number.

8747732.

A number as legendary as the Jinn Hunter who owned it.

'Congratulations, sir,' Mimi-Mo lisped.

Suavely, Epsilius smoothed back the flaming coiffure with the side of his hand.

'Thank you, Miss. Now, if you will take him off my hands, I'll go and get cleaned up. I've been in a hardwood tree for as long as I can remember.'

In an action later to be regarded as the cause of severe embarrassment, Mimi-Mo thrust all six of her arms at Epsilius. Pulling him forward, until he was flush with the desk, she smothered him in triangular kisses.

'I love you! I love you!' she swooned.

Extricating himself from the embrace, his composure unruffled, Epsilius stepped backwards. Bowing gallantly in the direction of Mimi-Mo, he handed the possum jinn to a liveried guard, standing to the left of the processing desk.

Without a word, the celebrated Jinn Hunter slipped off into the throng of hunters and captured.

Her eyes trained keenly on the fire, her mouth still pouting, Mimi-Mo let out a squeal of pained anguish.

'I love him more than he will ever know,' she sobbed.

Nineteen

WHILE QUICK TO grasp ideas, Oliver was challenged by the notion of what appeared to be the fantastical presented as fact.

'Why did you bring me here?' he asked Annis,

his expression knotted in confusion. 'To a palace in Sweden, centuries ago? Or to a war zone... or to...'

'To a desert, a world away in the deepest darkest depths of the Realm...?'

'Yes... why here, or there... or to any of them?'

The instructor peered out through the tall windows towards the landscaped gardens and the lake. His face gnarled and stern, as it had been in the Cadenta hall, he observed the distance.

'Because I want you to understand something very important,' he said.

'That you can travel through time?'

'*No*! Not that at all. The opposite in fact.'

'Wish I could say I understood,' Oliver countered.

'Listen and you may.'

Annis brushed a hand over the front of his frock coat. He was glancing down at the polished wooden floor, his beady eyes cold and forlorn.

'There's no such thing as time travel,' he said.

'I'm pleased to hear it!'

'You don't understand.'

'No, I don't.'

The chief instructor fluttered a hand back at the closest portrait, an oil of King Charles XII.

'There's no such thing as time travel,' he repeated, his voice more deliberate than before.

Oliver groaned.

'And why's that?'

'Because all possible times and all possible events are happening – all at the same time. Now. Tomorrow. A thousand years from yesterday, and in every fraction of a moment between them. Of course, time can advance and reverse, but that's different.'

Oliver groaned.

'You've lost me,' he said. 'But then again it would be right to say I was never quite with you.'

His small dark eyes glaring at the student, Annis said:

'All permutations of possibility... all times... and all places exist simultaneously.'

'You mean in some grand quantum multiverse?'

The chief instructor touched a finger to his chin.

'That's what the number crunchers at MIT call it,' he said. 'But I'm not talking about the kind of thing which is dreamt up by physicists to win a Nobel Prize.'

'Then what *are* you talking about?'

'Ultimate certainty.'

'Rather than...?'

'Rather than ultimate theory.'

'Can't you have a mixture of both?'

Annis pushed a hand into the air, urging Oliver to listen.

'You must free yourself from rigid theories and classroom models,' he said. 'Allow the way things really are to seep into you.'

'And how would that be?'

'Not in an abstract way, so much as an actual one.'

'Which means?'

'Which means if I were to throw you through this window, or to stick my thumbs in your eyes and hop round and round on one foot, or to strip down to my underwear and run through there into the throne room, screaming insults at the king, or...'

'*Or*...?'

'Or, if I was to materialize myself into another distant backwater of the Realm and set fire to a palace not unlike this – it would all be possible. Indeed, it would be much more than possible. It would be probable and yet well beyond probable. So much so, it would be absolute and ultimate certainty.'

Stepping back from the window, his eyes fixed on a patch of paisley silk on the wall, Oliver grinned again.

'Are you talking monkeys and typewriters?'

'Suppose so,' Annis retorted, reflectively. 'But monkeys eventually typing the works of Shakespeare would be the tip of the iceberg – an iceberg of outright possibility.'

'So what *is* possible?'

'Everything,' said the instructor.

'*Everything*?'

'Absolutely everything. But you have to forget damaged concepts.'

'Like what?'

'Like possibility and probability.'

'Huh?'

'They don't exist. There's no such thing.'

'Why not?'

'Because, the Realm is founded on what is definite – a vast and intertwined tangle of infinite certainty.'

'How can that be?'

'For once you just have to accept it.'

'Accept what?'

'That every permutation co-exists,' Annis said. 'Every arrangement. Every thought. Person. Place. Possible life form. All of it at the same time.'

'And where exactly is it all, this universe of certain possibility?'

The instructor almost smiled.

'Here. There. Everywhere. That doesn't matter. It's irrelevant.'

'So, what *does* matter?'

'That it all exists, overlaid on a canvas of ultimate infinity.'

Oliver frowned, his subconscious mind mapping the paisley patterns in the silk.

'Say I went along with this – with this canvas of ultimate infinity,' he said. 'How big would it be, this place where every thread of possibility was not only possible, but certain?'

Annis shrugged.

'Colossal,' he replied. 'Or, minuscule. Or, anything in between.'

Twenty

BEYOND THE GREAT Emerald Desert, in the fading light of dusk, Borbor found himself on an exposed mountainside.

His thoughts still firmly on the maraxa's hole and his body weary from days and nights of travel, he slumped down on a square-edged stone. His stomach grumbling and rumbling like an approaching thunderstorm, he was, as always, starving.

Borbor's mind flashed with a delicious mirage.

A plate sitting primly on the furry palm of his mother's paw.

A plate bearing a freshly baked wishwash pie.

Through a childhood devoted to gluttony, the dish had been his very favourite.

Drooling, Borbor swallowed once, then again.

Pining for his childhood village in the Kingdom of Molopus, he cursed himself for leaving home. The only reason he had ever done so was to track down a food said to be even more delicious than wishwash pie.

A fruit so appealing to the tastebuds it had been

known to drive even the most sensible jinn insane.

On an epic journey, the lemon-yellow jinn had travelled to the uttermost reaches of the Realm, searching for the most succulent food in existence. He had ventured to sunken kingdoms, had sought out hermits in cliff-top sanctuaries, and had even endured the ultimate in the unendurable – the Soothsayers of Hixx.

Following his gut, his spirits never waning, Borbor had eventually reached the one place where the prized fruit was said to grow in abundance.

The Caravanserai of Mishmak.

In the shadows of debauchery, at the tavern owned by Mr Ot, he had first experienced the vile taste of a smorop pod.

As Borbor pondered the wild adventures that had taken place in his search for the ultimate food, his stomach ached with terrible deprivation.

Had he not travelled to Zonus by land, rather than through supernatural means, he wouldn't have been sitting as he was, on a stone.

A stone lying on a barren mountain slope, on the far side of the Great Emerald Desert.

Borbor had no food.

But, as he pondered, there was always hope.

Closing his eyes, he imagined a shiny medal being pinned to his chest by the supreme leader of Councilus.

A medal hanging on a plush purple ribbon. A medal made from gold.

All of a sudden, Borbor's stomach grumbled, louder than before.

The idea of the medal melted away, and he found himself thinking of wishwash pie again. But, this time, it was different. He could smell it, as though it was actually there, his nostrils sucking in the subtle aroma, his taste buds feasting on the sophisticated flavour.

Borbor looked up.

The scent of wishwash pie seemed to be coming from behind the stone on which he was seated. Swivelling around, he sniffed hard, nostrils flaring at the ends. Sniffing again, he squinted downwards, his nose tracking the scent, apparently emanating from a stone slab set into the ground.

In the middle of the slab was an iron ring.

Without giving it adequate thought, Borbor hurried over and wrenched the handle hard.

As though weighing nothing at all, the stone slid away.

An entrance was revealed, steps descending into a chamber floodlit by fiery lanterns.

Crouching down on all fours, Borbor made out the scent of wishwash pie all the more keenly. Mouth salivating, he dropped into the hole, and hurried down the steps.

A moment later he was in the underground cavity, the walls covered in sheets of jagged blue ice.

His profuse fur ample protection against the most severe cold, Borbor hardly noticed the drop in temperature. He sniffed again, his nostrils anxious for more of the delicious scent.

Yes, yes, he thought, there it is – the pie just like his mother used to make.

The aroma was pungent, and was getting more so, as though the food was right there in front of him.

But, other than the smell, there was no sign at all of wishwash pie.

Pacing into the ice-bound cave, the ceiling hung with lanterns and icicles, Borbor came to a wooden table.

On it was not a pie, but a bowl.

A silver bowl half-filled with water, a veneer of crisp ice glazing the surface.

The smell Borbor so adored was apparently emanating from the bowl.

Following what his gut was urging him to do, he picked up the silver bowl, cracked the ice, and slurped every last drop of the liquid.

An instant later, the lemon-yellow jinn had collapsed, paralysed from the tip of his hairy toes to the top of his horns.

Even before his head had struck the stone floor, the scent had vanished, replaced by another.

The aroma of raw fear.

Although he was lying on his side, and unable to move, Borbor could still hear, see, and smell perfectly well.

Lying there, befuddled and dazed, he felt the floor thawing. It did so slowly at first. As it grew warmer, and warmer still, the ice began to melt.

Fused to the cavern's walls and ceiling, the sheets of ice dripped, cracked, and broke away. The melted ice drained through special channels cut into the floor.

His ears keenly honed, his eyes ranging left and right for the best possible view of what was going on, Borbor lay there motionless.

In his travels and during his time at the Mishmak Lodge, the lemon-yellow jinn had experienced a great many things. Priding himself on an inability to be easily surprised, he wouldn't blink while others collapsed in astonishment in the face of utter horror.

But Borbor was stupefied at what happened next.

As the blue ice sheets melted, they released an army of imprisoned dreq ghouls, entombed for centuries in its frozen walls.

Seeking refuge after a battle, the creatures had crept into the cave in ancient times, lured there by a mouth-watering fragrance. A stream cascaded over the walls, cooling the ghouls. All of a sudden, the stone slab had sealed the cavern shut, and the temperature had plunged. In the briefest of moments, the gruesome army had become entombed in glacial ice.

Now free, the ghouls stretched their sore limbs, cackling in glee as they warmed themselves on the lanterns, their shadows playing over the damp stone walls.

Grotesquely deformed, and all covered in warts, dreq ghouls were widely regarded as the most unsightly life form found anywhere in the Realm. An official committee, once established to locate the most hideous living creatures, had rated dreq ghouls as the absolute pits.

The verdict was later overruled, when a small group of unusually inbred ifrits were discovered wandering the Plains of Insipid Twilight. So ugly were they, that anyone who ever looked at them collapsed stone cold dead.

It made the business of verifying their ugliness almost impossible, and was the explanation as to why the committee had disappeared without trace.

As time passed, the dreq ghouls set about thinking how they might escape. Exploring the cavern, one of them noticed the entrance was open. He was about to leave, when he smelled something.

Something delicious.

Something no ghoul could pass up.

The scent of an underripe smorop pod.

Following his nose, he discovered the prized fruit, packed in straw, tied to the end of a cane. Beside it, grunting, vexed, and unable to move, was a lemon-yellow jinn.

The irony of the situation was lost on Borbor, just as it was on the ghouls. For, the scent that had lured the army of grotesque creatures down into the cavern in the first place, was none other than the succulent smorop pod. The cavern attracted its prey by reading the minds of passing creatures, enticing them below with their ultimate fantasies.

The smorop pod was devoured in the blink of a wart-covered eye.

Once they had consumed the fruit, the ghouls licked their warts, and sharpened their claws on the walls, as they tended to do after feasting.

They couldn't believe their luck.

Smorop pods may have been the preferred fare of dreq ghouls. But the rare delicacy was followed closely by the subtle flavours of lemon-yellow jinn.

Sneering and leering with delight, the ghouls gathered around, as they loomed down over the main course.

Bloodshot eyes wide with terror, Borbor took a last breath, and prayed for a miracle.

The chief ghoul's emaciated body bore down, trembling with unrestrained glee. Unhinging its jaws, the creature's mouth opened extra wide, as it prepared to crunch off Borbor's head.

Pressing forward, the band of ghouls were impatient for their leader to make the kill.

Silence.

Not a breath could be heard.

The only sound at all was the shrill lilt of a canary bird far away.

Twenty-one

GAZING OUT THROUGH the long windows at the gardens, Annis was preoccupied, as though something heavy was weighing on his mind.

'What's wrong?' Oliver asked.

'Hmmm?'

'You look worried.'

'Do I?' the instructor replied absently, his stare fixed on a stone fountain in the middle of a low geometric maze.

'Want to share it?'

'What?'

'The reason why you're worried?'

Slowly, the leader of the Cadenta allowed his line of sight to shift from the fountain, across the gardens, and back to the corridor.

Glazed, his eyes were touched with fear.

'As we stand here in idle reflection,' he said softly, 'Nequissimus is wreaking havoc throughout the Realm – throughout *your* world – and throughout so many others as well.'

'Can I ask something?' asked Oliver, puzzled.

'If you like,' Annis replied. 'But I can't promise you'll get the answer you wish for.'

'How does the world fit in to it all?'

'What do you mean?'

'Well, the world – *my* world… how does that fit in with everything else?'

Annis shrugged, as though it was the simplest of questions.

'You have to change the way you see things,' he replied.

'See what?'

'*Everything.*'

The chief instructor beckoned Oliver to follow him.

Turning, he strolled down the long corridor, crowned heads peering haughtily from their frames.

'Think of an onion,' he said, as he walked. 'The world in which you were born and have lived so far is a layer. If you didn't know any better, you might have thought it was the only one. In reality, it's just a layer in a far greater whole. As it happens, your world is no more than a backwater.'

'But is it the outer layer, or an inner one?' Oliver

asked, the heels of his buckled shoes clattering over parquet, as he hurried to keep up with Annis.

'You're doing it again,' said the instructor.

'Doing what?'

'Making the same mistake. It's a question of perception. Using the analogy of an onion is simplifying it to the point of absurdity. The Realm's absolute. It's everything. Millions, billions, trillions of dominions – worlds like your own and all kinds of others – all intertwined and coexistent.'

Annis stopped, his expression solemn.

'Everything you could imagine,' he said. 'Every fact, fantasy, unbridled possibility, or combination of them all – it's happening right now.'

'But where is it happening?'

'*Everywhere.*'

'Everywhere – all at the same time?'

'Yes.'

Oliver choked with laughter.

'Are you making this up?'

The leader of the Cadenta Academy scowled.

'The canvas of infinity is the Realm itself,' he replied irritably. 'But that's not the good part.'

'There's something better…?'

'Yes!'

'What could be more amazing?'

'That if you know how to do it, you can move between the layers with remarkable ease.'

'How do you do that?'

The instructor sighed.

'With experience,' he said.

Twenty-two

THE DREQ GHOUL'S repugnant mouth enveloped Borbor's entire head, row upon row of serrated teeth pressing down around his neck.

Crushing into the flesh beneath the yellow fur, the teeth took hold, as the creature's mighty jaws locked on.

Eyes dilated, body paralysed, Borbor's mind slipped back into the comfort of his childhood.

He thought of a river meandering through summer fields, of the little toy boat he had made from scraps of bastipok wood, and of feeling truly content.

As the ghoul's teeth clamped down all the tighter, drawing first blood, Borbor thought of what happened when he got to the water's edge.

A turquoise jinn had fallen into the river, and was floundering about, unable to swim.

Without giving it a passing thought, Borbor ripped down a branch from a nearby willow tree, and thrust it in the jinn's direction. Pulling the creature to safety, he saved its life. Once recovered, the jinn thanked his saviour and promised to return the good deed, were he ever to be in need of help.

The ghoul's teeth now tearing into his flesh, Borbor forgave the turquoise jinn for not coming to his rescue, even after he'd wished for him in the form of a miracle. His eyes rolled upwards, the circle of ghouls pressing closer behind.

At that moment, something unexpected happened.

A little yellow canary bird flew down into the cavern. Chirruping loudly, it transformed itself into the bulky form of a turquoise jinn – the very same jinn saved by Borbor long before.

Sliding its palms over one another, the jinn caused a flash of brilliant light.

Instantly, the dreq ghouls collapsed.

Dead.

Prising the jaws away, the turquoise jinn prevented imminent decapitation.

Another flash, and Borbor was sitting upright.

His debt having been repaid, the turquoise jinn transformed back into the guise of the canary, and fluttered away.

Twenty-three

AT THE END of the corridor, the instructor paused beside a suit of armour, his lips tight as if holding in a secret.

Reaching into the visor, he yanked it upwards.

The armour pivoted around to the right, creaking on rusted hinges.

Lost in darkness, a flight of narrow stone steps was revealed behind it.

'Follow me,' said Annis.

'Where does it go?'

'All you do is ask damned questions! No more... understand?!'

'Why not?'

'There you go again... yet another question!'

'But why?'

'Because the best way to learn is to work things out for yourself!'

Pacing along a short corridor, no wider than a barrel's length, Annis halted at the end. There were no lights, or burning torches, or windows but, the passageway was bright. As if in a dream, the lighting was an irrelevant detail, yet it was one that puzzled Oliver.

He was about to ask how it could be so they weren't in total darkness, when Annis dug a hand into his frock coat's pocket and pulled something out.

'Got a little gift for you,' he said.

Oliver leaned forward.

'What is it?'

The instructor pressed an object into his palm.

Even before he'd seen it, Oliver knew what it was from the shape.

A penknife.

Thanking Annis, he held it up to his face, to check out the tools. There was only one... a whistle.

'Oh,' he said, disappointed. 'I thought...'

'You thought there would be cooler stuff...?'

'Well, er, yeah, I guess so.'

Annis, too, seemed disappointed.

'The simplest of tools can be very useful in the right circumstances,' he replied.

'Thank you,' Oliver said again, his gratitude sincere.

The chief instructor tapped the back wall. Camouflaged into the stone, the outline of a door became visible.

'You're to go through there,' he said.

'To another dominion?'

Annis winked.

'Go find out.'

Opening the door, Oliver found himself back in the middle of the Cadenta hall. Alone, and dressed in dark-blue overalls once again, he wondered whether the journey had actually taken place.

Digging a hand into his pocket, Oliver's finger touched steel.

The penknife with the whistle.

As he caressed it, Zelgar and Amarath sidled up. Oliver was about to describe his visit to the trenches and to the palace in Sweden, when he stopped short.

'There's something I just don't understand,' he said.

Zelgar shrugged.

'What?'

'Why do they bother keeping them prisoner?'

'What else would they do with them?' Amarath asked.

'Kill them.'

The alpaca seemed anxious – so much so he didn't reply.

'Some questions are better forgotten,' Amarath riposted caustically.

'Really?'

'Yes.'

'Even such a simple question – one that would surely command a straightforward answer?'

'Especially simple questions.'

Before Oliver could respond, his attention was drawn downwards, to the black and white labyrinth traced over the floor.

Square upon it, was an object.

A jewellery box fashioned from indigo-coloured glass.

Twenty-four

THE DEAFENING WAIL of a siren ripped down Fifth Avenue.

The noise was coming from the lead vehicle in an armoured convoy of high-ranking military personnel – speeding to a secret command centre beneath Central Park. The streets were strewn with burned-out vehicles, garbage, and the general detritus left over from the lunacy.

As for people, there were almost none at all.

Most deranged New Yorkers had already been rounded up and taken to holding units outside the city.

Toiling round the clock on Presidential orders, a clandestine cell of the nation's top scientists had made a breakthrough.

A correlation between the epidemic of still unexplainable lunacy and the amino acid, tryptophan. Naturally occurring in the body, the chemical appeared to have an effect on the brain when administered in massive doses. Patients exhibiting advanced lunacy, and even blindness, were found to have their symptoms reversed when treated with the amino acid.

The discovery was made at a top-secret laboratory six hundred feet under the Central Park Pond. A throwback to the Cold War, the bunker had been hastily brought back into commission. Gathered from both military and civilian units, the scientists understood the only hope of finding a treatment was to be based at the lunacy's epicentre.

That meant Manhattan.

Within hours of the discovery, tryptophan production began on an industrial scale. Normal trials were shunned. Instead, the amino acid was handed out right away – starting with those who had gone blind.

A secondary breakthrough found that, when taken in a half dose, the same amino acid appeared to prevent the onset of lunacy altogether.

Sequestered in their own bunker south of the White House, the President and his senior advisers met in closed session. The medical officer in charge of the discovery had flown down to Washington to host the briefing.

In a short presentation he outlined the disease's pathology, detailing how tryptophan appeared to block the neurotransmitters. When he was done, General Brockmill leapt to his feet.

'Mr President, I can only beg you in the strongest terms, sir,' he exclaimed, 'to refrain from making this public. For the first time in the history of our great nation we've got a leading edge.'

'A leading edge…?' said the President softly.

'An edge over every third-rate despot from Caracas to Canton! We'll be invincible – in air, on sea, and land!'

The President pressed his hands together in thought.

'I like to think we're a nation that helps others,' he replied. 'A nation that gives before it takes.'

A senior adviser leaned over and whispered something discreetly in his ear.

'On second thoughts,' the President said, 'I guess it may well be prudent to delay the announcement of our discovery until the right time arises.'

Twenty-five

EXPERTLY CRAFTED FROM indigo-tinted glass, its sides etched with an intricate geometrical motif, the jewellery box was fastened at the front by a delicate silver clasp.

Unable to contain his curiosity, Oliver kneeled down and released it. As soon as he did so, the sides sprung outwards, transforming the box into a flat sheet.

In the middle of it was a little crystal – the shape of a snowflake.

Cautiously, Oliver picked it up.

Like the box that had contained it, the snowflake was engraved with a lovely pattern, repeated over and over.

Captivated, Oliver examined it, taking in the extraordinary craftsmanship.

All of a sudden he sensed a shadow fall over him.

The Bill Lewis alpaca, Zelgar.

'It's a seed,' he said anxiously.

'How can it be? It's made from glass.'

'Seeds can be made from anything. This one's crystal, from the Lake of Frozen Tears.'

'It's so beautiful.'

'Yes, it is, but deadly. You've got to be careful when handling seeds like that.'

'Why?'

'Because they tend to grow.'

Oliver grinned.

'Into what? A lake of frozen tears?'

'No, nothing as innocent as that.'

Just then, Oliver sensed the crystal warming.

As it warmed, it began to feel heavier.

A moment later, it weighed twice as much as it had done only seconds before.

Then four times… eight times…

Soon, it was too heavy to hold.

Oliver dropped it.

Still quite small, the crystal tumbled to the labyrinth floor with a *clink*!

Leaning down to check it wasn't damaged, Oliver saw the reason for the change in weight.

The crystal was growing.

Stooping low on his knees, Oliver watched the glass snowflake.

Like a living organism, its cells splitting, it was dividing and subdividing at an alarming rate.

'Look at it!' he said. 'It's getting bigger!'

The alpaca grunted.

Unlike Oliver, he wasn't impressed.

At first, the growth took place almost silently – no more than the faintest click-clicking sound. But, as it grew, and grew, so the noise was amplified.

Within a full minute, the crystal structure was the size of a family car.

A minute more, it was fifty feet high, the sound thunderous.

'Can't believe it!' Oliver yelled, falling back. 'Look at it!'

Standing well away, Zelgar covered his face with his front hooves.

'It'll lead to tears,' he said.

'Frozen tears?'

Before the alpaca could answer, the crystal shot up... transforming into an enormous glass fortress.

A fortress glinting in candlelight, its drawbridge poised over a crystal moat. Beyond it, lay a fortified bulwark, crenellated battlements running the full length of the perimeter. At each of the eight corners were watchtowers, each one adorned with crystal gargoyles.

Even more imposing than the fortress's size and shape was its inner structure, visible from the outside.

As it grew, the bastion developed vaulted passages and dungeons, cellars, banquet halls and private chambers. A warren of secret tunnels connected each individual area.

Scaling the moat's outer wall, Oliver gazed up at the structure, every inch of it crystal.

'How could all this have grown from a seed?' he questioned incredulously.

'Because it was no ordinary seed,' the alpaca replied.

Oliver looked round at his fellow cadet, who was now standing beside him on the moat wall.

'Think I grasped that,' he said.

'You're acting like you've never seen one before.'

'Well, I haven't.'

'*Really?*'

Oliver glowered at his friend's face on the alpaca's neck.

'So, how many crystal seeds have *you* come across?'

Zelgar shrugged.

'Dozens, I guess.'

'You've seen dozens of seeds just like that one?' Oliver quipped, his questions spat in annoyance.

For the first time, Zelgar seemed stern.

'You've never been deep into the Realm, have you?'

'Er, um… well…'

'Yes, or no?'

'Suppose not.'

'Thought so.'

'Have you?'

'Yup.'

Oliver took in Zelgar.

'What's it like?'

'Gigantic, and yet smaller than anything you've ever imagined,' the alpaca answered. 'Intricate and, at the same time, totally bare. Both confusing, and quite clear all at once. Beautiful, and utterly grotesque.'

'I don't quite believe it exists,' said Oliver.

'The Realm?'

'No, *that*…!'

'The fortress?'

'Yeah. Bet you anything I'm imagining it.'

Closing his eyes, Oliver found himself standing beside his father on the riverbank, gazing at the rainbow dolphin as it danced through the water.

'It exists if you believe in it,' Zelgar said.

'The line between fact and fantasy…?'

'Exactly.'

'But how can it be both?'

'Easily.'

'All right. But how do you get your head around it?'
The alpaca shrugged again.

'To understand it you have to rewire your mind,' he said.

Twenty-six

AT EXACTLY SIX p.m. Herbert Morlib wound the steel shutters down over the front of Morlib's Optical Inc., checking the tiny silver pill-box was in place.

Since Operative Zeliak's visit he had been on edge, never having imagined the great jinn's soul could have been stored in the holding zone beneath his family's shop.

Born into the service of Zonus, Herbert was schooled from earliest childhood in the ways of guarding the souls of jinn. He'd studied the ins and outs of the business, mastering the mass of information provided through official channels.

The most useful knowhow of all was that revealed to him by the members of his own family. Passed down from mother to daughter, and father to son, it took the form of stories and fables, anecdotes and riddles. Laid layer on layer, the information had taught Herbert how to act and react in any given situation.

As he had been told a thousand times, the holding

zone his ancestors guarded was once located on an insignificant little island – of no interest to anyone. Herbert often pondered how someone, or something, must have known that Manhattan's metropolis would eventually force out the tangle of rivers and forests. The little he knew about Zonus was that nothing at all ever happened by chance.

Pacing back through the darkened shop, Herbert caught a flash of himself as a boy, quizzing his grandfather on whether there were other such holding zones. Turning to the child, the old man was disturbed by the question.

'It's none of our business,' he replied in a severe tone. 'Just as it's none of our business who or what the birds down there are. We are guardians and that's all. Nothing more. Nothing less.'

Sniffing, Herbert Morlib wiped a cuff to his nose, let out a burp, and thanked Providence for not giving him a family. He had no one to judge him, or to tell him how to behave.

He sniffed again.

With his demise the unbroken line of duty stretching back since ancient times would be breached. After that, the powers in far-off Zonus would have to find a new line of guardians to watch over their precious birds.

Padding through to the back room, Herbert opened the store cupboard and took out the remains of a putrid scalica cake. His entire life had been spent in the Dominion of Men. But, as his departed parents used to constantly remind him, he was a wartle ogre in disguise.

As such, nothing was so sacred as feasting twice daily on scalica cake. Not even venerating the tufts of hair that grew in the inner curl of his right ear.

Twenty-seven

HIS FEET SPLAYED wide on the Cadenta's floor, Oliver made out the cries of a woman screaming for her life.

Looking up fast, he scanned the fortress's glinting façade.

Zelgar thrust a hoof upwards.

'Up there!'

'Where?'

'High on the battlement.'

Craning his neck back, Oliver made out a figure high on the north-east battlement, arms gyrating frantically.

'Oh my, oh my,' exclaimed the alpaca anxiously, biting his lower lip. 'It's Amarath!'

Oliver caught a flash of the blond cadet with six fingers on either hand, the one who had savaged him.

'What's *she* doing up *there*?'

'We have to save her!' cried the alpaca desperately.

'And how the hell do you plan to do that?'

'We have to think of something!'

'*We*?'

'Who knows what'll happen if we don't?!'

Oliver held up a hand, the fingers splayed.

'Wait a minute. This looks like just another good ol' fantasy to me.'

'No, no… not this time.'

'How can you be so sure?'

The alpaca motioned a hoof towards the crystal battlement.

'Because of *that*,' he said.

Oliver squinted.

Poised on a crystal parapet way above, a few feet from where Amarath was crying out, a gigantic creature was looming down. Glowing red-hot, it was a fire jinn.

The screaming grew all the louder.

Pleading for someone to rescue her, Amarath fell onto her knees.

'We *must* help her!' Zelgar bawled again. 'She's one of us. It's the code of the Jinn Hunters. *Whatever the circumstances, always save one of your own!*'

'OK! OK!' Oliver griped. 'I get it!'

Mind racing, he examined the outer wall.

The moat was peppered in glass spikes, impaled

with the bodies of ill-fated invaders. Some were no more than skeletons. Others were fresher – their ragged clothing drenched in blood.

Amarath's exclamations increased in pitch and volume.

Oliver evaluated the situation.

No way to breach the moat or lower the drawbridge.

No equipment with which to vault over to the fortress walls.

No time to waste with plans that stood no chance.

As he climbed up onto the moat wall, Oliver thought of something.

A memory from childhood.

Seated cross-legged on the floor at the carpet shop, his uncle was teaching him how to fit a wooden puzzle together. However hard Oliver tried, the blocks wouldn't join up. All afternoon he forced them together – his fingers bruised, patience at breaking point.

Just as he was about to give up, his uncle whispered something – something Oliver had never forgotten:

'Change the way you're doing it,' he'd said.

'But they don't fit!'

'Try again, but not in an obvious way.'

Oliver put the blocks down on the carpet. Observing them from a distance, he imagined them turning in his mind.

All of a sudden, he noticed something.

The blocks' sides were numbered with tiny Roman numerals. Join the corresponding numerals, and the blocks fitted together.

Climbing down from the moat's supporting barricade, Oliver stepped back.

Behind him, the expanse of the Cadenta hall was hauntingly empty. Ahead, rising up like a great glass citadel, was the crystal fortress.

High on the battlements, Amarath was screaming, even more stridently than before.

Detaching himself from conventional thinking, Oliver considered the problem in a new way, just as he had done with the wooden blocks.

Rather than focussing on the immediate hurdle – the moat filled with glass spikes – he turned his attention to the fortress wall.

Like everything else connected with the fortress, it was fashioned from crystal. Carefully, Oliver examined the individual blocks, and the supports which jutted out into the floor of the Cadenta hall.

Something caught his eye.

A misshapen crystal block.

Much rougher than the others, it was engraved with a motif that didn't quite fit.

Hurrying over to it, Oliver gave it a heave.

It was loose.

Quickly, he kicked it away, and discovered a

channel behind. Wasting no time, he clambered in head first, crawling full speed down a crystal passageway. Sinking down below the ground, it ran beneath the moat, before coming up sharply on the fortress's west side.

Knees chafed, Oliver climbed out.

He was past the moat.

High above, Amarath's screams were more strained, as though the fire jinn was roasting her alive.

Once again, rather than rushing headlong as he might usually have done, Oliver considered the next steps. By concentrating, he found he could see into the fortress's inner structure.

The more he focussed, the more layers he perceived.

At the left side of the channel through which he had emerged, he spotted a duct, spiralling up to the battlements.

Running over to it, he started climbing, hands and feet making use of the little niches carved in the spiral's sides.

A good many times he lost his footing.

As he climbed higher, Oliver wished the niches were bigger.

Miraculously, they enlarged.

But, the higher he ascended, the further away the battlements became. Hands and feet dug into the crystal, Oliver threw his head back.

The screams a world away, there was no hope of ever reaching Amarath.

Hanging there desperately, like a mountaineer on a cliff face, Oliver caught sight of his Uncle Sinan in yet another of his lessons.

The old carpet seller was telling his nephew to follow his gut – to always do the unexpected.

Oliver got a flash of inspiration.

If climbing hand over hand was the expected route – what would the unexpected be?

'Let go,' his uncle's voice whispered in his mind.

'But I'll fall.'

'How do you know unless you try?'

So, with closed eyes, Oliver confronted his fear, and let go.

He fell.

And fell.

…And fell.

But, the curious thing was that he didn't fall down…

…but up.

Twenty-eight

BORBOR MAY HAVE been redeemed from the dreq ghouls, but he wasn't content.

Far from it.

Heartbroken, he slumped into a state of despondency.

The idea of presenting the smorop pod to the supreme leader of Councilus had been not only agreeable, but important.

Through a sense of dutiful gratification, it had filled him with utter joy. Now it was gone, he had no fantasy with which to while away the hours of laborious trudging.

So, he did what every lemon-yellow jinn did when it had time on its paws.

He thought of food.

Not the kind of modest meal that would satiate a normal appetite, but one of vast proportions.

Mounds of gruluq from the Glens of Steeped Loathing.

Barrels of s'baw as great as a green poliak jinn's ego.

Platters of fried makkam, drizzled with maroob juice, sliced into slivers no thicker than a verum monkey's arm.

With each stride, Borbor grew hungrier and hungrier.

Until his stomach squealed and screeched.

Well aware how injurious to health prolonged deprivation could be, he resorted to emergency action.

The kind of action one would only consider when not in the presence of others.

Checking no one else was near, Borbor scanned the horizon, spinning round three-sixty.

Emptiness.

Holding still, he urged a claw into his left ear.

Scooping it round and round, he excavated the delicious harvest.

A dollop of wax, the size and shape of an orange.

Rapturously, he scraped it onto his tongue, closed his mouth, and gulped it down.

Twenty-nine

As HERBERT MORLIB's mouth swallowed the last chunk of scalica cake, his taste buds tingling with satisfaction, his ears recorded a faint knocking sound.

The slow, cold noise of metal knocking against wood.

Padding back through the shop, the optician checked the front door, as he had done every evening for as long as he could remember. Then, glancing down at the pill-box, left in position by Operative Zeliak, he let out a relieved sigh.

Three seconds passed in which the clock mounted on the back wall stopped.

297

Twisting round, Herbert cocked his head to the side, and listened.

At the precise moment the clock fired up again, Nequissimus materialized.

Fulminating with teeth, barbed scales, and serrated claws, he seemed to suck out all the air. Eyes leaden with evil, nostrils distended, he faced the optician as his executioner.

Like a mousetrap snapping into action, the little silver pill-box exploded open.

Within a fraction of a second, a legion of warriors stood where the cabinets had been. A hybrid between ogres and something far more fantastical, each was armed with a crusader sword.

The great jinn held still, as if summarizing the situation.

He blinked slowly, signalling for the battle to begin.

Surging forwards, the warriors slashed and cleaved with their swords, slicing at the jinn's scales and limbs. Wave after wave of them advanced, whooping and roaring as they went.

Rather than fighting back, Nequissimus simply ebbed into translucence. Smirking at the frailty of the onslaught, it was almost as though he was enjoying it.

The warriors made no discernible progress, their blades slashing at thin air. Tiring of them, the great jinn exhaled, reducing the ogre legion to oily grey dust.

The only sound now was the clock on the back wall.

Herbert's eyes were locked onto the jinn's face, his thoughts racing as he recalled official protocol. Closing his eyes, he cleared his mind, and tore through the secret code sequence reserved for attack.

As soon as it was received by the Department of Caged Souls, backup would arrive.

Plucking an image from the deepest recesses of Herbert's mind, the great jinn imagined a perfectly square scalica cake, dripping with juices and all putrid with worms. After that, he imagined the cake being sliced diagonally across the middle, and the two halves being worn as hats by wartle children on a summer afternoon.

Every emergency code in Zonus was paired with a deactivation one – a code devised by the mind where it was destined to lie.

Herbert Morlib's face trembled, its features spinning around.

His mouth was where his forehead had been; his eyes were near his chin, and his nose was upside down. The veteran guard might have protested, but he wasn't himself any longer.

Having slipped into the wartle's body, albeit

disguised as an elderly creature from the Dominion of Men, Nequissimus descended into the holding zone.

Thirty

TUMBLING UPWARDS, ROUND and round, Oliver hit the battlements with a *thump*!

Winded, choking, he struggled to pick himself up.

Close by, Amarath was crouching, her face spattered in blood, eyes ringed with fear. Her screaming ceased, she was trembling, like an animal resigned to death.

As Oliver sprinted over the short distance between them, a tower sprung up, incarcerating Amarath.

Crystal block laid on crystal block.

At the base of the tower was a transparent door, through which Amarath could be clearly seen. Down low on her haunches, she was rocking back and forth, whining hysterically, blood gushing from her face.

'Hold on! I'm almost there!' Oliver yelled.

'Hurry, please hurry!' Amarath sobbed. 'Can't bear the pain.'

Vaulting over the last stretch of battlement, Oliver reached the tower, hunkered down, and peered through the window.

'You... you... you OK?' he whispered.

'I've been terribly burned,' Amarath lamented, her voice pitiful and weak.

'Gonna get you out of there… I promise!'

'Thank you, dearest friend. Thank you.'

Oliver was about to attack the crystal door, when something coaxed him to stop.

His gut.

'What's the matter?' Amarath moaned. 'My dearest, please free me before I bleed to death, or before the fire jinn returns to slay us both!'

Oliver caught a flash of his first meeting with Amarath, way below in the Cadenta hall.

'Do you love me?' he asked.

'Oh, yes, yes! I absolutely adore you my beloved!' Amarath exclaimed.

Oliver stepped back from the tower.

Concentrating, he considered not what he was seeing and hearing, but what his gut was telling him.

A stream of blood spouted from Amarath's head.

Befuddled, Oliver stepped backwards along the edge of the parapet.

'Where are you going, my darling? Please, set me free! I beg you! We must escape!'

As he retreated, Oliver imagined an image.

Not like a photograph, or even a painting, but more like a carpet – a carpet woven from twisted woollen yarn. The more he focussed, the more detail he discerned, and the richer the colours became.

Although he didn't understand how it worked, the carpet's pattern seemed to be linked to the situation in which he found himself. He was part of it, just as Amarath was, as was the crystal fortress, the Cadenta hall, and the fire jinn, too.

As he observed it in his mind, a pang of sensation shot up his spine. Agonizing, intoxicating, and strangely passionate all at once.

Crouching, Oliver peered towards the window, spying the outline of Amarath. Her silhouette blood-red, she was pleading even more frantically than before.

Instead of sensing the same urge to help, Oliver now felt disconnected, as though her predicament hardly mattered at all.

An unrelated thought made him remember the penknife.

Delving a hand into the pocket of his overalls, he fished it out. Then, flipping open the whistle, he blew with all his might.

A shrill, swirling blast of sound spewed out over the battlements. Warm and cold, salty and sweet, it was both ferocious and compassionate.

As Oliver blew full force, the blocks of crystal began to shudder.

Far below the parapet and the battlements, Oliver made out a series of muffled exclamations.

Down at the moat, Zelgar the alpaca was

gesticulating. He was warning that the fortress was rocking from side to side.

Without pausing, Oliver continued to blow the whistle.

As he did so, the ribbon of sound soared up and down in peaks and troughs, cascading through the firmament, as if on a journey.

All the while, Amarath crouched in the crystal tower, shaking, whimpering, bleeding.

Moments passing, her condition changed.

First, her skin began to peel away, flaking off in shavings, like those from a carpenter's plane.

Growing larger, the flakes of skin blew away.

Instead of blood vessels, organs, or a skeleton, Amarath's body was made from sparks and flames.

Again, Oliver took in the pattern, a pattern woven into a carpet.

This time it was overlaid on what his senses were reporting. The whistle still pursed between his lips, he blew with all his might.

Although he didn't understand how it worked, the carpet pattern gave a structure to the sound.

The more Oliver blew, the more unruly the fire grew, flames glinting and refracting through the tower and far beyond.

Suddenly, the song of a red-breasted robin could be heard above the whistle. It was fresh and lovely, like something from a late summer meadow a world away.

Still whistling, Oliver looked around for the source of birdsong. But there was no sign of it. Focussed even harder than before, he wove the situation's details into a pattern. From it, he whistled a solution – a solution devised in the design of a tribal rug.

Gradually, the flames began to die down, and the robin's song grew more shrill.

Jerking the whistle from his lips, Oliver took a deep breath. He was thinking of the basement below Ozymandias.

Of the eye.

The thought was sucking him inside.

The more he tried to obliterate it, the stronger the image became. The stronger it became, the more dazed he felt. Eyes clouding, he witnessed the projection once again – each image filed away in his subconscious.

As the images raced through his mind, one at a time and all at once, he felt himself getting warmer and dizzier.

…and dizzier.

The heat wasn't coming from the flames, but from inside him, as though his blood was boiling.

Disorientated, his face gushing with sweat and muscles cramping, Oliver collapsed – his body striking the crystal battlement.

Far down below, petrified of heights, the alpaca was yelling warnings and encouragement.

Doubled in pain, his eyes rolled up into their sockets, Oliver was in no state to do anything.

Arranged in the fiery outline of a man, the fire jinn melted the crystal tower without a second thought, and stepped out onto the battlement.

Like the rest of him, his mouth was pure fire.

The flame smile thundered with laughter. Its form flaring, the fire jinn leant down over Oliver.

'How dare you imagine yourself worthy to spar with me?!' he wailed. 'What kind of an insignificant wretch are you?'

Silence.

No sound, except for the crackle of flames.

Then a voice. A woman's voice:

'He's a Jinn Hunter!'

The fire jinn turned, and found himself facing a woman with a mane of blond hair, and six fingers on each hand.

'And who are you?' he asked with curiosity.

'I'm the one who has come to do what *he* was supposed to do.'

'And what is that?'

Amarath glowered.

'To trap you, so you can be locked in the Prism where you belong.'

The fire jinn exhaled. Its red-orange inferno turned blue, then into a single platinum-white flame, like a welder's torch.

'Pray tell,' he replied briskly, 'how do you plan to catch me?'

Undeterred by flames or heat, Amarath strode boldly forward.

'By using your stupidity against you.'

Piqued by the insult, the jinn held out a hand, a hand shaped from flames. Tracing a blazing arc around Amarath and Oliver, he exhaled a gentle breath of blistering air.

Instantly, the arc turned into a prison cell, a cell walled in fire.

Leaning down, Amarath shook Oliver hard.

'Hey, you!' she scolded. 'Time to wake up!'

Grunting, Oliver felt the back of Amarath's hand slapping his face. He came to, opened his eyes, jolting wide awake.

First he focussed on the mane of blond hair.

'I came to save you,' he said tenderly.

'Yeah, well you didn't do a great job!' Amarath retorted. 'Next time, remember that I'll never need your help! Not *ever*! You couldn't save a fly drowning in a glass of milk!'

'I knew it!' Oliver scoffed.

'Knew what?'

'That it wasn't you in the tower over there.'

'Course it wasn't me!' Amarath spat. 'I wouldn't be so stupid as to get myself trapped up here!'

Oliver rolled his eyes.

'So, you're far too smart to get in a jam like *this*?'

Reaching into her pocket, Amarath pulled out a six-fingered glove. The surface was shiny and wet.

She slipped it on.

'What're you doing?'

'Close your eyes and count to ten.'

'It's no time for hide and seek!'

'Just do it!'

'OK. OK.'

Oliver shut his eyes and started counting.

'...Eight... nine... ten...' he paused and blinked. 'Here I come, ready or not!'

Amarath was standing ten feet away.

In one hand was a birdcage, a robin perched on the bar. In the other was a sphere of compressed fire in a mesh net, the size and shape of a bowling ball.

Oliver did a double take.

'*I... I... I....*'

'Don't understand?'

'Something like that.'

Leaning down, Amarath picked up the penknife.

'If you're smart, you'll never lose this again,' she said, pressing it into Oliver's palm.

'How are we gonna get down from here?' he asked. 'I got up here by falling upwards. So do we jump up to fall down?'

Amarath sneered.

'You really are an imbecile, aren't you?'

Before Oliver could muster a reply, the fortress began shaking, as if quaking back and forth on its foundations.

That was the problem.

The fortress having been constructed on the smooth floor of the Cadenta hall, there weren't any foundations.

As the crystal sheets began to collapse, the clatter of glass cracking and fracturing was deafening. The towers were the first to go. Followed by the battlements and staircases, the banquet halls, private chambers, and everything else.

'It's coming down fast!' Oliver hollered. 'We've gotta get out!'

Spinning round, Amarath scanned the crumbling crystal structure. Unlike her fellow cadet, she was unruffled, and was working on a plan.

'What are we gonna do?' Oliver cried.

So as to free up her right hand, Amarath passed him the birdcage.

'Take this!'

'Shall we jump for it?'

'Are you crazy? We'd fall to our deaths.'

'But…'

'Just shut up and follow me!'

Amarath slipped on the six-fingered glove, and the surface came alive with thousands of droplets.

Amarath motioned a circle around Oliver and herself, creating a tube – black and empty – like the outer limits of space.

Corkscrewing down from the ruined battlement, it led all the way to the ground. Amarath took care to stuff the glove back into her pocket. Having stepped up to the edge of the tube, she bowled the fire jinn into the blackness.

Clenching her knees, she jumped down after it.

Sheets of crystal cascading around him, Oliver stepped forward and found himself at the edge of the tube. He had so many questions. But waiting for an answer would have meant certain death. Still smarting from failure, he was fearful at the thought of jumping into an empty void.

Oliver leapt after Amarath.

Spiralling round and round, up and down, and back on itself, the tube was more than a simple escape slide. It was a world within a world, the warped walls a rollercoaster of motion and emotion.

All of a sudden, Oliver collided with the Cadenta hall's floor, his face slamming into the labyrinth. Miraculously, he had managed to keep hold of the caged bird.

The alpaca was waiting for him.

'Well done for saving Amarath!' he applauded, clapping his front hooves together.

Oliver regarded his fellow cadet frostily.

'It was she who saved me, as she's sure to tell you – if she hasn't already.'

'That's not what she told me.'

'Oh yeah?'

Zelgar held up a hoof.

'She said you kept your cool in a heated situation.'

'Is that a compliment?'

Bill Lewis's right eye winked.

'Count it as lavish praise.'

Taking a deep breath, Oliver looked behind him.

The Cadenta hall was silent.

A vast empty space, devoid of almost anything but candelabra dripping wax down onto the labyrinthine floor.

Except for he and the alpaca, there were no other students.

'Where did the fortress go?' he asked.

'Gone.'

'Gone where?'

'Gone where everything goes.'

'Where's that?'

'Back into the Realm.'

'What about Amarath… where's she gone?'

'To the processing hall, to log the fire jinn.' The alpaca cocked the side of his head at the robin inside the birdcage. 'They'll be waiting for that,' he said.

'Why?'

Zelgar frowned.

'Because it's the fire jinn's soul.'

'Is it?'

The alpaca frowned a second time.

'You've really just started here, haven't you?'

Oliver nodded.

'Fresh off the boat.'

'Then the first thing to know is a jinn without its soul is snorp putty in your hands. That's why Amarath separated the two. Keep them apart and you'll have peace. Put them back together and...'

'*And*...?'

The alpaca's eyes widened with fear.

'And you get a wild rumpus,' he said.

Thirty-one

CAGED UP IN Holding Zone J5D/Z, the birds were rarely peaceful when Herbert Morlib did his rounds.

But, as the great jinn descended the ladders to the basement complex, they erupted into a cacophony of unrestrained commotion. Squawking and chirruping, screeching and wailing, they flapped in their cages as though the end of time had come.

Herbert tramped along the cold stone floor, his

face still upside down. Pausing there, the elderly optician's body divided lengthways, like a banana being peeled down the middle.

Stepping out of the unwanted skin, Nequissimus flexed his muscles, cleared his throat, and scanned the interminable rows of cages. Relishing the moment, he listened to the birds – each of them certain their end had come.

All but a small, blue-feathered bird in a uniform cage on a high row. Unlike all the other jinn souls, the little blue bird was not protesting, but rather tweeting in jubilance.

The muscles of his legs clenching, Nequissimus sprang up into the air, wings soaring until he reached the cage...

Its bars melted like wax.

The little blue bird was absorbed.

And, for the first time in three thousand years, the great jinn was complete once again.

Thirty-two

THE LANDSCAPE CHANGING from Crushed Glass Desert to scrubland, and to Crushed Glass Desert again, Borbor struggled frantically to keep his mind off food.

In order to divert his attention, he replayed

every conversation he had ever participated in. An unusual characteristic of lemon-yellow jinn was their ability to remember even the longest conversations, verbatim.

He reminisced about sitting beside the open fire on his mother's knee, his young blond fur freshly shampooed and brushed before bed. He couldn't have been more than an oroking, an infant jinn. She'd told him a tale from *The Book of Jopolos*, part of the sacred myths of lemon-yellow jinn.

Borbor lived with his mother in a freezing cave, halfway up a precipice. Walled in purple grick moss, it was bedded with fastulam leaves.

Replaying the story line by line, as he trudged towards yet another horizon, his lips mumbled the words:

'...And then, King Corbor of the yellow jinn took off his crown and hurled it over the edge of the dark cliff, into the waves of the Eternal Ocean.'

'But, mother, why would the king have done such a thing?'

'Because King Corbor was so wise he had no interest in governing any longer.'

'Didn't his people miss him though?'

'Expect they did,' Borbor's mother cooed gently, running a paw over her young son's shoulder and down the damp fur on his back. 'But King Corbor had to help himself before he could help anyone else.'

TAHIR SHAH

'How would he do that, mother?'

'By walking the Xerex lines.'

'Oh, yes,' said Borbor, 'as I shall one day do.'

'Of course you will, my little smorop pod,' his mother cooed, squeezing her son tight in a loving embrace. 'Because no lemon-yellow jinn can grow to manhood without walking the Xerex lines, and singing them well.'

'*Mother*?' whispered Borbor solemnly.

'Yes, my little marmul fish?'

'Did my father walk the Xerex lines and sing them very nicely?'

Gazing down into the fire, a glint of orange in her eyes, Borbor's mother sighed deeply.

'He walked the lines like no one else,' she said. 'And he sang them more perfectly then even the sisligulets.'

'*Really*?'

'Yes, my dearest. But I have told you so many times before.'

'I know, I know,' little Borbor replied.

'So why do you ask again?'

'Because I like to hear you speak of him.'

Gazing into the flames, deeper than before, the mother jinn smiled.

'He is always with us,' she said.

'But...'

Borbor was about to mumble the next line of

conversation when he spotted something way in the distance.

A totem pole.

Thirty-three

LED BY ZELGAR, Oliver made his way from the Cadenta Academy through into the processing hall.

As before, it was packed to the gunwales with creatures, noise, and uproar. Indeed, it seemed as though there was twice as much activity as the first time that Oliver had experienced it.

Every inch of floor space was taken up with jinn and Jinn Hunters, with officials and administrators, auxiliaries, factotums, and throngs of 'oolaks' – lowly subordinates.

Unlike the others, oolaks were notable because of their ability to stand in for almost anyone or anything else. As well as being able to shape-shift, the oolaks could also become the space around a creature or a thing.

Some of the jinn were shrunk to the size of bowling balls, but a great many others were manifested in full form. More still were doing their best to evade captivity through last-ditch efforts in shape-shifting.

Holding the birdcage high above his head, Oliver weaved his way through the hordes. He was about to

TAHIR SHAH

step over a little fluffy pink creature when, without warning, it ballooned up in size, squeezing out everything else around it.

'Over there!' the alpaca bellowed.

'What is?'

'The processing counter.'

'Where?'

'There... beyond the swarm of butterfly jinn.'

Practised at moving through the fluttering mass of life, Zelgar pushed ahead. Approaching the butterfly jinn, he pressed his front hooves to his ears, and ploughed straight through them.

A few strides behind, Oliver followed.

Even before he reached the cloud of butterflies, he heard them.

It sounded as though they were laughing.

As he pressed into the middle of the swarm, he started to giggle, then to laugh as well. It was contagious. Struggling to hold on to the birdcage, he collapsed to the floor, wailing with laughter.

Losing sight of Oliver, the alpaca worked out what had happened. It was what always happened the first time novice cadets encountered butterfly jinn.

Hurrying back, Zelgar pressed his hooves to his ears once again.

'Get up quickly!' he chided. 'Or we'll never make it for processing in time.'

Rolling back and forth on the ground, his right

316

hand clamped to the cage's handle, Oliver wiped the tears from his eyes.

'They're so funny!' he howled.

The alpaca nudged him up with his horns.

'They're a damned pain in the rump!' he shouted, leading the way ahead.

Oliver was still giggling.

'Haven't laughed that much in years! I didn't even hear a joke!'

'That's because they don't tell jokes,' Zelgar replied.

'Don't they?'

'No, of course not. Butterfly jinn detest jokes. Everyone knows that.'

'*I* didn't.'

The alpaca stopped dead still. He looked at Oliver, then at the birdcage, the robin inside it and, finally, at the commotion all around them.

'You don't belong here, do you?' he said.

Thirty-four

EVEN THOUGH THE totem pole was perfectly vertical, towering more than a hundred feet into the sky, the shadow it cast was coiled, twining and twisting for miles over the Crushed Glass Desert.

Approaching with caution, Borbor felt an

immediate and desperate twang of sympathy, in the pit of his ever-famished stomach.

A twang which reminded him of the droves of wanton jinn at Mishmak. Jinn addicted to smorop pods and unspeakable vice.

As he grew closer, Borbor noticed that the totems which ran the entire length of the pole were living heads. Spanning the full spectrum of imagination, some were ghoulish. Others were delicate and quite lovely. More still represented the wildest margins of crazed fantasy.

One thing united all the heads.

Their expression, each locked in a tortured mask of outrage, as though terribly wronged.

Stooping, Borbor walked around the pole, taking in the many faces. He was struck by the tranquillity, and by the sense of desperation.

Only after making a full circumnavigation did he realize the reason for the silence.

The heads were dumb.

Those that had once possessed tongues had been relieved of them.

Although repulsed, Borbor found the totem pole compelling. He couldn't stop looking at it, or wondering why it was there. The more he scrutinized it, the more desolate he felt.

All of a sudden, he noticed the shadow was moving.

Twisting clockwise and anticlockwise both at once, it was uttering incantations.

Incantations absorbing Borbor, as they seemed to connect with his innermost thoughts.

He found himself thinking of Mr Ot, of the derelict regulars at the Mishmak Lodge, and of their addiction to smorop pods.

Then he thought of the turquoise jinn which had come to his rescue, and of the sound of the wind howling over the Mountains of False Hope. As the shadows twisted, and as his mind turned, the sky above him changed colour.

From blue to red.

Red to jade green.

Jade green to black.

Ears filled with chanting, Borbor sensed his tongue loosening – which was in itself perhaps the oddest feeling in the entire Realm. Just before his great furry yellow bulk collapsed onto the surface of the Crushed Glass Desert, Borbor remembered something.

A scrap of unfinished conversation.

A glass jinn at the Mishmak Lodge was begging for another slice of juicy ripe smorop pod. Although a regular, the jinn was impecunious, and had no way of summoning wealth of any kind. So, instead, he had tried to amuse Borbor with tales of his adventures, in the hope of being rewarded. But, on the strict orders of Mr Ot, Borbor knew better than to bend the rules, especially when it came to smorop pods.

Worked up into a frenzy of craving, the glass jinn had uttered something Borbor had been unable to forget. It was stored in the back of his head, along with all the other conversations.

'Beware the Shadows of Reflection,' the penniless jinn had said. 'For they will swallow every word of your memories, and everything you ever plan to say.'

'So what?'

'As a yellow jinn it would surely worry you especially, am I not right?' the glass jinn had asked.

'Perhaps,' Borbor had replied, ruminating. 'Where are they anyway… the Shadows of Reflection?'

'Thrown across the Crushed Glass Desert by the pole.'

'*Pole?*'

'The Pole of Silent Faces.'

'You're not getting any smorop pod for this information,' grumbled Borbor, eyeing the glass jinn sideways.

'I'm not expecting any hand-outs.'

'So what's your motive?'

'Friendship,' the smorop-addicted jinn had uttered unctuously.

'All right then… what's the secret to avoid the dangers of the totem pole?' he asked out of curiosity, after a prolonged silence.

'You must think of a four-billed platypus passing wind for the first time.'

'That makes no sense, no sense at all,' Borbor had grunted.

'When did making sense matter?' the glass jinn had replied.

The Caravanserai of Mishmak tended to bring out the very worst in jinn, as a result of their insatiable greed for smorop pods. And, greed was something which Mr Ot regarded as the lowest and most despicable quality imaginable.

There was irony in this fact, of course.

For Mr Ot's own existence had been shaped by suffocating avarice.

'I've been taught not to like greedy customers,' Borbor had said. 'My employer regards greed as something more detestable than anything else. He says the greed for smorop pods is worse than any other.'

'Alas, I am powerless,' the glass jinn had replied. 'A prisoner to its charms. In any case, it seems to me the proprietor of this respected establishment has done very well on the need for ripe smorop pods.'

Borbor had been about to shoo the jinn away, when something coaxed him to give pity. Cutting up a good-sized chunk of smorop pod, he tossed it towards the traveller.

As the morsel of fruit was swallowed in a single

gulp, the conversation eased its way back into the recesses of Borbor's mind.

Back at the Pole of Silent Faces, Borbor's memory may have been working well, but his throat was not.

It was choking, as his tongue loosened.

Both paws clamped up to his neck, he struggled urgently for breath.

The faces set into the totem pole leered and jeered, cackling in a communal chorus of mute taunts. As they did so, the shadows spiralled around all the faster, in a stroboscopic chequerboard of light and dark.

Desperately, Borbor struggled to imagine the secret:

A four-billed platypus passing wind for the first time.

Having never encountered the creatures, he didn't have a reliable reference point. The more he tried to imagine one, the more his tongue loosened. And... the more his tongue loosened, the more bizarre the thoughts that came to mind.

He thought of a gilded sparrow perched on the face of a noseless ogress.

Of a green-hoofed snail in the Zopopo Mountains.

Of a rock made from pink antimony, all covered in lava beans.

He thought of the fragrant scent of the purple grick moss on the walls of his childhood cave.

Of fluorescent fighting ants doing battle.

Of Xerex lines, and of his feet walking them, backwards.

His tongue now almost entirely detached, he thought of an egg.

A mottled bronze egg, in a nest fashioned from weathered dodo bones. Warm and greasy, the shell was cracking apart.

Watching in his mind's eye, his mouth filling with blood, Borbor saw it...

A baby four-billed platypus emerging into life.

Emaciated and skeletal, the little creature had diminutive stumps around its mouth. Stumps that would one day grow into two symmetrical pairs of bills.

As he listened, Borbor heard the infant platypus grunt and groan.

All of a sudden it passed wind.

In all his wanderings and wonderings, Borbor had never heard anything like it.

Poignantly tender, it was like an opera of lost love.

Borbor reached into his mouth to remove his tongue, which was hanging by a thread.

But, his mouth was tingling.

One at a time, the tongue's connective fibres began re-joining. The more Borbor thought of the four-billed platypus passing wind, the stronger the muscles became. The stronger the muscles became, the more the faces on the totem pole jeered in silent rage.

Thanking the glass jinn, Borbor brushed the dried blood from his face, swallowed in delight, and walked on.

On towards the crushed glass horizon.

Thirty-five

AT THE PROCESSING counter, the clerk – whose name was Ursulus – took in Oliver, the birdcage, and the robin tweeting inside.

She had worked in the processing hall longer than almost any other clerk, and had once had ambitions of dancing on the stage. But her mother, a stern wartle from the Inner Sanctum, had said she would be ruined by all the attention.

So Ursulus had learned to process rogue jinn instead.

'Name of species?' her husky voice queried fast.

Oliver swallowed.

'It's the soul of a jinn,' he said gravely.

Her six hands counting out the forms, Ursulus looked at Oliver tetchily. She could tell from the cleanness of his overalls that he was a new cadet.

Nothing riled the processing clerks more than new cadets.

'Name of species?' she repeated.

'I'm not quite sure,' Oliver said.

'Previously registered?'

'I don't know.'

Ursulus was losing her patience. It was nearing shift change, and that meant mountains of paperwork to get through.

'Well, is it already tagged?'

Oliver peered at the robin vacantly.

'Don't know,' he said again.

The clerk's six hands began to shoo Oliver away.

Zelgar stepped up to the counter. Although fearful of administration, he strained to appear brave.

'The soul of a fire jinn,' he said.

'Where is the corpus?'

'Recently logged by…'

The alpaca had Amarath's name in his mouth, but couldn't speak it. He was too frightened. Not of the clerk, but of the figure now standing beside him.

For, to his right, between himself and Oliver, was Amalorous.

'Send the fire jinn for incarceration,' the leader said in a cold even voice, 'and the paperwork to my office.'

Smoothing down the lilac tuft of hair at the front of her wide flat head, Ursulus gushed thanks. In all the time she had logged in rogue jinn, she had never known the leader of Zonus to preside over menial paperwork.

325

'At once, your honourableness,' she crooned, fluttering her lashes.

Swinging an arm around Oliver's shoulder, Amalorous led him away through the hall.

'I am proud of you,' the leader declared as they walked.

'But... but... but I didn't capture the fire jinn,' Oliver said quickly. 'Amarath did.'

'That's not the point.'

'She saved my life.'

The leader of Zonus caressed a hand down his tangled white beard.

'Were you frightened?' he asked.

'Terrified,' Oliver said.

Amalorous grinned.

'Thank Providence for that!'

'Wouldn't it be braver to have no fear?'

The leader wagged an index finger, left then right.

'Of course not,' he said.

'Why?'

'Because fear is the metronome that makes us all tick. Without it there'd be no bravery. You see, bravery is merely fear used in the right way.'

'So being scared out of your wits is OK, then?'

'Of course it is... if it allows you to keep your head in the face of uncertainty.'

Oliver held up a hand.

'There's something I want to ask you,' he said.

The leader of Zonus regarded him warmly.

'Of course, anything.'

'Why are rogue jinn imprisoned?'

'To punish them, and to urge them to change their ways.'

'But why imprison them when it would be simpler to just kill them?'

The leader appeared a little anxious and a little disturbed.

'Surely that would be a monstrous way of behaving,' he said. 'And, we are not monsters.'

Clarifying the remark with a fatherly smile, he gesticulated towards the far end of the hall.

'There's something rather unusual I want to show you,' he said.

'More unusual than all of *this*?'

'Oh yes,' the leader replied dreamily, 'far more unusual.' He paused. 'See that little doorway over there?'

Oliver craned his neck.

Between the leader's fingertip and the doorway was a sea of creatures and life.

Jinn formed like giant caterpillars and jinn in the shape of feathered giraffes.

Jinn that looked like blocks of sandstone.

Blue snail-like jinn with purple spots.

Jet-black jinn no bigger than fleas clinging to wowips' backs.

Jinn with ten heads, and others with none at all.

Jinn with beaks on their feet, and jinn with hooves sprouting from their faces.

Many were too ugly or downright peculiar to describe.

Where there were jinn, there were hunters.

Like the prey they tracked through the furthest limits of the Realm, they themselves came in every conceivable form.

Some were bloodied, covered in sores, or still hidden in camouflage – exhausted and weary after weeks of pursuit. Others were immaculate, suave like knights embroidered into a medieval tapestry. The one thing common to them all was the emblem worn so proudly by one and all.

The dragon's eye.

A badge of honour, respected and feared.

'Do you see it, the doorway?' the leader of Zonus repeated.

Again, Oliver craned his neck.

'Think so,' he said. 'That low door all covered in silvery spikes?'

'Yes, that one.'

'What is it?'

'Come and see.'

Thirty-six

THE SHOP WINDOW of Ozymandias & Son was vibrating gently, soft crimson light streaming through.

Inside, stacked carpets, and the collection of objects gleaned from a lifetime of adventurous travel lay in silence, untouched since the lunacy had begun.

Uncle Sinan wasn't there.

His walking boots and favourite cane were missing from just inside the door.

Despite the mayhem outside, the shop itself was calm.

Most other stores had been plundered, or even burnt to the ground. But, despite the fact its door was unlocked, Ozymandias & Son had been spared.

The crimson light swelled in intensity and gradually waned.

As it died away, the shop itself was filled with a pungent stench, as though a thousand rotting eggs had been trampled underfoot. The odour seeped into the corners, beneath the floorboards, and into every carpet. It filled the shop, the basement, the apartment above the showroom, and the top-floor attic as well.

The vibrations, the crimson light, and the overpowering stench of sulphur, were manifestations of a rogue jinn.

A rogue jinn reunited with its soul.

Thirty-seven

As AMALOROUS REACHED the door, a jade jinn slipped its shackles and charged headlong through the processing hall.

Rogue jinn transported to Zonus were prevented from using their powers by a kind of mesmeric field, known as the 'xylotroc'. The field also thwarted jinn planning escapes and acts of revenge from breaking into Zonus.

The only species that could disrupt the mesmeric field was a rare form of oak jinn. Commonly referred to as 'livictons', they had anti-mesmeric qualities, allowing them to alter into virtually any shape – although they tended to favour hexagonal forms.

The jade jinn had broken new ground, not by shape-shifting, but by swallowing an oak jinn moments before being captured in the Grey Forest of Walalala.

Turning itself inside out, it wrapped the oak jinn around it in a kind of hexagonal wheel, and rolled at speed through the hall.

As his hand approached the spiked door, Amalorous heard a commotion behind him.

Swivelling around, he was knocked off balance by the speeding hexagon.

In the same moment, the jade jinn transformed

itself back into a towering mass of sea-green flesh.

Its immense bony tail swung full tilt at Amalorous, who was clambering to his feet.

Lurching to the right, Oliver thrust out, pushing the leader down.

Within the blink of an eye, fifty Jinn Hunters had encircled the area and were closing in, Epsilius at the front.

In a last desperate bid for freedom, the jade jinn barged towards the door.

Instantly, the silvery spikes transformed.

Into razor-sharp points.

Then, into sunflowers.

'What's happening?!' Oliver cried out.

'The door's arming itself,' Epsilius responded.

'With flowers?'

'Of course,' responded the legendary Jinn Hunter. 'How would *you* protect yourself against a rampaging jade jinn?'

As if time had slowed, the sunflowers contorted into mouths which snapped ferociously at the jinn.

Coolly, Epsilius took out a penknife, identical to the one Oliver had been given by the leader. He flicked open a tool.

A little plastic loop.

Holding it out at arm's length, he blew into it gently.

A transparent bubble billowed out.

Catching the light as it breached the few feet between himself and the jade jinn, it enveloped him.

As soon as the wayward creature was trapped inside, the bubble began shrinking.

Within seconds, the jinn was compressed into the size of an apple.

Epsilius stooped down and picked it up. He and the other Jinn Hunters ebbed away, back to their work.

Amalorous got to his feet.

'Thank you for shoving me out the way,' he said.

'You're welcome,' Oliver replied.

'That happens from time to time,' the leader grunted. 'Oak jinn have a lot to answer for. They may be well-meaning, but they cause havoc.'

'You've lost me, again,' said Oliver.

Amalorous motioned to the door handle. As he did so, the sunflowers transformed back into spikes, and then melted away entirely. In their place was a dazzling surface of polished brass.

'After you,' the leader said.

Oliver stepped forward.

His mind was not so much on the door, but what might lie beyond it. Rotating the handle, he caught a glimpse of himself in the door's polished surface, half an arm's length away.

As the handle turned, the reflection seemed to

change.

The more Oliver twisted it to the right, time itself seemed to advance. By turning the handle clockwise, he scrolled the reflection forward; and turning it anticlockwise scrolled it back.

The reflection of Oliver's life.

'I don't believe this,' he said warily.

'Believe what?'

'*This*... look...'

Oliver rotated the handle anticlockwise.

His face scrolled back, mirroring a decade and a half in random snapshots of childhood.

Milk teeth. Scraped knees. Clothing that never quite fitted right.

Twisting the handle clockwise, he scrolled forward – back to the present.

Then, on... into the future.

Unlike the measured order of his past, what was to come was tumultuous.

But, far worse, it was short.

Terrifyingly short.

Oliver scrolled forwards from the present through the remaining span of his life. Twisting the handle by a few degrees was all it took for his youthful face to age, to become grotesquely injured and deformed.

'Some things are better not known,' Amalorous said under his breath, as a last frame of the reflected life was captured freeze-frame.

His fingers releasing the handle, Oliver recoiled.

'You're sending me to certain death, aren't you?!'

The leader of Zonus cleared his throat awkwardly.

'Nothing's certain.'

'Not even the fact you're planning to sacrifice me like a worthless pawn?'

Amalorous turned, his ancient eyes locked on Oliver's youthful ones.

'This isn't a game of chess,' he snapped.

'But it is about sacrifice, isn't it?'

Amalorous sighed. He squinted down at the floor.

'It's about treading the right path,' he said.

'I don't believe you. And I definitely don't trust you!'

'I can see that, so....'

'*So*?'

'So I promise never to ask you to trust me again. As for believing... I suppose that's up to you.'

Coaxing Oliver to step aside, the leader grasped the handle. Rather than rotating it, he jerked it inwards.

An invisible clockwork mechanism chimed twice, and a pleasing smell was heavy in the air.

The scent of Christmas...

Crushed cinnamon.

Mulled wine.

Gingerbread men.

The door swung open.

Curiously, Oliver peered through.

'Is that it?' he said, puzzled. 'Is that what you wanted me to see?'

Thirty-eight

FOR SIX HORIZONS, Borbor the son of Torbor pressed on over the Crushed Glass Desert.

And, for six horizons, nothing of any interest passed under his feet.

No trees or plants.

No birds or any creatures, and certainly no jinn.

The emptiness didn't lower Borbor's spirits in the least. He found himself buoyed by the solitude, and grateful for the opportunity to reminisce and to ponder. His stomach growled interminably from emptiness, and the pads of his feet were painful from the shards of glass. But, as he mused, a journey was a time of reflection.

The longer an expedition, the more reflecting could be done.

After tramping over crushed glass for a very long time, Borbor began to hope for a change... for something a little less uniform. He was about to think of the Caravanserai of Mishmak, as he tended to do, when another thought popped into his mind.

A bowl of orange-flavoured jelly, all wobbly and good.

The more he tried to replace the image with another, the more it began to preoccupy him. He found himself thinking of trees whose branches were made from orange jelly. Of ships fashioned from it, plying across oceans swelling with it. He thought of distant lands where all forms of life were orange jelly, and where the sun and the moon were orange jelly, as well.

To take his mind off the increasingly preposterous apparitions, Borbor recounted a conversation. It had been with a blind ogre traveller who had arrived unexpectedly at the Mishmak Lodge one evening.

A traveller who had spent a fortune on smorop pods, and who claimed to have set all three of his unsighted eyes on the Querilis Stone.

By any standards, it had been an unusual conversation and had stuck in Borbor's thoughts – even though every conversation stuck in his thoughts, whether he wanted it to do so or not. By repeating the ogre's story to himself, the preoccupation with orange jelly subsided.

Borbor was about to mumble the next line of the traveller's dialogue, when he spotted something on the crushed glass ground.

A little brass button.

A little brass button embossed with a coat of arms.

Without thinking, Borbor picked it up, placed it on his palm, and lowered his face towards it...

The most lovely thing he had ever seen.

Unable to contain himself, he was overcome. Gazing at the dusty object, held a few inches from his enormous eyes, he began to weep. Within a moment or two, the flood of tears had washed the button clean.

Suddenly, the little brass disc began to quiver and shake.

A riotous flash of silver light was followed by the scent of rose water.

Tossing the button onto the crushed glass ground in fear, Borbor jumped back.

Ramrod-straight before him, dressed in a pristine uniform, was an admiral. His head was crowned in a navy-blue bicorn hat, the stout body below cloaked in a matching frock coat – a set of the same brass buttons running down the front. Both shoulders were adorned with heavy tasselled epaulettes, and the name 'AMAR' was embroidered in gold thread on the left side of the breast. Upon the figure's feet was a pair of sharkskin boots.

His expression sombre, the officer withdrew a telescope and surveyed the desert.

'A pity,' he said austerely. 'A great pity indeed.'

Bowing out of respect, Borbor introduced himself,

and enquired how the admiral might have come to be lying as a button in the middle of the vast Crushed Glass Desert.

'The Great Campaign,' the sailor replied with a snarl.

'Which one?'

'The campaign to reach the bottom of the Emerald Sea.'

Turning in a full circle, Borbor peered out at the horizon.

'And where exactly is it?' he asked.

'Where is *what*?'

'The sea?'

The admiral stamped the heel of his boot down on the ground, crushed glass grinding beneath it.

'We appear to be at the bottom of it,' he said with disgust.

'But where are the waves?'

'Drained.'

'How?'

Forlornly, the sailor folded up his telescope.

'Through my own blunder,' he said.

'*Blunder*?'

'So impatient was I to reach the sea floor,' the admiral explained, 'that I wished a careless wish.'

'What did you wish for?'

'That the last drop of emerald water would disappear.'

'When did you make the wish?' Borbor enquired.

'An eternity ago,' the admiral replied. He scowled. 'Or rather I suppose it was.'

'But how did you end up as a button just lying there?'

'By the same artifice that drained the waters.'

Enthused at the thought of having someone to chat to, Borbor realized he was asking a lot of questions. But he was curious by nature. Pointing to where the Crushed Glass Desert became the sky, he said:

'I am going over there.'

'Where?'

'To the end of this, and to the beginning of that.'

'Are you indeed?'

'Yes, I am. If you would like to join me, we could walk together.'

Admiral Amar held up an index finger, as though testing the wind.

'On one condition.'

'What is it?'

'That you never speak of the sea,' he said.

Thirty-nine

THE ROOM BEYOND the door was circular, very ordinary, and painted gloss white.

Except for a little patch of neatly clipped grass

lawn in the middle, it was entirely empty. After the hullabaloo of the processing hall, and the outlandish portal that had led to it, Oliver regarded the room as something of an anticlimax.

'Oh,' he said, stepping inside.

'Not what you expected?' Amalorous probed.

'Well, er, no… not really.'

'What *did* you expect?'

'The unexpected,' Oliver responded quickly.

'Well, isn't this just that then?'

'I suppose it is. But I expected something…'

'…*bizarre*?'

'Yes, I guess so.'

The leader of Zonus tugged off his shoes and stepped onto the patch of lawn.

'Not all the Realm is weird and wonderful,' he said. 'There are great swathes of ordinariness… the kind of thing that might put you instantly to sleep.' Knitting his fingers together, he pressed them back against themselves. 'And, don't think for a moment that all jinn are remarkable. Because they're not.'

Oliver wasn't listening.

He caught a flash of East 8th Street covered in snow.

The snow made him think of Japanese cherry blossom, and that led him to consider the fallout of a nuclear blast. The fallout made him reflect on a ticker-tape parade and that, in turn, led to a memory of the Yankees winning the World Series.

The World Series coaxed him to imagine snow out on 8th East Street again.

The associations ending where they'd begun, Oliver realized that all five of his senses were acutely honed.

He could smell the air around him more keenly than he had ever imagined possible. It was tinged with the faintest trace of cardamom. He could hear in a way he never dreamt possible, his ears picking up the faint sound of the grass growing. His other senses were heightened, too.

Amalorous reached down and plucked a stem of grass. Holding it to his nostril, he breathed in.

'Most of us go through life blinkered to what is really happening,' he said. 'We like to think that we notice things, but most of the time we are incapable of real perception.'

'Why's that?'

'Because we are taught how to perceive. In being taught how, we lose the ability to see, to hear, smell, taste or touch.'

'You mean we become diluted versions of ourselves, or of how we're supposed to be?'

'Precisely,' Amalorous replied. 'That is the essence.'

'What is?'

'That we must relearn. If we do so, the possibilities

TAHIR SHAH

are infinite.'

'But how to do it – *relearn*?'

'By looking beyond the obvious.'

Oliver's expression hardened as he remembered the reflection on the door.

The reflection of his own end.

'Will looking beyond the obvious save me?' he asked coldly.

'It could do far more than that.'

'As in…?'

The leader of Zonus scrunched his gnarled old toes into the grass.

'You've learnt about the Realm through unconnected fragments,' he said. 'It's the best way to understand anything. A little at a time, through pieces of a puzzle that don't seem to fit. Wherever there are pieces of puzzle, there are patterns. Where there are patterns, there are answers.'

'I'm pretty good with patterns,' Oliver said, not wanting to boast.

'Of course you are,' Amalorous replied, 'but no pattern is going to save you if you can't think zigzag.'

'You mean, if you can't think straight?'

The leader wagged a tapered finger, left then right, as he liked to do when making a point.

'No, no, no. A straight road never got anyone anywhere.'

'Of course it did.'

Again, the finger wagged.

'Remember when you came in here. The white walls made you think of snow, and that led you to think of blossom, and the blossom of a nuclear war, and the war of a ticker-tape parade.'

'How did you know any of that?'

'Because I know everything,' said Amalorous. 'Or rather everything worth knowing.'

'So what of zigzag?'

Scrunching his toes into the grass as he spoke, the leader smiled.

'Zigzag's the answer to everything,' he said. 'It's the way the Realm works. You already know how everything's connected to everything else.'

'Through conduits?'

'Yes, but, what you must now understand is how the lines of possibility snake out, criss-cross, and ultimately converge.'

'Annis told me that every possibility was probable,' Oliver replied. 'And that even the improbable was certainty – somewhere.'

'That's right,' said Amalorous. 'It's more than right. At the same time, it's utterly wrong.'

Oliver scoffed.

'What does it matter, anyway?' he asked. 'The world's gone nuts, and I'll be dead in no time.'

'Of course you won't.'

'Won't what?'

'Won't die... not right away. Well, not necessarily, anyway.'

'I told you... I don't trust you,' Oliver countered.

The leader stepped off the grass, the shoes having reappeared on his feet.

He held out a hand.

In its fingers was clutched a black hood, the kind an executioner puts on the condemned.

'For you,' he said.

'Has the end come already?'

'Put it on.'

'Why?'

'Because I want you to see something.'

'Another unremarkable white room?'

Oliver slipped the hood on. He found that as well as blocking out the light, it blocked all his other senses as well.

But there was still a voice in his head.

Amalorous's voice.

'Clear your mind, and think of your room at Ozymandias & Son,' he said. 'Lying on your bed there's a patchwork quilt. It's always been there, but you know it so well that you hardly notice it.'

'My mother sewed it,' said Oliver gently.

'Imagine that you are stepping down into it.'

'Into the quilt?'

'Yes, into the pattern… into the threads.'

His senses blocked, Oliver descended into the design as instructed.

Instantly, he made out a spectrum of colours and shapes. As he did so, he began hearing unfamiliar sounds, and tasting rare flavours. His sense of touch perceived fabulous textures, even though his hands were empty. His nostrils picked up overpowering aromas. His consciousness bombarded by a kaleidoscope of sensation, Oliver felt every permutation of sensory possibility overlaid upon itself.

Endless parallel sights, sounds, smells, touches and tastes.

'*This* is the Realm,' said Amalorous. 'Not the detail, but the framework. Learn to perceive its spectrum, and you'll surpass all expectations… even your own.'

Oliver's concentration was suddenly broken.

Ripping off the executioner's hood, he found himself back in the gloss-white room.

'If every permutation of possibility is out there,' he asked, 'why can't I just slip back into the life I used to live?'

Amalorous peered down at the grass.

'Because the great jinn has reunited with his soul. A terrible tragedy. He's more powerful than he ever was… and he will be waiting for you.'

'Waiting in *every* permutation?'

'I'm afraid so… even in the one where you're a left-handed reindeer-fish.'

'So what choice do I have?'

The leader of Zonus answered with silence.

Oliver's hands clenched into fists, his face gripped uncharacteristically in rage.

'All right!' he yelled. 'If this is what it takes to get my life back, I'll go get your damned Nequissimus!'

Amalorous's despondence lifted.

'We'll do our best to protect you,' he said limply.

Oliver shot him a vexed look.

'How very reassuring,' he said.

FINIS

THE STORY CONTINUES...

JINN HUNTER

BOOK TWO

THE JINNSLAYER

TAHIR SHAH

JINN HUNTER

BOOK THREE
THE PERPLEXITY

TAHIR SHAH

SUPPLEMENTARY MATERIAL

DRAMATIS PERSONAE

Amalorous	Leader of Zonus and its penal system.
Amarath	Polydactylic member of the Cadenta Academy, known for her beauty and her sharp tongue.
Annis	Leader of the Cadenta Academy.
Bellissima	Maraxa with a penchant for devouring lemon-yellow jinn.
Bill Lewis	Oliver Quinn's best friend since childhood.
Borbor	Clusot species of lemon-yellow jinn, in the employ of Mr Ot at the Mishmak Lodge; loves almost any food in abundance except for smorop pods.
Epsilius	Most celebrated living Jinn Hunter.
Fred Moss	Oliver's professor at the Courant Institute.
Herbert Morlib	Veteran owner of Morlib's Optical Inc., and guardian of Holding Zone J5D/Z hidden beneath it.
Jaspec	Young malbino guard in training.
King Corbor	Legendary monarch whose deeds are recorded in *The Book of Jopolos*.

King of Frastilas   King famed for his immense wealth.

King Solomon   King who could control jinn through the power of a magical seal.

'Mad' Max Brockmill   Seasoned US Army's Chief of Staff.

Marcie Spark   Chief reporter on ABC News.

Mimi-Mo   Clerk in the Processing Hall.

Morrock   Most senior malbino.

Morsius   Supreme leader of the Order of Councilus.

Mortimer Baskart   Night guard at the Bank of England's bullion vault.

Mr Ot   Sinister and sometimes cruel owner of the much-fêted Mishmak Lodge at the Caravanserai of Mishmak. Although known as Ot, his real name is 'Yreashöœuplj' – which is deemed to be so unpronounceable, that he changed it by legal deed to Ot.

Nequissimus   Most evil jinn in existence, captured by King Solomon, and imprisoned in the Prism.

Oliver Quinn	Protagonist, from the line of Jinnslayers, supposedly the one person alive with a chance at capturing Nequissimus.
Sinan Quinn	Oliver Quinn's uncle and guardian, carpet aficionado and owner of Ozymandias & Son.
Soothsayers of Hixx	Diviners known to be boring beyond belief.
Soothsayers of Mūlch	Unreliable and exceptionally rude oracles whose popularity is matched only by their inability to correctly determine the future.
Soulia	Wayward aduxa jinn with an obsessive greed for gold.
Spowla	Veteran malbino guard.
Tameleth	Girl in charge of the legal conveyances in Zonus.
Ursulus	Long-serving wartle clerk in the processing hall at Zonus.
Zelgar	Alpaca-like cadet at the Cadenta Academy.
Zeliak	Operative in the employ of Zonus with high-level clearance.

KINGDOMS, DOMINIONS & EMPIRES

Dominion of Astrip-Pi

Dominion of Capual-så

Dominion of Droliw

Dominion of Fāā

Dominion of Farlippia-Ox

Dominion of Gogolo

Dominion of Grim Feet

Dominion of Gūuüu

Dominion of Lapopopo

Dominion of Lû

Dominion of Men

Dominion of Quex

Dominion of Red Revenge

Dominion of Sacred Glass

Dominion of Scall

Dominion of the Serpent Queen

Dominion of Spoo

Dominion of Sqzzzi

Dominion of Tranquillity

Dominion of Xoliam

Kingdom of Alphot

Kingdom of Aoör

Kingdom of Avenged Hope

Kingdom of Blazing Tides

Kingdom of Boör

Kingdom of Griliap

JINN HUNTER

Kingdom of Gròósol
Kingdom of Kríx
Kingdom of Masticula-Plik
Kingdom of Molopus
Kingdom of Sarax-Ga
Kingdom of Smod
Empire of Woz-woz
Vanished Empire of Trystia

SPECIES OF JINN

Aduxa jinn
Blood jinn
Bluebottle jinn
Butterfly jinn
Crestula jinn
Crush jinn
Death jinn
Desiccated jinn
Diamond jinn
Finkel jinn
Fire jinn
Fossil jinn
Fox jinn
Garble jinn
Glass jinn
Goose-footed jinn
Ink jinn
Jade jinn
Jester jinn
Lemon-yellow jinn
Libertine jinn
Lice jinn
Midian jinn
Mouse jinn
Oak jinn
Plague jinn

JINN HUNTER

Portrait jinn
Possum jinn
Prowling jinn
Pygmy jinn
Rimulam jinn
Sabatine jinn
Snark jinn
Stealth jinn
Tower jinn
Turquoise jinn
Wart jinn
Wixula jinn
Wrath jinn

PLACES WITHIN THE REALM

Archipelago of Trill
Blackened Islands
City of Imaginary Minds
Courant Institute
Crushed Glass Desert
Den of Bitter Temptation
Desert of Secret Wishes
Drottningholm Palace
Fazzisti Mountains
Forest of Gryn
Forest of Silent Fear
Frozen Zone
Garden of Dwaldiak
Glens of Steeped Loathing
Grarpï
Great Emerald Desert
Green-Green Sea
Grey Forest of Walalala
Hall of Sanctity
Inner Sanctum
Island of Aoldrœm
Klozross
Lake of Frozen Tears
Listermot
Mercuric Sea
Mines of Slanted Beams

Mishmak
Mount Zylovos
Mountains of False Hope
Mountains of Kastilash
Ocean of Fecund Fear
Plains of Insipid Twilight
Sacred Well of Hestiac
Sea of Green Wind
Slaked Slew Forest
Speeg
Spöom Chamber of Zolīk
Swamps of Slōnt
Terranean Sea
Wipiliā
Zipiad
Zonus
Zopopo Mountains

GLOSSARY

Afafula tree
Type of tree whose cured bark is used to bind legal documents in Zonus. Although much prized, the bark is known to make those working in the book-binding department go cross-eyed. No reason for why this happens has ever been proposed.

Ainu
Ancient people of Japan, who fashioned clothing from the fibre of tree bark.

Antiquitas
Ancient times, especially before the Vanished Empire of Trystia disappeared.

Antraxa Code 33/Q
Alert code relating to a state in which one of the most dangerous jinn prisoners has escaped from Zonus.

Arabian Nights
Greatest treasury of stories existing in the Dominion of Men. Also known as *The Thousand and One Nights*. Thought by humans to have originated in medieval China. In actual fact the collection was written by a travelling maraxa who burrowed into the Dominion of Men and then out again as soon as he realized what an abominable place it was.

Aslaik Sensory Absorption
Established methods by which incredibly boring information may be read, appraised, or learned – originally developed by a blind mole that wanted to commit to memory all the works of her favourite poet.

AZAZAZAZ/998152
System of Consistent Administration that calibrates and configures information to the cranial and mental frequencies of the one taking advantage of it.

Ballad of Eternal Winter
Tongue-twisting song featured in the game of vosssuk. The ballad is made notable for the fact that when sung backwards, the consonants turn to vowels, and the vowels into consonants.

Barking moot
Species of creature living in Listermot, known for their crazed behaviour, and for dropping everything they are doing when a freshly baked gramzel pie is offered to them. Their communal obsession with the delicacy, which turns them twice as mad as usual, is one of the reasons barking moots and their civilization have never amounted to anything at all.

Barmyal cage
Apparatus used to punish anyone divulging secrets relating to the *Jinn Hunter's Handbook*. The cage is designed to configure itself to the exact proportions of the offending creature – while ensuring that the maximum amount of pain is exacted.

Bartle snort wood
Exceptionally greasy wood that dissolves books and other material of a fragile or sensitive nature.

Base manifestation
Default setting of a jinn's corpus, to which it returns when subdued or separated from its soul.

Bastipok
Light-weight wood found in the Dominion of Lû, whose grain has been likened to that of zebra stripes. The wood, which is highly prized, can be added to warm water as an aromatic tea for the treatment of certain forms of leprosy.

Blind zothula fish
Incredibly lazy marine species devoid of fins, found in subterranean wells. Celebrated in some dominions for their ability to sing short poems in staccato. Blind zothula fish cannot swim, probably because they are too lazy to do so.

Bobastia trees
Trees said to have magical properties, including the ability to reverse time. One of 539,281,762 known species of tree with mysterious properties that have never been studied. A reason for the lack of academic interest is that when the trees are observed closely, they emit a poison gas which instantly kills whoever is attempting to observe them.

Book of Jopolos
Treasury of tales popular with lemon-yellow jinn, famed especially in the culture of clusots. Most of the book's tales feature a waxed king who has wings made from sliced acorns. Those that do not, tend to be homages of lost love and tranquillity. *The Book of Jopolos* is reviled by makkam lizards as greatly as it is adored by lemon-yellow jinn.

Bottle snake
Species of serpent widely feared in dominions in which it exists. Known to bring misery on those who set eyes upon them, they have the peculiarity that they can double up usefully as tent poles and short sticks. The fact bottle snakes bring such misfortune means that they have rarely been able to be of assistance to others – a point that consumes them. For, bottle snakes are by nature one of the most kind-hearted species found in the Realm.

Brass elk leather
Fine leather used for binding rare and valued books. The covering eventually emits smœl oil, a point that generally makes the leather impractical.

Brolloc bone
Hard bone carved in intricate patterns and used for shoes in Zonus. No one has ever managed to work out where the bones come from. All that is known of their source is that a ready supply can be procured on a beach in the Kingdom of Alphot. When tapped with the back of a spoon, the bones chime like miniature hand bells.

Bronichiat crisis
Much-discussed catastrophe in antiquitas in which a clear lack of procedure led to a domino effect. During the crisis a great many kingdoms were destroyed, among them the Kingdoms of Aoör and Booör, as well as the intermediary states of Aax, Bsx, Cdx, Dfx, Egx, and Zhx.

Broose prunes
Type of dried fruit found in the Dominion of Red Revenge, which grow on a bush made from glass. Packets of broose prunes bought in neighbouring dominions have been discovered to be favoured hiding places for rogue jinn. No one is quite certain why.

Brotherhood of Invincible Jinn
Hailing from the most fearful and dangerous secret Order of which Nequissimus is leader. Merely thinking of the Brotherhood is regarded as such bad luck that no more than the briefest entry is provided here.

Buck beetle
Cursed species of beetle whose furry pelt is regarded as exceptionally dark. Buck beetles are disliked by most species of slug, but are adored by all varieties of sloth dogs on account of their fantastical sense of humour.

Caapi
Vine used by the Shuar tribe in the Dominion of Men, to enable them to fly into what they regard as the 'real world'. Sometimes referred to as the 'Vine of the Dead', Caapi's effects depend very much on the admixtures stirred in to it during preparation.

Cadenta Academy
School in Zonus where Jinn Hunters are trained. The most celebrated educational institution in the Realm, the Cadenta Academy is the one place in which good manners and intelligence can be assured. Jinn Hunters who graduate at the Academy protect the Realm by capturing rogue jinn.

Cadet

Trainee Jinn Hunter at the Cadenta Academy in Zonus. Cadets undergo a long, complex and secretive training period. During training they are provided with a redacted version of the *Jinn Hunter's Handbook*. The full text is awarded on graduation.

Calamitous occasion

Event that occurs by a freak of nature, in which certain species of creature, including goose-footed jinn, are overcome with exalted elation. During such situations no amount of calming can reduce the accompanying sense of terror, the only solution being that the victim must be left to realize its foolishness. This can take anything from three seconds to four thousand years.

Candlemas

Annual festivity held in the Kingdom of Smod, in which the inhabitants – especially wart jinn – like to feast on bowls of thick, lumpy porridge known as 'mos-mot'.

Clusots

Species of lemon-yellow jinn, celebrated for their good manners, kindness to strangers, and for the ability to remember even the longest conversations verbatim. Exceptionally hungry all the time, clusots are regarded as the best travelling companions one might hope to encounter.

Conduit
Invisible connections between everything in the Realm. Conduits have been studied at various times by special commissions. Despite this, almost no one has ever come up with a plausible reason why they exist. One thing known for certain is that isolated conduits emit ripples that, when tasted, are said to be very delicious indeed.

Corpus
Physical body of a jinn, as opposed to its soul. Many species of jinn can shape-shift into any form they wish, but they almost always have a 'base manifestation', regarded as the 'corpus'.

Corticac
Group of nine wasp slugs, regarded with universal affection for their sense of humour and their ability to turn almost anything into first-rate manure.

Curse of Zimilia-Po
Epic spell comprising 18,752,422 couplets, each of which has sixteen different meanings depending on the intonation used to speak them.

Dance of Humiliation
Various types of ritualistic dance occurring in different parts of the Realm, the Dance of Humiliation occurs when an auxiliary clerk oversteps his mandate, and is punished. Although the punishments meted out through the dance vary greatly, they tend to involve stripping off clothing or layers of furry skin (such as in the case of klunials) and parading or dancing about while the audience jeers and jests at the sight.

Dancers of Supreme and Insidious Liberty
Troupe of roving performers whose 'Ritual of Day and Night and In Between' forms part of the reprimand meted out to anyone who divulges the contents of the *Jinn Hunter's Handbook*.

Decimus bird
Small red-hued bird with feathered hands rather than wings, in whose nests rogue jinn like to take refuge. The reason for their selecting this hiding place is a point of speculation, and has led to feuds and even to wars at various times through recorded history. The reason, it seems, is that decimus birds line their nests with quilts made from their own ancestral songs – the notes of which are appealing to jinn.

Department of Exceptional Danger & Predicament
Department at Zonus recording certain events of

extraordinary peril that have taken place or are about to occur. When hunting certain species of rogue jinn, a Jinn Hunter is required to obtain a licence from the department before initiating capture.

Desolation Archive
One of many special archives at Zonus reserved for particularly complex documents, or those written in an inverted language. The Desolation Archive is so restricted, that showing an entry pass has been found to be a reliable way to impress female clerks in the administration.

Dok-kod
Species of cow, the tanned leather of which is used for binding books in the Dominion of Scall in particular; favoured on account of its ability to massage the hands of the reader while the book is being held.

Dominion
Group of kingdoms, likened to a galaxy as opposed to a single planet. Ranging in size and variety, some dominions are small enough to fit under the fingernail of a mouse jinn. Others are so large that their size has never been measured.

Dragon's eye motif
Symbol of the Jinn Hunters, feared by a great many

jinn, and said to contain the ability to ward off zem wasps, swarms of which have been known to paralyse entire kingdoms.

Drap
Vosssuk piece worth 119 points.

Dreamstate
State of mind known to indigenous people of the Australian Outback in the Dominion of Men, in which a connection to the ancestors is maintained.

Dreamtime
Type of sleep employed in Zonus as a way of instructing cadets, in which the pupil is exposed to a vast and multifarious gamut of experiences and conditions. One second of 'dreamtime' has been likened to an entire year of conventional study.

Drem-drem tea
Turquoise-coloured beverage regarded as a delicacy by malbinos, containing a variety of bizarre and rare ingredients, which include: a spoonful of ear wax from a spatula whale, a jar of fermented pioaha cream, six leaves plucked at night from a marmary bush, a sprig of lavender grown secretly on the southern slopes of Mount Zylovos, and a wart from the left cheek of a souloulou bear. Foul-smelling and

distinctly unpleasant to anyone or anything that is not a malbino, drem-drem tea has been known to cure whooping cough and various forms of plague.

Dreq ghouls

Race of terrifying ghouls widely regarded as one of the foulest life forms in the Realm. They inhabit mines and cold damp caves, especially those that are upside down. Grotesquely deformed, and all covered in oily warts, dreq ghouls believe they are exceptionally attractive, which is definitely not true by any stretch of the imagination. Their main characteristics are being mercenary, boring, impatient, cruel, rude, wretched, and greedy. Their favourite foods are underripe smorop pods, toothpicks, and lemon-yellow jinn.

Drima stones

Small lumps of stone carved in antiquitas by three-finned fish in the Mercuric Sea. Drima stones are used as a currency across the Realm because of their abundance, and on account of the fact that they cannot be easily forged.

Drüp

Language spoken by certain species of deep-rooted tree, praised for its melodious tone, especially when uttered in an accent from the Kingdom of Alphot.

Dwarf albino mole
Species of mole noted for its peculiar ear wax, which tends to be vermilion in colour, except during eclipses when it is shocking pink.

Epoch of Obscurity
Time in which all life is expunged by a series of unrelated coincidences. Only once in the ancient history of the Realm has such an era occurred. To speak of it, or even to think of it, is regarded as a treasonable act.

Era of Despotic Bleakness
According to the Soothsayers of Mūlch, this era will occur when Nequissimus perishes.

Fala-fala curse
Jinx that in rare cases turns unfortunate communities to stone. To be effective, the fala-fala curse must be spoken backwards and inside out, and uttered by a pilgrim crawling across a desert overlaid with dried scarab beetles. Only when the curse is recited correctly is the effect delivered. If a single syllable is intoned incorrectly, the fala-fala curse is cast on the pilgrim delivering it, rather than upon his intended opponent.

Fala-fala stone
Type of stone into which the fala-fala curse turns the target. Harder than almost any other form of stone found in the Realm, fala-fala is so heavy that a piece the size of a bottle cap would require an entire army to carry it.

Fastulam leaves
Used as bedding in some kingdoms, the leaves from the fastulam tree are highly regarded for their ability to release warmth in winter. The leaves have the added benefit of reading the thoughts of the person sleeping upon them, ensuring that their dreams are fabulous in the extreme.

Festooned slime gourds
Long colourful gourds growing in bogs and fetid swamps – a habitat prized by certain rogue jinn as a perfect hiding place from Jinn Hunters.

Féxx ghoul
High-spirited race of ghouls living in the Dominion of Gogolo, celebrated for their shrill voices and for the anthem sacred to their faith. Singing the anthem is off limits by anyone or anything not a Féxx ghoul, for fear of being charged with treason and sentenced to life incarceration in the Prism.

Figglewist fruit
Delectable fruit, popular in various parts of the
Realm, prized by certain species of jinn and non-jinn;
the juice of which is regarded as the best pickling
agent for corporal appendages.

Folizz-nü
Medical condition in which the joints stiffen and
the eyeballs fall out. In some cases, the afflicted
individual levitates, before falling like a stone into the
nearest pool of uncovered liquid.

Fopula slugs
Species of slug regarded as possessing extraordinarily
good memories. It's said that only once has a fopula
slug ever forgotten anything, and that happened
when he had been hypnotized by an oolak that was
doubly insane.

Forlock
High-speed legal conveyancers employed in Zonus,
they are experts in drafting documents of astonishing
complexity in the blink of an eye. Blessed with five
hands, dainty feet, and elongated ears, they smell of
overripe prunes.

Fostula geese
Species of haughty self-important geese well-regarded

for their skill in sharpening knives. Historically employed before battles and duels.

Four-billed platypus
Creature featuring in the antidote for those succumbing to the danger of the Pole of Silent Faces. The four-billed platypus has never been studied and so almost nothing is known of it. The lack of knowledge surrounding this curious creature has occurred not for it being tedious, but rather because every time an expedition has embarked on making an investigation, it has been swallowed by a vaux vulture – an unlikely coincidence in its own right.

Frax poetry
Discordant form of rhyme despised by a great many jinn, including Nequissimus, and said to have been indirectly responsible for the destruction of entire kingdoms in ancient times. Even though most varieties of frax poetry are now banned, the memory lives on.

Friz
Vosssuk piece worth 58,667,752,431 points.

Frozen martep flats
Grassy expanses running east–west between certain deserts, frozen martep flats are popular with jinn as

hiding places for their treasure, as well as with rogue jinn who tend to hide themselves in the hidden hoards.

Fugian wind
Breeze powering the sails and thence the mechanism of the Prism; it is expelled from the lungs of a pair of bottle jinn who take it in turns to blow into the iron sails as punishment for their crimes.

Fusilia
Unctuous slime secreted over the fur of malbinos, known to have numerous effects. These include cooling the fur and the skin beneath it, as well as protecting it from lice. Fusilia slime has been said to glow bright red once in the lifetime of a malbino – a sign that death is near.

Ghost venison
Species of deer found in the forests of Wipiliā that, by royal decree, may only be hunted by the king and his retinue of ancestral servants. The monarch provides gifts of the prized meat twice yearly to the malbinos at Zonus, in return for guarding an especially wicked wart jinn that once terrorized the kingdom. The nocturnal ghost jinn earned their appellation for the fact they become almost completely transparent

in moonlight, thus making them exceedingly
challenging to hunt.

Golden waziz
Creature known to be extremely loud and discordant
in its death throes. A hybrid between a fish and an
enormous bird, the golden waziz has a pair of bills,
multiple fins, and as many as sixteen interwoven
tongues.

Grall
Vosssuk piece worth 888 points.

Gramzel pie
Putrid baked fermented pie considered to be a luxury
in certain dominions, prized for its sour taste, and
regarded as peculiar for the way it tends to turn those
who gorge on it utterly insane.

Grangula
Burrowing creature known to swallow entire cities
and small kingdoms whole by dislocating its jaws.
Although relatively small and stout in stature,
grangulas have the ability to envelop the most colossal
spaces before devouring their contents.

Gras-grot surgeon
Medical practitioners entrusted with handling autopsies in certain cases; considered to be adept in the art of dissection – except when the dissected form is boil-blooded.

Green poliak
Species of snow jinn with an unusually pronounced ego, said by at least a dozen dwarf ghoul races to be so conceited that they eventually turn to stone.

Green-hoofed snail
One of more than 387 species of snail bearing cleft hooves, twin tails, and iridescent shells.

Grick moss
Purple moss growing on walls of high-altitude caves, that keeps in the warmth during winter.

Girid bear
Symbolic mascot of otter heralds; regarded as purer than pure, except when feasting on beetle dung – at which time they are regarded as indecent in the extreme.

Gristial rainbow
Rainbow believed by all ghouls to be imaginary, and by jinn to be not only real, but the most real

occurrence ever to take place. Folklore regarding the gristial rainbow differs from location to location. In some dominions, it is said to contain the souls of those slain in battle; while in others it's believed to be linked to the reason why clouds float as they do.

Grix stick
Sacred to dreq ghouls, grix sticks attract lightning, and are exceptionally magnetic. Although the properties of this curious wood have been studied at various times, the students investigating it have always succumbed to inebriation and have never filed a report that made any sense at all.

Grollow
Bloodied and pustular.

Group think
Capability of insects, certain species of jinn, and some trees, to reason and ruminate in a communal way.

Groyl
Vosssuk piece worth unlimited points.

Grulac ointment
Fungal cream used for a variety of medical afflictions; regarded by many forms of ghoul as a delicacy when spread on wafer-thin squares of toast.

Gruluq
Food favoured by certain species of jinn, made from fermented roots harvested from bobastia trees, particularly in the Glens of Steeped Loathing.

Grumple gas
Noxious kind of sour-smelling vapour thought at one time to cure insanity, and at another time to bleach whale bones. In actual fact, grumple gas has no uses, except that of delighting sloth jinn, who are amused by almost anything at all.

Gumble
Lower half of the fin structure of various species of cave-dwelling shark, that forms part of a popular expression of madness – 'fluted to the gumbles' – the actual etymological meaning of which has long since been lost.

Gwalipa juice
Juice made from the berries of the fig-like gwalipa bush; bottled in special flasks and sold for a high price in emporiums at certain crossroads between dominions. The bottles have been known to be favoured hiding places for rogue jinn.

Heriz
Persian rugs crafted on the Slopes of Sabalan, in the south-west region of the Caspian Sea.

Holding Zone
Protected warehouse under the remit of the Department of Caged Souls in which the souls of imprisoned jinn are housed. In normal circumstances, holding facilities are sited far from Zonus, so that – if a jinn were to escape – it would not easily be reunited with its soul.

Hollow-backed toad
Classification of toads existing at the bottom of certain dank and miserable wells. Although the toads constantly wish for an end to their unfortunate situation, they are always blessed with extremely long lives – a point that troubles them greatly.

Hosolica lizards
Species of lizard with an intensely pungent smell. The aroma has been likened to that of a mouse jinn burping, although that particular smell has never been accurately studied.

Hupp
Vosssuk piece worth 62,077 points.

Ifff
Vosssuk piece worth 76,654,983,448 points.

Ifrit
Race of creatures similar to jinn; believed by some to actually be jinn or death spirits, they are blessed with supernatural powers.

Ikat
Form of tie-dye found in central Asia and Latin America in which individual threads are dyed to produce colourful textiles.

Inventory of Outstanding and Pressing Questions
Encyclopaedic archive of answers on etiquette and general behaviour, made available to officials at Zonus.

J5D/Z
Secure holding facility for rogue jinn souls located beneath Morlib's Optical Inc. on New York's West 72nd Street. When constructed after the last Ice Age, the unit was in a remote region of jungle – the reason for its original selection. With the development of Manhattan, however, the wilderness was replaced by urban sprawl – and J5D/Z found itself in a basement adjacent to a busy thoroughfare. More than once there had been plans to relocate the facility from

Manhattan, and indeed from the Dominion of Men, but such was the slowness of bureaucracy that a replacement location was never found.

Jaguar ice
Exceptionally hard form of ice grown in laboratories and prized for its perfect structure and luminescence.

Jinn
Parallel life form said to have been brought to life from smokeless fire, they exist throughout the Realm. As ancient as any other species, jinn are believed to be born, live, and die, like any other creature. When they are good, they are very good, but when they are bad – they can be wicked in the extreme. The bane of the Realm since the moment of their creation, jinn are monitored by the Order of Councilus, with rogue jinn being imprisoned in the Prism. Innumerable sub-species of jinn exist, falling into seven broad classifications. Jinn are capable of all manner of feats, such as shape-shifting, spontaneous travel, colossal and immediate destruction, as well as performing acts of anonymous kindness.

Jinn Hunter
Warrior who hunts rogue jinn in the service of the Order of Councilus. Regarded as the bravest legion in existence, they comprise jinn and half-jinn, as well

as a wide number of other species. Through training at the Cadenta Academy at Zonus, they acquire the skills needed to identify and trap rogue jinn, before entering the esteemed Fraternity of the Jinn Hunters.

Jinn Hunter's Handbook

Secret dossier of information relating to jinn and in particular to rogue jinn. The *Handbook* is made available in full to those who have passed out from the Cadenta Academy, and in redacted form to cadets. The pages of the *Handbook* constantly change as the information is checked, double-checked, amended and augmented.

Jinnslayer

Most celebrated line of ancestral Jinn Hunters, the Jinnslayers are regarded as the only line that would ever have a chance of trapping Nequissimus. The most famous Jinnslayer of all, King Solomon was responsible for capturing the great jinn three thousand years ago.

Jistipimas

Constellation used for navigation by lemon-yellow jinn, believed erroneously by various species of tree frog to have the magical power of being able to turn trees into gold, and gold into stone.

Jool
Vosssuk piece worth 45,002 points.

Jostixill fish
Species of fish living at the bottom of the Green-Green Sea whose wits are sucked out during the birthing process, and replaced by a highly potent form of insanity. In rare cases, when the fish have been caught on the lines, the curious blend of lunacy has been carried from the hook into the fisherman himself. Insanity and psychosis from the jostixill fish has, at some times in the distant past, turned to plague – infecting vast swathes of the Realm.

Kilim
Style of carpet from the Near East formed from a type of distinct tapestry weaving.

Kingdom
Subsection within the Realm, a number of which form a dominion. Kingdoms may not have a reigning monarch, but do usually possess some form of command structure. One notable exception are the regions of the Frozen Zone, which are ruled over by a species of glass marbles in a complex system of democracy.

Klunial
Creatures that ensure jinn do not abuse their powers, especially in gaining vast wealth for themselves. Raven-black, they are generally well liked, except when they allow their authority to get the better of them. In certain cases, klunials have been trapped, forced to strip out of their fur, and to dance round and round in an act known as the Dance of Humiliation.

Krill choir of Spî
Creators of one of the most pleasing sounds in all the Realm; said by some to be capable of transforming any expression of misery into the most superlative demonstration of beauty.

Lisping wasp kings
Line of ruthless monarchs who speak with a lisp so pronounced that they are misunderstood by anyone not born with ears that can make sense of what they say. At the point of writing only three creatures in existence are known to possess such ears – two of them are sea slugs and the third is an unremarkable brown lump of stone.

Livicton
Species possessing anti-mesmeric qualities, livictons have been used in many rogue jinn escape attempts from Zonus. Obsessed with hexagons, livictons are

masters of shape-shifting. Less known is their ability to drink sixteen times their own body-weight in seaweed beer.

Locāxula

Otter-like servants in the service of Mr Ot at the Mishmak Lodge, the creatures were bred in antiquitas to be loyal and polite in the extreme. Never once has a locāxula ever behaved in a way that would displease their master, or anyone else, and for this reason they are universally liked.

Maestro

Archivist in the service of Zonus. Maestros are small, nimble creatures with overly large eyes, and with astonishing memories. It's said that they never forget anything – an advantage for their role as archivists, but a disadvantage for their general well-being. Hailing from the Dominion of Xoliam, the maestros are employed at Zonus in shifts of 333 years, and wear coarse black capes embroidered with feathers from the aromatic qavak bird.

Magi

Deriving from the Order of the Magus. A secretive sect known for their enthusiasm for turning wartle ogres into mice, and for their ability to walk over oceans and seas.

Makkam
Hybrid of lizard and rodent regarded as quite delicious when fried in mô oil, and as the most revolting food imaginable when cooked in anything else.

Malbino
Ancestral guards who oversee the inmates at the Prism, malbinos live up to 300 years. Short in height, they possess nine eyes of varying sizes set around the circumference of their heads. Their hands bear five fingers and a pair of thumbs, and their bristly white fur is bathed in a lilac slime known as 'fusilia'. Malbinos do not have ears, but instead communicate by a form of telepathy.

Mall
Vosssuk piece worth 0 points.

Maragor
Judges who preside over all legal cases brought before the courts at Zonus, they are expected to be utterly impartial – except in cases where the defendant is descended from a snarling bot-bot. In such cases, maragor judges are expected to throw the book at them whether they are guilty or not.

Maraxa
Blend of a parrot and a dog, maraxas tend to burrow

under the ground, or take advantage of empty caves and caverns, where they delight in entrapping travellers by luring them with promises of wonder and delight. Maraxas are amused by treasure, by stories, and by reducing their prey to a paranoid state. Although not known to humans, it was maraxas that seeded the so-called treasury of the *Arabian Nights* into the Dominion of Men. Fortunately for humans, maraxas disliked the dominion very greatly, and left soon after arriving on account of the weather, the limited variants in language, and the food.

Marmary bush
Fragrant plant, the aromatic leaves of which are used in drem-drem tea. Marmary bushes have at times been regarded as sacred, idolatrous, comical, shameful, and sordid. In at least one dominion they are thought to be capable of reading the minds of anyone or anything that does not believe in the power and the musings of a zonnial stone.

Marmul fish
Marine creature that squeaks like a child's toy when squeezed.

Marmus water
Liquid that tattoos the skin and drives the sane insane with absolute shame.

Marmut
Species of animal in the service of Zonus, employed for all manner of menial tasks.

Maroob juice
Juice from the maroob fruit, regarded as one of the sweetest and one of the bitterest foodstuffs in existence.

Marshmak bird
Flightless fowl prized by a great many jinn for the bags of succulent flesh hanging from their throats. The golden variety is especially valued because as soon as it has been devoured, the bird reappears, allowing itself to be consumed a second time.

Marsimus juice
Form of sap used for pickling in some regions of the Realm; thought to be an extraction made from the sweat of ointment geese.

Mô oil
Type of oil used for frying certain species of lizard, including the makkam, a hybrid of rodent and lizard. Mô oil is much appreciated for the way it dissolves the outer scales of especially chewy reptiles and amphibians.

Moöl
Sentient state into which imprisoned jinn slip, moöl
has been likened to a kind of hypnotic hibernation,
which allows jinn to serve time while imagining acts
of unspeakable depravity.

Morlib's Optical Inc.
Quiet shop on New York's West 72nd Street, beneath
which Holding Zone J5D/Z – for the caged souls of
imprisoned jinn – is located. Run by the Morlib family
of wartles since the Upper West Side was developed
in the late 1800s, the optical store had once boasted
celebrity clientele, with customers queuing down the
block to avail themselves of its services.

Morning of Unknown Dawn
Start of a day widely believed never to have existed
except in folklore. Despite this, certain species of
jinn fervently insist the Morning of Unknown Dawn
does exist and, that if blessed in a certain way, it will
lead to treasure.

Morsiminal hour
Sacred measurement of time used by malbinos.

Morsolog
Species of rodent found in subterranean dominions,
regarded as the finest wrestlers found anywhere

in the Realm. Morsologs are so preoccupied with wrestling, that they find it almost impossible to hold down employment of any kind. For this reason they are scorned in a great many dominions, although regarded highly for their advanced wrestling techniques.

Morsolog neck hold
Wrestling move favoured by morsologs, the Realm's greatest wrestlers, said to be so sturdy that there is no way of breaking free.

Mortle bark
Rigid tree bark used for binding official ledgers in Zonus. The supply of bark has in recent times dwindled on account of the fact it is ground into a powder and taken as snuff by miscreants and scoundrels at ports on the Sea of Green Wind.

Mos-mot
Variety of porridge favoured in the Kingdom of Smod, especially by wart jinn during the season of Candlemas. Mos-mot is poisonous to most other jinn, unless sprinkled with saliva extracted from the spittle glands of spatula whales.

Neee
Vosssuk piece worth 1,222,464,131,776 points.

Nemalila
Singularly poisonous plant whose berries are so toxic that even looking upon them leads to paralysis, before an extended and agonizing death.

Nequissimus
Most evil of all jinn in existence, Nequissimus was trapped by King Solomon, and sentenced to live out his days at the nadir of the Prism, the great revolving penitentiary at Zonus.

Ointment geese
Species of bird prized for the fact that their beaks are lubricated with an ointment containing medicinal extracts. The feet of the geese, which are not webbed but rather similar to bovine hooves, stream with perspiration often used in the pickling process.

Oolaks
Lowly shape-shifting subordinates employed at Zonus, regarded as useful because they can stand in for almost anyone else.

Order of Councilus
Highest division of administration of Zonus and the Realm, the Order of Councilus consists of fourteen members, each one of whom is selected by a secret ballot process, the details of which are known only to themselves.

Orlibs
Judges in Zonus, overseeing the trials of rogue jinn, orlibs are regarded as impartial and utterly unbribable – even by the charms of swans, for which they hold a great affection. Resembling human toddlers, at court they wear intricate robes made from waxed pink taffeta and mealy grub silk.

Oroking
Word for an infant jinn, especially one whose horns have not yet broken through.

Otter herald
Proclaimers of official information, otter heralds are trusted, intelligent, funny, and believe they are better than average at playing vosssuk.

Ozymandias & Son
Celebrated emporium of Oriental carpets in Greenwich Village, New York.

Parsilimus pods
Pungent fruit of the parsilimus tree, used by some
species of ghoul to cure stomach disorders, and by
various forms of slug as an aphrodisiac.

Patrax dust
Fine powder that drives spatula whales mad with
desire. The dust is produced by sloth jinn when they
sneeze. Fortuitously this fact has never been revealed
to spatula whales, as the creatures despise sloth jinn
more greatly than anything else in existence.

Phynx
Species commonly employed as stenographers in
Zonus on account of their curious physiology. Feathered on one side and devoid of plumage on the other,
they possess a funnel-shaped ear on the top of their
head, as well as twenty-four hands, with between a
hundred and a hundred and fifty fingers on each.
Capable of typing simultaneously in six hundred and
twelve languages, phynx were bred over centuries for
the administrative position in which they excel.

Pioaha cream
Type of rancid cream which, when fermented, is one
of the constituents of drem-drem tea.

Plague ghoul
Variety of ghoul once thought to spread pandemics, but now regarded as one of the least likely creatures to have anything to do with plague or pestilence. Despite this, the unfortunate appellation has stuck, even though immense sums have been spent on publicity to correct it.

Pole of Silent Faces
Totem Pole in the Crushed Glass Desert, covered in an astonishing range of heads – each one bearing a tortured mask of outrage. The incantations uttered by the heads cause the tongues of passing travellers to loosen and then detach. The only known remedy to ward off this unpleasant consequence is to imagine a four-billed platypus passing wind for the first time.

Poll Monk
Minor factotum charged with officiating in certain traditional ceremonies and punishments.

Popofof fish
Found in mercuric oceans, popofof fish are large, jet-black, and prized for their teeth, which are exceptionally sharp.

Portmanteau bear
Species of animal famed for the extraordinary flexibility of its stomach which, at certain times, has been used as a place to keep important documents safe.

Pozulz
Appellation given to the inhabitants of the Dominion of Slaked Thirst, which means 'melancholic' in their native dialect.

Prism
Great jail at Zonus in which rogue jinn are kept. Fashioned from sheets of impenetrable glass, and designed as a vast inverted pyramid turning on its own axis powered by the fugian wind, the Prism is protected by legions of malbino guards.

Pygmy marmolous
Swarthy species of frog-bear that often carry a satchel fashioned from carved aardvark bones.

Qavak bird
Classification of bird whose feathers are highly prized, used as quills and for cloaks in Zonus. Other than being valued for their feathers, the birds are fêted for their melodious cry when in the presence of royalty.

Quastular bats
Genus of bats found in the tunnels leading to the
Prism, and known for the high-pitched squealing
sound they emit.

Querilis Stone
One of the rarest objects in all existence, the Querilis
Stone has spawned religions and faith groups, been
the reason for military campaigns, catastrophic
disasters, plagues, jubilation, invention, and led to
the greatest work of literary fiction being written –
Querilis My Querilis.

Red slime frogs
Functionaries in the bureaucracy of Zonus charged
with ensuring that perilous expeditions are executed
correctly.

Reindeer-fish
Ordinary marine creature existing in oily oceans,
with a fondness for stories about crescent moons.
Its six pairs of antlers are believed to protect against
all manner of psychological disorders, although very
little research has ever been done on them.

Rimulam
Type of jinn with a considerably advanced folklore,
and a belief in certain animistic objects – such as that

which decrees all marbles to be gods, and various forms of paperclip to be angels.

Ritual of Day and Night and In Between
Bizarre rite enacted by the Dancers of Supreme and Insidious Liberty, regarded by roaming troubadours to be the most sinister yet sublime ceremonial occurrence to take place anywhere in the Realm.

Rogue jinn
Jinn culpable of misdemeanour, particularly those currently free and licensed to be hunted. Once trapped and separated from their soul, they are sentenced in the law courts at Zonus. Rogue jinn found guilty of wrongdoing are incarcerated in the Prism.

Ropes of Mazumagat
Knowhow needed to be a Jinn Hunter which is taught at the Cadenta, and regarded as one of the great secrets of the Order of Councilus.

S'baw
Type of spongy pulp, regarded in some kingdoms as a prized delicacy, and in others as the most revolting thing in existence. Wars have raged on for centuries between kingdoms holding strong views on s'baw.

Salafass moon
Lunar occurrence which desiccates lands touched by its light.

Saliani
Fabulously decorative carpets of varying size and shape from Azerbaijan, they are celebrated for their rich colours and geometric designs.

Sarvel curse
Belligerent form of curse that tends to involve the recipients being turned to chalky powder. Fines and other penalties are meted out to jinn casting a sarvel curse without permission. Lengthy sentences in the Prism are handed down for this thoroughly unpleasant crime.

Scalica cake
Putrid baked product made with bovine bile, and served only when rotten and thoroughly infested with worms. A variety of kingdoms pride themselves on preparing the very best scalica cake, and have at times come to blows in competing with one another. An annual competition for the very best example of scalica cake was held at one time, but had to be stopped because of underhand behaviour, ill-feeling, and sabotage.

Seal of Solomon
Magical seal that provided Solomon with power over all jinn. Regarded as the ultimate object of jinn repression, the seal's whereabouts is currently unknown. In some dominions, there are religions dedicated to worshipping the seal. In others, groups have protested that the seal never existed at all. Fortunately, the 'pro' and 'anti' Solomon's Seal factions have never come into contact.

Secrets of Dorsalim
Inventory of clandestine and top secret information provided to Jinn Hunters during training and never permitted to be revealed.

Seep juice
Pungent extract introduced into a barmyal cage, regarded as both cleansing and exceptionally perilous. Nothing good has ever come to anyone or anything anointed with it.

Seven States of Mind
Belief that seven types of thinking exist in those who follow a creed of sacred knowledge. Although now antiquated, the concept has at certain times been regarded with reverence, so much so that it appears in a significant number of administrative documents.

Shuar
Tribe of former head-hunters in the Upper Amazon,
known at one time for shrinking the heads of their
enemies to the size and shape of grapefruits.

Silitia
Class of worms living in the Slaked Slew Forest,
known for the sound they make when slithering over
rocks, and for the taste they give to certain varieties
of venison stew.

Sisligulets
Form of snail hailed for singing the Xerex lines very
well, and for their ability to glow in time with the
music they create.

Slaked bones of Kramuläia
Legendary collection of rune-like bones mentioned
frequently in folklore, and believed to have been
conjured into existence by a spatula whale that was
bored out of its mind.

Slink moss
Reddish-brown moss found in various regions of
the Realm, slink moss is unusual in that it sets fire to
itself in times of danger – or during an eclipse.

Slippery Slope of Cursed Imagination
Psychological concept that the more one thinks of
something that is utterly malevolent, it sucks one in,
and leads to the most wretched state of melancholy
imaginable.

Sloke mullet goot
Cave-dwelling invertebrate employed in certain
jurisdictions for acts of vengeance.

Slom pear
Pithy green-brown fruit with a glazed carapace and
abundant seeds. Slom pears are not prized for their
taste, but rather are used across the Realm in the
making of decisions, such as who shall start a game
of vosssuk.

Slop stick
Sharpened baton used for knitting socks and for
taunting prisoners.

Sloth dog
Hybrid between a dog and a lizard, known for a
high-pitched howl that resembles hysterical laughter
but is in actual fact an expression of remorse.
Misunderstood by almost everyone and everything
that encounters them, sloth dogs are the most
sensitive creatures found anywhere in the Realm.

Smarm geese
Elongated species of geese, prized for their golden beaks, hunted in a great many jurisdictions under strict licence. Representatives of smarm geese frequently protest that they are set upon by all and sundry. In more usual circumstances they would receive a fairer hearing. But, the fact that most judges and legal clerks secretly collect smarm geese beaks means that they are hunted without restriction, in the most ruthless ways imaginable.

Smarob House of Translation
Widely regarded as the finest translation organization in the Realm; used by officials at Zonus, and a byword for the highest quality.

Smílc grub
Administrative assistant charged with selecting updated information for use in the *Jinn Hunter's Handbook*. Smílc grubs are regarded by most as impartial, hardworking, polite, and unusually good-looking considering they are infested with lice.

Smish-smish cloth
Waxy fabric used for polishing and cleaning metallic surfaces, imbued with an astonishingly rich folklore of its own. Worshipped in certain kingdoms after a

complex misunderstanding featuring a blind elf, a bottle cap, and an albino maraxa.

Smœl oil
Malodorous oil tapped from the glands of certain jungle trees, which by coincidence is also secreted by brass elk leather used in book-binding.

Smorlak state
Ambient state of hypnosis especially difficult to translate accurately into any language not understood by violiss snails.

Smorop
Tree whose fruit – the smorop pod – is universally regarded as one of the most delicious of all foods. Such is the widespread preoccupation with the fruit, smorop trees have at times been regulated by authorities, and even driven to obliteration, as a way of curtailing the obsession with smorop pods.

Smox fleas
Minute fleas that plague the lives of vermilion jinn, known for their communal obsession with the penalties and punishments meted out by the Order of Councilus.

Snall
Vosssuk piece worth 9 points.

Snark herald
Long-limbed administrative courier entrusted with certain lowly tasks, including those involved with the punishing of wayward Jinn Hunters.

Snarl beetle
Hereditary witnesses given far more importance than they are worthy of and universally disliked as a result – but so socially connected that they are unlikely ever to be replaced.

Snarling bot-bot
Small meek species of incarnate pebble, found in various corners of the Realm, and regarded by many as the rudest and most obscene of all living creatures. In actual fact, snarling bot-bots are kindhearted, but are the victims of a communal character assassination unleashed in antiquitas.

Snarling foxes of Dribâ
Slender fox-like beetles with a gleaming carapace, which emit a dull thumping sound from their hooves when stressed.

Snoring Judge at Filleêegm

Narcoleptic magistrate overseeing sentences relating to the Spöom Chamber of Zolīk. Usually falls asleep during judgements, much to the irritation of the legal counsel and the clerks, but not the defendant.

Snorp putty

Pleasantly scented compound used in the glazing of opaque windows, and for hypnotizing certain varieties of warty fish.

Sosuala fish

Fat-tailed fish known for its exceedingly peppery smell when dried slowly over a naked flame.

Soul of jinn

Usually manifested as a bird, a jinn's soul must be trapped if the jinn itself is to be caught and then imprisoned for a crime.

Souloulou bear

Species of bear whose cheeks tend to be afflicted by warts in summer months. The bears are curious for the fact that they survive almost entirely on eating worms gathered by night in forests believed by others not to exist.

Spatula whale
Species of whale found in certain oceans, whose ear wax is added to drem-drem tea in order to give a nutty flavour.

Species of jinn
Belonging to the seven distinct classifications – ranging in intelligence and physical development – jinn are exceptionally diverse.

Suzani
Decorative Central Asian embroidery, celebrated for its bright colours, motifs, and fine needlework.

Swamisiod
Fleshy creature found in oceans and bodies of dark water, known for their wish to have amputated appendages fused into their underbellies so as to ward off a particularly virulent form of plague that they believe incorrectly to be stalking them.

Sworp-sworp soap
Type of soap made from fat extracted from the underbelly of certain species of frogs; regarded highly for the way it cleans filth from between the toes, and for its scent – which has been likened to the smell of a snark jinn with incurable diarrhoea.

Syfetic leeches
Leeches that suck the memories from their victims,
rather than blood. Famed for the ability to grow
inside out, and for the fact that they communicate to
one another in poetic couplets and rhyming slang.

System of Consistent Administration
Respected arrangement of administrative matters,
revered by most for its exceptional order – notably
that of the AZAZAZAZ/998152 system.

Sythostic dream
Order of dreams and dreaming in which Jinn Hunters
may perceive certain future events by following a
complex series of instructions precisely.

Telepathic musing
System by which life forms may absorb relevant
information and ideas. Although practical, the
system is regarded by many as a shortcut, and has
therefore been banned, in a variety of kingdoms, on
pain of dissection.

Thuya
Tree from the desert of Morocco, prized for its
aromatic wood.

Tørqular pattern
Geometric arrangement in which various uniform pieces are clustered around a central point, causing a sense of wonder in those who set eyes upon it.

Treasure Repatriation Department
Otherwise known as the TRD, the department is responsible for getting hoards confiscated from captured jinn back to their rightful owners. Exceptionally and unnecessarily bureaucratic, the TRD has been ordered time and again to increase efficiency on pain of being shut down.

Trost moss
Form of sooty moss that builds up in ducts and certain pipes, hampering effective movement of gases and liquids.

Turcoman
Tribal people residing in the region east of the Caspian Sea, whose culture is celebrated for creating intricate carpets and rugs.

Vaux vulture
Big-boned scavenger found in various deserted regions of the Realm, the birds have shocking pink plumage, razor-like bills, and delight in picking off scientists sent to investigate them – especially on

the third day of their expeditions. When boiled and stuffed into a cloth bag, the vultures have been said to stave off the xirid plague. No information exists on whether this is accurate, however.

Vector moon
Invisible lunar occurrence given far higher status than it deserves.

Verum monkey
Monkey known for its paper-thin limbs, and its ability to withstand excruciating pain. On one occasion on which a verum monkey was witnessed being torn limb from limb, it emitted nothing more than a single muffled groan of hysterical puzzlement.

Violiss snail
Species of snail conjured into existence by a rogue jinn during the reign of Solomon, celebrated for the way it falls into a smorlak state, and for the fact that it dissolves in warm water upon which a dreq ghoul's shadow has fallen.

Vosssuk
Impossibly complicated board game, popular at Mishmak and elsewhere, vosssuk is one of the most prized and challenging games ever devised. Beginning with the 'vouch' in which the players agree to abide

by all the rules on fear of harsh punishment, the game itself is so complex that almost no life form in the Realm has ever been known to excel in it.

Vosssuk Adjudication Unit
Specialized division established to monitor cheating in the revered game of vosssuk; thought at one time to be impartial, the Vosssuk Adjudication Unit recently lost much of its credibility during a case involving a hamster and a fire jinn in the Kingdom of Woz-woz.

Wart frog hog
Despite their designation, wart frog hogs are not amphibian but rather a hybrid of horse and lion. The fact that they have exceedingly bad breath has led to rogue jinn hiding in their mouths, in the soft tissue to the right of their tongue.

Wartle
Six-handed ogre with a fondness for scalica cake, known for reliability and for possessing advanced clerical skills.

Was-swas ointment
Fluorescent green salve used for rendering exposed dermatological surfaces impervious to attack.

Wasp slugs
Manure-obsessed slugs that are highly prized and equally adored for their sense of humour and their ability to turn almost anything into fine manure.

Wicilian
Tribe of people who reside on the shore of the Terranean Sea; notable for their swarthy appearance, their webbed feet, and for the fact they can juggle up to 122 live mice when blindfold.

Wishwash pie
Type of pie favoured by jinn, many of whom embark in adolescence on a rite of passage centring around a search for the perfect example. When performed correctly, the rite ought to lead the traveller straight back to his own home – for it is widely believed that no wishwash pie tastes better than that cooked by one's own mother.

Wowip
Repugnantly flea-infested ghoul known for its inability to tell a plausible lie. Wowips sweat yellow liquor from glands under their knee joints when they tell falsehoods – an unfortunate occurrence, since they rarely tell the truth. A second misfortune is that the liquor secreted as sweat is greatly liked by the diminutive fleas that live on wowips' backs.

413

Xerex lines

Invisible lines of magical energy on which lemon-yellow jinn walk and sing. Said to have been conjured in antiquitas, the lines were supposedly materialized by a great wind that ripped through the entire Realm, leaving a trail of energy in its wake. Other species of jinn also walk the Xerex lines, but only the lemon-yellow variety regard it as a sacred act.

Xirid plague

One of the most despicable forms of pestilence known to exist, xirid plague has been feared from antiquitas onwards, with no known cure. The only way thought to stave off the affliction is by preparing a vaux vulture in a certain way and wearing it in a simple bag around one's neck.

Xorrk grubbe

Notary charged with certifying documents and doing so without unnecessary fuss.

Xylotroc

Mesmeric field preventing rogue jinn escaping from Zonus, as well as preventing jinn within the Realm from breaking into Zonus to free family or friends, or those set on revenge. The xylotroc is so complex that an entire department was created to ensure it operates at maximum efficiency. A little-known fact is that the engineer who devised the xylotroc was put up for an award at one time. Despite being the winner, he was not permitted to accept the prize on account of his singularly bad breath.

XYP-55

Experimental medication thought to partially cure a patient from the harmful effects of Nequissimus's whispering. Among its shortcomings are a total loss of memory, and the point that the drug jumbles the patient's senses around – so that the eyes sense smells, the nose senses touch, the ears see, and the hands sense taste.

Zarid

Word used in all manner of descriptive ways, including 'cooling to the feet', as well as offensive, brash, naughty, ugly, grey-green, pungent, and so hilarious as to be indecent. In malbino dialect, zarid tends to be used to mean 'so slippery and unctuous that it is shocking and rather amusing as well'.

Zem wasp

Particularly annoying species of wasp that form colossal swarms and infest open spaces in which self-absorbed and arrogant creatures live. One of the only known ways of warding off zem wasps is to display the dragon's eye motif of the Jinn Hunters.

Zonnial stone
Type of stone found at the bottom of certain oceans and said to exhibit extraordinary powers, such as the ability to control jinn through what is known as 'zonnial musing'.

Zorl
Class of limbless mice that, despite all odds stacked against them, live exceedingly long lives. Accurate information on the exact length of an average zorl lifetime varies, but it is said by the leading scholar on the subject to be sixty-two times as long as a hollow-backed toad.

EXTRACTS FROM

THE JINN HUNTER'S
HANDBOOK

TAHIR SHAH

A NOTE ON THE JINN HUNTER'S HANDBOOK

Rudimentary Information

The *Handbook* was first prepared after what became known as the 'bronichiat crisis', in which failings in elementary practice were made – failings leading by numerous connected and interconnected results to the destruction of the Kingdoms of Aoör and Booör, as well as the intermediary states of Aax, Bsx, Cdx, Dfx, Egx, and Zhx.

While the *Handbook* is provided in limited and redacted form to trainee Jinn Hunters, it is reserved in entirety to those who graduate from the Cadenta Academy.

The *Handbook* is available in all languages, dialects, sub-dialects, argots and vernaculars – except for those found in the Den of Bitter Temptation, as it was agreed in antiquitas that its inhabitants are not worthy of such elevated and consequential information.

Each *Handbook* operates on the AZAZAZAZ/998152 System of Consistent Administration – disposing itself to the cranial and mental frequencies of the one who is reading it at the time. The text may be absorbed in all the major forms of Aslaik Sensory Absorption – including through osmosis, inhalation, telepathic musing, taste, smell, as well as through acoustic and visual stimuli.

The *Handbook* alters constantly depending on information selected and prepared by the smílc grubs. It does not at any time pretend to be encyclopaedic. Indeed, any shortcomings may be counted as proof that it is a bona fide document, and not a fraudulent rendition prepared in the Mines of Slanted Beams.

Please note that copies of the *Handbook* in brass elk leather ought to be bound again every 19½ years, or as and when the leather shows first signs of emitting smœl oil.

JINN HUNTER

Where Not to Keep the Handbook

The *Handbook* must on NO account be kept in any of the following places:

1. In a satchel that has been owned by a pygmy marmolous.

2. In a box lined with bartle snort wood.

3. Beside a fire kindled with grix sticks.

4. In a hole where drem-drem tea has been spilt.

5. In the stomach of a portmanteau bear.

6. Under salt flats baked dry by a salafass moon.

Common Superstitions Relating to the Handbook

1. That it is an amulet against the poison effects of the nemalila plant.

2. That kissing it in a certain way will lead to true love.

3. That it glows in shades of phosphorescence when the shadow of King Solomon is near.

4. That it can recite poetry in the dialect of dreq ghouls.

5. That it holds any affection at all for its owner.

6. That it can provide winning moves in the game of vosssuk.

Standard Penalty for Divulging Information Connected With the Handbook

It goes without saying that the *Handbook* and its contents are secret to the Fraternity. Divulging any information will result in the P/12871/23/AAA/Z Penalty, and an unlimited span of incarceration in the Spöom Chamber of Zolīk.

419

For those in need of being reminded of the details relating to the P/12871/23/AAA/Z Penalty, it comprises thus:

1. The offending Jinn Hunter is forced into a barmyal cage, with the slam spikes sharpened the morning before by twelve pairs of retired fostula geese.

2. The ducts at the top and bottom of the barmyal cage are opened and aligned with the Vector moon. Once open, the ducts are cleaned with a smish-smish cloth, and checked for trost moss. Then, slowly, a quantity of seep juice is introduced, before the ducts are closed.

3. The barmyal cage is rotated through 234 degrees clockwise, and then by 11 degrees in an anticlockwise direction, or until the confined Jinn Hunter makes a sound like that of the snarling foxes of Dribâ.

4. The small window at the base of the unit is unfastened, and the offending Jinn Hunter is poked with a slop stick.

5. The crimes of the Jinn Hunter are read out in the relevant language by a snark herald.

6. Once the seep juice has been seen to take effect, the liquid is drained, and the barmyal cage is turned to the upright position.

7. The offending Jinn Hunter is removed from the cage, and the skin is peeled off its head, limbs, and feet. Once this has been achieved to a satisfactory degree, incisions are made into the muscles of its tongue, neck and principal limbs.

8. Grulac ointment is rubbed into the incisions, so that the now-fetid flesh turns grollow.

9. It is at this point that the Dancers of Supreme and Insidious Liberty are called for. When they arrive they are asked to perform the Ritual of Day and Night and In Between. Note that, depending on the schedule of the Dancers of Supreme

and Insidious Liberty, it may be necessary to pause the punishment process until they are available.

10. When the Ritual of Day and Night and In Between has been performed, and approved by the administrating poll monk, the offending Jinn Hunter is doused in marmus water, ridiculed by sloth dogs, and shamed with the Curse of Zimilia-Po.

Once the entire process has been completed, checked and double-checked, the offending Jinn Hunter is taken to the Snoring Judge at Filleêegm, who will determine the length to be served in the Spöom Chamber of Zolīk.

TAHIR SHAH

OATH OF THE JINN HUNTERS

By the blood, bile, and sinew of my corporal form, and by the slaked bones of Kramuläia, I vow with stooping and utter subservience to uphold the secrets, laws, codes, charters and jurisprudence of Zonus, pledging myself from toe to topknot to the service of the Order of Councilus and – swearing by all that is holy in the Garden of Dwaldiak – to refrain from depravity and to live by a code of duteous and biddable surrender. Every moment of every day, night, and limbo, I pass henceforth, shall be passed in the realization that I am worthless, and that my existence is but a wretched and insignificant reflection of that which is true and right. Never shall I deviate from the Path, and never will I shirk my responsibilities, even when affected by the fog of disconsolate and interminable desolation, or any other manifestation of the Seven States of Mind. By signing this document, and entering the Fraternity of the Jinn Hunters, I shall be now and evermore a fragment of dust on the plains that are reality. By deviating from the righteous Path of the Jinn Hunters, or by merely giving a passing thought to such an indecorous route, I shall be open for admonishment, and be willing for the ultimate punishment to be meted out. Further, I agree that in the event of my untimely demise in the course of my chosen craft, I permit what remains of my corporal form to be dissected by gras-grot surgeons, in the hope that medical and other pertaining advancements may be gleaned from my expiration. And, I give full authorization for the nineteen wasp slugs, otherwise known as a 'corticac', to use my remains for manure, and/or for cooling themselves in the long dry summers of their kingdom, as was agreed by convention and rite in far antiquitas. On the off-chance that one, both, or all, of my feet are not wanted by a corticac, I give full and resounding permission for the said appendages to be fused onto the underbelly of the swamisiods, as is their ancestral and undisputed right. Lastly, in the event that I happen to win the great and most remarkable lottery in the Dominion of Capual-så, I agree with absolute and most

JINN HUNTER

fervent delight that the Order of Councilus may benefit in entirety from the proceeds.

Jinn Hunter signed   [Full Name]

Number   [Jinn Hunter's Number]

Witnessed by   [Name of Witness]

Certified by   [Name of Legal Administrator]

Note: to be legally enforceable, this document must be sealed with vermilion wax scooped from the inner ear of a dwarf albino mole.

THE 7 GOLDEN RULES OF JINN HUNTERS

Rule One

A Jinn Hunter's allegiance is to the Order of Councilus, and it is to it that they ultimately report.

Rule Two

Whatever the circumstances, a Jinn Hunter must always save another Jinn Hunter in distress.

Rule Three

A Jinn Hunter never on any account believes anything a rogue jinn says – not even if the creature in question has been serenaded by the Krill choir of Spî.

Rule Four

A Jinn Hunter never allows a rogue jinn entry into their sythostic dreams.

Rule Five

A Jinn Hunter always separates the soul of a jinn from its corporal form at the earliest opportunity.

Rule Six

No Jinn Hunter is more important or valued than any other.

Rule Seven

Jinn Hunters obey the Sacred Code of their Order, and take the Secrets of Dorsalim with them to their grave.

JINN HUNTER

THE DOMINION OF MEN

A point worth drawing to the attention of all Jinn Hunters is that the human race believes it is superior to any other life form. Despite this, humans have almost no comprehension of either the dominion in which they live, or those that exist beyond its borders.

At the time of this edition (777654E-YY) of the *Handbook* all attempts at civilizing this imbecilic and downright arrogant species, have ended in nothing. The indescribable wretchedness of human civilization has enabled jinn to take advantage in the most extraordinary ways.

Jinn Hunters are advised to have as little as possible to do with the Dominion of Men. Interacting with humans will lead to extreme frustration, annoyance, and a possible case of folizz-nü.

Note that if the latter is contracted, Jinn Hunters must report at once to the medical centre on level LH998AAA-B, and provide ocular swabs for immediate examination.

The human species engages in a wide and perverted range of behaviour. Most members of this race consider they are alone in what they term to be a 'universe'. Those who are found to support other beliefs – such as that of 'alien life forms' – tend to be incarcerated in psychiatric units. In some cases, however, they are embraced as visionaries, and given wealth and power beyond their wildest dreams.

Throughout human history, we have attempted to affect elements of their society, so that life in the dominion might be far more melodious, and so that the future of this wretched and insignificant backwater might not be so terribly doomed.

Note: all Jinn Hunters planning to hunt jinn in the Dominion of Men, must report to the red slime frogs before they embark, and again immediately on their return. They must refrain from interaction of any substantive kind with local humans.

TAHIR SHAH

Guidelines on behaviour in the Dominion of Men can be found in document DP-iii-P776156, filed in the Desolation Archive at Zonus.

Any Jinn Hunters planning on spending an extended period of time in the Dominion of Men may wish to seek out answers to the questions on the Inventory of Outstanding and Pressing Questions on Form XYT221-999.

Current sample questions include:

1. Why do humans take such interest in deviations in the tone of their skin?

2. What is the thinking behind giving such value to small rectangles of printed paper?

3. How are humans affected by the phases of their moon?

4. Why do humans so value members of their societies with pleasing voices?

5. What reason accounts for humans' obsession with scaling mountains?

6. Most importantly of all, what accounts for the human species' need to exterminate itself in such a ready and obsessive fashion?

JINN HUNTER

JINN IN THE DOMINION OF MEN

Note: the human species is particularly partial to believing in spurious or irrelevant phenomena. Throughout their recorded history they have exhibited an alarming desire to follow that which is clearly gibberish. They regard the most idiotic ideas, objects, and people, with unreserved attention and glee.

During their short and mediocre rise, humanity has squandered far too much time in following false beliefs, and in arguing about so-called 'monsters' that, in most cases, are evidently jinn. At the same time, they appear to be blind to the fact that certain members of their own kind are jinn, just as objects that surround them are jinn as well.

The ease with which jinn are able to conceal themselves in plain sight in the Dominion of Men is itself an explanation as to why so many jinn choose to reside in such an unimportant, bland corner of the Realm.

Examples of jinn manifesting as monsters, objects, and humans in the Dominion of Men follow.

Jinn Manifesting as Monsters

Behemoth

Jinn of considerable size which, like a great many jinn inhabiting the Dominion of Men, is largely tranquil, except when disturbed during ritualistic hibernation.

Chimera

Oppressed by humanity in ancient times, chimera typically resemble lions, though with the head of a goat rising from its back. In more recent times, chimera have adapted their form so as not to stand out as prominently as they once did.

427

Kere

Blood-craving jinn, the kere is known for carnal preoccupations, and for tearing the spirit of their enemies away from the corporal form. In recent times they have migrated to the sewers beneath Manhattan, where they live in abundance in the guise of ordinary brown rats.

Minotaur

Persecuted jinn particularly from the era of the Greeks, minotaurs are generally peaceful, although depicted in human folklore as malevolent. Their current form is in the guise of stage hypnotists, especially those with the initials D.B.

Ouroboros

Circular serpentine jinn, depicted in human culture since ancient times as swallowing its own tail. Ouroboroses have made a fortune for themselves by fashioning handbags and other accoutrements in the luxury leather line.

Werewolf

Common species of jester jinn lying low within the Dominion of Men, werewolves are usually placid, except when their burrows are disturbed. More recently, they have been known to assume the guise of actors in television soap operas, and of janitors in late-night drinking haunts.

Jinn Manifesting as Objects

Ark of the Covenant, Axum

Venerated by humans, the Ark of the Covenant is in actual fact the reflection of a nest of five libertine jinn that lies in an iridescent swamp on the western border of the Kingdom of Sarax-Ga.

428

Centre Pompidou, Paris

Although plenty of humans residing in the French capital will swear blind they can remember when the Centre Pompidou was constructed, the building is a jinn – hailing from a minor sub-class of bottle jinn. Despite considerable investigations, no one at Zonus has any idea whatsoever why the bottle jinn in question configured itself into such an ugly and inappropriate form, or how long it is planning to stay there.

Leaning Tower, Pisa

Wart jinn that manifested itself into the shape of a tall building, the 'Leaning Tower of Pisa' is very much alive and well. Like many jinn shape-shifted into the guise of architectural objects or ornaments, the wart jinn is merely biding his time until the kingdom he has devoured has been digested.

Mona Lisa, Paris

Renowned portrait of the Mona Lisa at the Louvre Museum in Paris is a possum jinn disguised as a mouse jinn, which in turn is masquerading as a portrait jinn.

Monkey Puzzle Tree, Chile

Although known to have originated in Latin America in the Dominion of Men, monkey puzzle trees are found in numerous other dominions, especially in permutations featuring bluebottle jinn. In common with many barbed species of tree, the monkey puzzle is almost exclusively a variety of garble jinn. A significant exception are those examples with fuchsia bows, as well as the 'singing' variety.

Montgolfier Balloon, Ardèche

Although the Montgolfier brothers were not jinn, their first great balloon certainly was – a point that annoyed them greatly, but which they kept secret. The jinn's shape-shifting into the form of a hot air balloon was done as a bet between two fraternities of jinn resident in the Ardèche at the time.

Niagara Falls, Niagara

Technically a rogue jinn, the Niagara Falls was given a temporary pardon, unless he ceases from flowing in a continuous waterfall. Constantly monitored by Jinn Hunters and at least seventeen departments at Zonus, the jinn in question wants sorely to change shape, but knows he will end up in the Prism if he does so.

Opera House, Sydney

Another example of a jinn shape-shifting in recent times to a particular form that humans believe they witnessed being constructed. In the case of the Sydney Opera House, the fox jinn in question is merely cooling her limbs after being buried in baking sand – which is another story.

Sphinx, Giza

Female jinn in a profound state of hibernation for more than ten thousand years, the Sphinx is incorrectly believed by humans to have been built by their own culture.

Welwitschia mirabilis, Namib Desert

So-called 'fossilized' dwarf tree found in the Namib Desert in the Dominion of Men, Welwitschia mirabilis has long been a fascination for botanists. As is usually the case, however, human scientists have missed the point of major interest – namely, that the curious plant is actually a species of finkle jinn in a rather second-rate disguise.

JINN HUNTER

Jinn in Human Form

At the current time there are believed to be in excess of seventy million jinn of various species, classifications, and descriptions, living in the Dominion of Men. Most are peaceful by nature, and are disguised either as humans, or as creatures or objects within physical representations accepted by humankind.

Although most jinn disguised as humans have never been known to achieve anything regarded by their fellow jinn as worthy, a certain number have been noted in human history. They include:

Jane Austen

Celebrated for her literary oeuvre, Jane Austen came to the Dominion of Men while avoiding the unwanted solicitations of admirers. Although shape-shifting into the guise of a respectable young woman, Austen was in actual fact a tower jinn. Rising up to more than a thousand feet, her natural form was blotched with thick waxy fur, and her head crowned with sixteen pairs of sharpened horns.

Humphrey Bogart

One of several former rogue jinn, Humphrey Bogart moved to the Dominion of Men after being released from the Prism. He was sentenced for devouring at least three kingdoms, and for being rude to the maragor judge hearing his crimes. Having been freed, he repented his sins, and promised never to cause trouble again.

Julius Caesar

Celebrated Roman politician and statesman, Caesar first visited the Dominion of Men while suffering from stomach cramps after swallowing sixteen blind ghouls. The climate, prescribed by a glass jinn, was thought to be favourable to the condition. While recuperating on the Italian peninsula, he was mistaken for someone else and, before he knew it, had risen to an exalted status. Tiring of the position, and the shortcomings of humanity, he staged his own murder, and has not visited the Dominion of Men since.

Coco Chanel

Regarded as a beauty by her glass jinn family and friends, Chanel was tricked into leaving her own dominion by her sister's best friend – a wasp jinn filled from the tip of her horns to the end of her claws with jealousy.

Christopher Columbus

Fêted by humans as an expert navigator, Columbus was forced to venture to the Dominion of Men after being expelled from his own kingdom on account of his inability to hold down any form of sensible employment. By a long and unlikely series of coincidences, Columbus found himself in a position to make a great discovery – that of a land which had never actually been lost.

Charles Darwin

With a love of the ocean and an interest in the natural world, the man known to humans as 'Charles Darwin' was in actual fact a bluebottle jinn with penchants for feather pillows and custard flan.

James Dean

One of numerous snark jinn to have become celebrated Hollywood actors, Dean was an incurable thespian at heart, even though his snark jinn parents disapproved of the lowly line of work. Eventually, Dean was blackmailed into returning to the Kingdom of Griliap, where he married a pretty female snark jinn, called Filomia.

Albert Einstein

Hailing from a kindly family of prowling jinn, Einstein ventured to the

Dominion of Men after a dream. He dreamt that, by visiting at a certain time, he would be able to assist a change to occur that was sorely needed. Unfortunately, miscalculating the time of his arrival, Einstein was never able to make the mark he was supposed to have done.

Genghis Khan

Legendary Mongol leader, Genghis Khan was actually a female blood jinn named 'Vermalia'. Lying low in the Dominion of Men, she had been banished from her own kingdom for gross insolence, and for masquerading as the right eye of the queen.

George IV

Blessed with an immense appetite, matched only by his ever-expanding waistline, the Prince Regent (later George IV) was not only a jinn, but was a star pupil selected for the Cadenta Academy. On the advice of a maternal uncle, he did not enter the service of Zonus, but rather journeyed to the Dominion of Men, where he assumed a role in the British Royal Family.

Hatshepsut

Reigning as pharaoh, Hatshepsut, queen of queens, may have donned the livery of men but was neither a man nor a woman. Born to rogue jinn parents, she was sent to safety as an oroking in the one backwater where her family imagined she would be safe – the Dominion of Men.

Frida Kahlo

Despite attaining considerable fame during her sojourn in the Dominion of Men, Frida Kahlo was no human but rather belonged to a sub-class of diamond jinn. After her death, a formal investigation was commissioned by the authorities at Zonus to ascertain why she had moved to the dominion in the first place. The results are still classified and will not be made public until the year 3999. Certain details were published, however, including the point that Kahlo's paintings and other artistic representations are largely imprisoned portrait jinn.

Queen Victoria

As were many members of her ancestral line, Queen Victoria was a jinn devoted to the well-being of the small island on which she spent much of her life within the Dominion of Men. In her shape-shifted form she passed well enough as a human female, although the expansive triangular patch of snake skin on her spine never adapted as she would have hoped to the indigenous climate. On leaving the Dominion of Men under the guise of supposed death, Victoria, whose real name is 'Graggiap', returned to live at the bottom of the Mercuric Sea.

JINN HUNTER

THE GAME OF VOSSSUK

The Vouch

In all versions except that found in the Dominion of Scall, vosssuk is played by two opponents, both of whom pledge the 'vouch' before the game begins. If the players do not share a common language, the Vouch must be translated by a recognized clerk from the Smarob House of Translation.

If a smarob translator is unavailable, the players may request a translation to be made by a secondary translation house – but only if a snarl beetle has given permission, signing a letter providing approval in inversed quadruplicate.

Agreed Text for the Vouch

I, [name of first player], have agreed to play [name of second player] at a place called [name of place] and in the attendance of [name of third party] who shall act as administrator and referee. It is agreed that sixteen witnesses will observe the game, and will keep notes on the state of play and the condition of the players. On no account will there be any hostility, bribery, foul language, threats, deviation, debased behaviour or lewd talk. It is further agreed that both players shall allow for their oral cavities to be inspected before the outset of the game. In addition, if the game continues for more than 186 days (i.e. of a period of average time as found in the Dominion of Sqzzzi), then the referee and witnesses shall be liable to pay a fine of 119½ drima stones. If drima stones are not available, then it is agreed that the fine be paid in a currency of mutual inconvenience. Further, it is agreed that all weaponry will be surrendered before the outset of play, and that no teeth, claws, stomach juices, curses, hexes, or maleficence of any kind will be directed by one player to the other.

Signed on this day, the [date]

By

[Signature of first player]

And

[Signature of second player]

Witnessed by

[Signature of referee and all 16 witnesses]

Elementary Rules of Vosssuk

To decide who goes first, a slom pear is cut lengthways down the middle, and the first player to call 'krixxx!' at seeing a seed starts. If such a fruit is not available, then any fruit from the Dominion of Quex may be used.

Basic rules of play are as follows:

- The first player puts down their pieces in order of size and shape.
- The second player follows with their pieces.

- The first player moves 22 pieces while the second player sings the Ballad of Eternal Winter backwards.

- The second player then moves their pieces in the same way.

- The opponent's pieces may be captured by landing on a square on which 17 'blind' pieces have been clustered in a tørqular pattern.

- The winner is the first player to correctly guess what the next 55 moves will be – as refereed by an external and impartial member of the Vosssuk Adjudication Unit.

Value of Key Vosssuk Pieces

Mall	0 points
Snall	9 points
Drap	119 points
Grall	888 points
Jool	45,002 points
Hupp	62,077 points
Friz	58,667,752,431 points
Ifff	76,654,983,448 points
Neee	1,222,444,111,776 points
Groyl	unlimited points

TAHIR SHAH

SPOKEN CLUSOT

Clusot is known for the complexity of its tonal structure, and for the fact that when spoken backwards it sounds exactly the same as when spoken forwards. Despite this feature of pronunciation, written clusot is distinctly different from the spoken version.

The dialect is made additionally unusual by the fact that the numerical system is exceptionally irregular. This accounts in part for why clusots have little understanding of mathematics, and why they are universally trusted – because no clusot would ever bother trying to deceive anyone else by sharp accounting.

Common Clusot Expressions

Which way is the place where I can eat a huge amount of delicious food?

??Malu-malu ka ka rulala zik??

Why do I always feel so hungry?

??Bo na ru koooook malu-malu??

Please help me because my stomach is about to devour itself.

Haaaaaaaaaaaa lal yo yo dir.

My paws are trembling because I just remembered there was no food to eat.

Ti-ka k aka wam malu-malu waaaaa.

438

JINN HUNTER

My mother says I can't have any more food because I was rude.

Giq kio ka malu-malu tof fot.

I look forward to walking the Xerex lines soon.

Fif rop Xerex ba ba ba ba kop.

When I walk the Xerex lines I can taste smorop pods in my mouth.

Fif rop Xerex ba ba pa pa pa.

I can't wait for the smorop pod festival because it's a yummy time.

So so ma maj klip pa pa pa doooo.

Please do not talk to me about desiccated jinn because the thought of them makes my head swell.

!!Woooooooon!!

I thought I told you already: I feel sad when I think of barsiliam juice and other such food.

Hox xod kip malu-malu.

Where should I go to find some clusots like me?

??Qop po??

439

NOTES ON NEQUISSIMUS

On <u>NO</u> account should a Jinn Hunter approach the rogue jinn Nequissimus without informing the Department of Exceptional Danger & Predicament. Located on level 186A/F2, Room 29YYYQ, the department accepts communications made through all usual channels.

The following is a list of facts about Nequissimus which may aid a Jinn Hunter in the event of confronting the most wicked of all rogue jinn.

1. The day after his birth, Nequissimus swallowed his entire family, having bitten off their heads.

2. Although immune to most conventional methods of attack, he is known to possess a small patch of unprotected skin below his left nostril. Depending on the shape-shifted configuration, this zone may potentially be targeted with was-swas ointment.

3. Nequissimus is characterized by an indefatigable hatred of authority, with Jinn Hunters at the top of his list.

4. In the time of King Solomon, Nequissimus was known to have devoured an entire dominion because an unruly sailor's singing had woken him during a nap.

5. He loathes frax poetry very greatly, and has made it known that if he ever hears it again, he will hasten the end of time.

6. Among Nequissimus's favoured pastimes is that of chewing violiss snails until they fall into a smorlak state.

7. His favourite number is said to be:
   10972635478861.872526342.

8. He is believed to have once ground an army of plague ghouls into dust because they ridiculed the way he spoke.

9. Nequissimus can comprehend, speak, and recite poetry in almost any language, although he is said to prefer the sound and intonation of Drüp above all others.

10. The Soothsayers of Mūlch have said that when Nequissimus perishes, an Era of Despotic Bleakness will befall the Realm.

TAHIR SHAH

ROGUE JINN MOST WANTED

1.

NAME: NEQUISSIMUS

SPECIES: PLAGUE JINN

NUMBER: 1119876425/AB/I/PA

CRIME: Causing destruction, injury and devouring too many dominions and kingdoms to record here (see document GF/D/S123/9UYT/189.8 for a full list of his felonies). Most recently escaped from the great Prism.

STATUS: CURRENTLY AT LARGE

2.

NAME: SALIMAK

SPECIES: SNARK JINN

NUMBER: 9918844461/TP/Q/ZA

CRIME: Killing the celebrated Jinn Hunter Estiath in the Kingdom of Blazing Tides.

STATUS: CURRENTLY AT LARGE

3.

NAME: ZUZLIÄLAK

SPECIES: WRATH JINN

NUMBER: 2256436695/WW/F/PC

CRIME: Ingesting the royal family of Gūuüu and exterminating 187 law enforcement officers sent to capture him.

STATUS: CURRENTLY AT LARGE

4.

NAME: DRÏD-DA-DA

SPECIES: INK JINN

NUMBER: 9837451827/SQ/FQ/OO

CRIME: Ridiculing the King of the Dominion of Droliw and terrorizing the inhabitants by pouring liquid fire over them.

STATUS: CURRENTLY AT LARGE

5.

NAME: KOUSALIA
SPECIES: TURQUOISE JINN
NUMBER: 9862538427/XX/Q/AL
CRIME: Laying a sarvel curse on the Dominion of Grim Feet.
STATUS: CURRENTLY AT LARGE

6.

NAME: SOFULAT
SPECIES: STEALTH JINN
NUMBER: 9482641222/WY/K/PV
CRIME: Drinking from the Sacred Well of Hestiac.
STATUS: CURRENTLY AT LARGE

7.

NAME: ASTRIALM
SPECIES: LIBERTINE JINN
NUMBER: 9830006381/GH/J/NS
CRIME: Terrorizing aquatic life in the Mercuric Sea in the Kingdom of Sarax-Ga.
STATUS: CURRENTLY AT LARGE

8.

NAME: FÖ
SPECIES: CRUSH JINN
NUMBER: 7362555184/FH/D/SA
CRIME: Devouring 198,003 smarm geese without a licence.
STATUS: CURRENTLY AT LARGE

9.

NAME:	MILOUSIAD
SPECIES:	DEATH JINN
NUMBER:	97483999625/MH/L/JH
CRIME:	Escaping from the great dungeon of Zipiad, having been incarcerated for 2,873,526,272 offences.
STATUS:	CURRENTLY AT LARGE

10.

NAME:	NIMĀ-AX
SPECIES:	LICE JINN
NUMBER:	9826341538/UU/K/PP
CRIME:	Singing the anthem of Féxx ghouls in the Dominion of Gogolo.
STATUS:	CURRENTLY AT LARGE

JINN HUNTER

THE SACRED STORY OF RIMULAM JINN

(Certified as a true and accurate translation by the xorrk grubbe from the Smarob House of Translation, from the original Rimulam dialect.)

Once there was a land called the Dominion of Slaked Thirst where the ground was stained black with wicked tripe, and the air was tinged with the scent of grumple gas. The few inhabitants of the dominion were weathered, withered, and worn, and went by the name of pozulz – which meant 'melancholic' in their language.

No one ever visited that land because of the gas in the air and the wicked tripe on the ground. No one, that is, until the Morning of Unknown Dawn.

The day began as any other.

The putrid air hanging with a distinct chill, a chill that stank of dried sosuala fish.

Suddenly, the sky went dark as a buck beetle's pelt and, as it did so, a visitor arrived. Dressed in the livery of the otter heralds, on his head he wore a crown fashioned from carved jaguar ice. Emblazoned on the otter herald's tunic was a symbol – the sacred seed of the giririd bears.

Making his way into the capital's main square, the otter herald clapped his paws together, grinned, scowled, and declared:

'It is hereby announced that from this morning, night shall be day and day shall be night. Up shall be down and down shall be up. In shall be out and out shall be in. Sweet shall be sour and sour shall be sweet. Right shall be wrong, and wrong shall be right. And, let it be understood that if these wishes are not agreed upon by one and all, the most terrible and wrathful act of vengeance imaginable will be meted out by a sloke mullet goot.'

With that, the otter herald turned his ice crown round, so that the front was the back, and the back was the front. Then, thanking those in attendance for their time, he paced backwards from the square, and out from the Dominion of Slaked Thirst.

445

From that morning on, up was down and down was up; in was out and out was in; sweet was sour and sour was sweet; and right was wrong and wrong was right.

And, all was well until the seventh month of the lisping wasp king's reign.

JINN HUNTER

FAVOURED HIDING PLACES OF ROGUE JINN

1. In amongst packets of broose prunes in the Dominion of Red Revenge.

2. In wrecked whale ships off the coast of the Kingdom of Alphot.

3. In bottles of gwalipa juice bearing blue-and-white-striped labels.

4. In caravanserais and watering holes with the maraxa letter 'Ø' in their name.

5. In plain sight.

6. In the mouths of wart frog hogs.

7. In nests belonging to the decimus bird.

8. In bogs where festooned slime gourds grow.

9. In rings owned by piteous jinn, especially those in the Dominion of Tranquillity.

10. In treasure buried under frozen martep flats.

11. In bottomless mine shafts in the Empire of Woz-woz.

12. In concentric circles made from barbed wixula jinn.

A Request

If you enjoyed this book, please review it on Amazon and Goodreads.

Reviews are an author's best friend.

To stay in touch with Tahir Shah, and to hear about his upcoming releases before anyone else, please sign up for his mailing list:

 http://tahirshah.com/newsletter

And to follow him on social media, please go to any of the following links:

 http://www.twitter.com/humanstew

 http://www.facebook.com/TahirShahAuthor

 http://www.youtube.com/user/tahirshah999

 http://www.pinterest.com/tahirshah

 http://tahirshah.com/goodreads

http://www.tahirshah.com

Made in the USA
Middletown, DE
03 May 2021

38929443R00274